CW01082469

Which Of Your Sons?

Keith T Richards

ISBN: 978-1-917601-39-9

To those that suffered injustice
and to those who reveal it.

'I do not know how to thank you.'
'I can tell you,' said Obierika. 'Kill one of your
sons for me.'
'That will not be enough,' said Okonkwo.
'Then kill yourself,' said Obierika.

—Chinua Achebe 'Things Fall Apart'

Chapter 1

The Fixer Awaits

"Yeah I reside in Lagos
The city of hustlers
Everybody's in a hurry
Traders and customers
Walkers get picked on a regular
If you're not street
You gon' pop with your cellular
You're driving
I suggest you check your rearview
Be careful
Cos' an okada might just be near you
Knock one of them down
And rest just gonna tear you to pieces
Hey yooo
Welcome to the jungle!"

'Stylee' by Jimmy Jatt, featuring 2Face Idibia,
Mode 9 & Elajoe.

Francis was well known by everyone who worked at MMIA—
the Murtala Muhammed International Airport—in Lagos. If you
asked a random porter, Customs or Immigration officer, even a
tout, especially the touts, if they had seen Francis, you would
inevitably get a raised shoulder or a lifted eyebrow to accompany
a vague wave indicating the direction he was last seen. If there
was any hesitation, the addition of "Fixer" to his first name
would do. This confirmed that while there were countless people
in Nigeria ready to "fix" things for you, there was only one true
fixer in MMIA, and that was Francis. No one knew his true
surname.

Francis called himself a Protocol Officer. He was a man employed by companies and individuals to escort expatriates and VIPs through the labyrinth of MMIA's immigration, customs, health, drugs and firearms, and currency control checkpoints, all designed to procure a "dash" from the unsuspecting and the unprepared. From the entitled avoidance of long queues, to the prevention of the worst of the extortion rackets, Francis was your man.

The first sight of Francis did not inspire confidence. Round shouldered with a unique shuffle that made it appear as if his feet were somehow attached to the ground by magnets, he gave off a distinctly world-weary air. Invariably, a plastic supermarket shopping bag which contained his office filing system, would be hanging at his side. At any point in time, the bag contained photocopies of passports and personal documents of several of his clients, alongside a collection of blank forms and certificates. Entrusting private details and credentials to an unlicensed, freelance operator would have breached any company security officers' code of conduct but such was Francis' reputation that he was the go-to guy for many multinationals.

Robert Railsford and Terry Armstrong had never met. Both were employed by different companies whose travel policies meant one was spread comfortably in business class and the other was squeezed tight in steerage. But both were destined to have Francis welcome them to Nigeria.

Even for an old hand, any trip through Nigeria's borders had the potential for stress. The first experience was seldom forgotten. As you stepped out of the plane, the first thing that smacked you in the face was the astonishing physicality of the damp heat and the speed with which your skin became sticky with sweat. The second shock was the smell. It is hard to describe that smell, not least because after the first few times you no longer registered it. It was so prevalent that it was absorbed into your consciousness and you noticed it no longer. Until you left and came back again. It was the cumulative smell of a million kerosene stoves, the exhausts of countless generator sets, of rotting vegetables and open sewers, clogged storm drains, atop traffic fumes. It was the sweetish, sickly dead fish smell of twenty million people densely packed onto three small islands

2

and a small ribbon of land surrounded by creeks and swamps. Lagos! As your feet followed the sticky red matting that was once a carpet, you noticed how rundown the airport was. Cracked windows, walkways that were not moving, air conditioning that was on but palpably not cooling, and people lolling about on benches everywhere.

As Robert was in Club, he was ahead of Terry in joining the melee. Adept at picking out fresh fish, Francis spotted the lone innocent quickly enough.

"Mr Railsford?"

Robert paused and nodded.

"Wait here," he was told flatly. "We have one more person."

Robert blended in, dressed as he was in chinos and a polo shirt but when Terry staggered out in a Millwall FC shirt and matching tracksuit pants, he was unmissable.

Francis did not blink. "Armstrong?"

Nothing about White people would ever surprise Francis.

"Alright?"

Robert was somewhat taken aback. Terry spoke in that unmistakable south London accent, more fluid and lazier than cockney, almost a drawl.

"Oh hello," he said, offering his hand.

Terry looked at him before he nodded his crew-cut head. It took him a few moments before he took Robert's offer of a handshake.

Francis was a man of few words and when he held out his hand, his gesture managed to imply irritation, impatience, and resignation, in one simple movement.

"Papers," he said.

The newbies meekly handed over large envelopes with documents required for processing residency permits.

"Oya."

Francis turned and started walking.

For a split-second, Robert and Terry hesitated before realising that "oya" was a command. Francis marched to the head of one queue then turned and beckoned tetchily at the two Brits who had stopped at the back of the line. Robert and Terry both felt uncomfortable as, under Francis' instructions, they squeezed up

3

to the front of the queue doing their best to ignore dozens of glaring eyes. Their discomfiture was not just the heat and humidity but something deeper. Beyond it was the feeling of helplessness, of having no clue what they were supposed to be doing.

For Terry, his uneasiness was obvious. He had never been anywhere with so many Black people around. Even after six years in the army, he was intimidated.

Robert's response was more complicated. Being Black with Nigerian heritage, he had not expected to feel so alien. As their British passports were passed from hand to hand with various stamps applied and initials added on, he noticed that none of the immigration officers even glanced at him. He felt invisible as he was fast-tracked past the noisily waiting Nigerians. He felt their irritation firmly on his back; this was no warm cultural embrace. He hadn't known what to expect but it had not dawned on him that he was as much a stranger to this environment as the tall, slightly overweight, football-kitted, White bloke walking beside him.

The baggage collection area was the waiting room to hell. One moment, the crowd waited in the stuffy, gecko-green hall. The next, the instant the first cases started to drop haphazardly onto the creaking conveyor, there was an explosion of energy bordering on the manic as two planeloads of impatient Nigerians fought to retrieve their belongings. Whether smart designer suitcases, cardboard boxes held together by various forms of tape, or Ghana Must Go bags, everything was collected with a maximum of mayhem.

Eventually, the ingénues, sweat dripping down their backs, dragged their cases behind a waddling Francis, past more checkpoints and into the arrivals hall. Terry was limping from the impact of a luggage trolley a woman had rammed into his ankles.

Out in the public area, the trio was joined by one of Francis' acolytes who ran errands, carried luggage, and interpreted his more complex intentions. Much younger and less confident than his boss, he introduced himself as Sunday.

Sunday picked up both suitcases and started towards the exit with a nervous look over his shoulder towards a version of

4

Francis far removed from the controlled torpor of the last hour. Francis had become far more animated and was yelling into a battered Nokia cell phone, gesticulating as he did.

"Oga Francis says the car is late and you should wait in that bar," said Sunday, pointing towards a small group of plastic tables assembled around a couple of Coke-branded fridges.

As Sunday parked their suitcases by a table, Robert and Terry gratefully sat down. Francis wandered by still shouting into his phone.

"Beer?" the boy asked. Followed by, "Money?"

Robert pulled out a $20 note that was swiftly grabbed, pocketed, and was soon replaced by three bottles of Star beer and three tumblers. Sunday took out a grimy handkerchief, wiped one glass, and poured his foamy lager into it. He raised his glass, beaming.

"You are welcome to Nigeria!"

Robert and Terry were still in culture-shock suspended animation. The delay in their transportation and the chance to sit, drink a beer and take stock, was welcome. Robert managed a smile and raised his glass to Sunday.

"Thanks."

Terry took the bottle to his lips warily. On finding the contents to his liking, his shoulders visibly relaxed.

"Fucking hell!"

There was a short pause.

Then, Sunday, looking at Terry's shirt, observed, "Millwall are not in the Premier League."

In Nigeria, there was little concept of supporting a local team. Invariably, everyone supported Arsenal, Manchester United, Chelsea, or one of the Spanish giants. As if anything else would simply be unthinkable.

"We just got to the FA Cup finals, mate."

"Yes, but we stuffed you 3-0." Robert was a Man U fan.

Terry's natural response would have been a curt 'Fuck off' but being so far out of his comfort zone, he restrained himself to a cursory shrug.

"Your Dennis Wise was a good player, but is too slow now," Sunday explained.

Terry considered this an acceptable assessment.

5

Sunday continued, "Arsenal is the best team in Europe."

This time, both Terry and Robert responded simultaneously with "Fuck off", looked at each other, and laughed. The Star beer and football conversations created a sense of normalcy and the two newcomers were able to relax a little and look around.

MMIA is the proverbial Piccadilly Circus and as the "meeters and greeters", company protocol and security officers, touts, drivers, well-wishers, and ne'er-do-wells milled around waiting for their prey, Terry began to realise he had swapped New Cross for something more akin to New Delhi. He looked at Robert.

"So, just asking mate, are you Nigerian?"

Robert stared directly at him. "No mate, British." Then less defensively, "Though I do have Nigerian heritage on my mum's side."

Sunday perked up. "Oga, you be omo ile?"

Getting a blank look, he followed up with, "You are one of us, a son of the soil?"

Robert smiled. "Well, not really. Isn't that Yoruba? My mother's family is from the East. I have never been there but Mum is nagging me to visit them."

"Yes o!" Sunday declared. "You must!"

"I think that's where my granddad spent some time just after the war," said Terry.

Robert was surprised. "Really? Was he in the oil business?"

"Nah," Terry was hesitant. "I dunno really. He never spoke about it, but I don't think so. Most of his family were in the Old Bill, you know, coppers, in Glasgow."

"But you're not from Glasgow?"

Terry snorted, "Ha, well spotted, mate!"

At this point, Francis slouched back to the table, muttering something to the effect that only one car had turned up and they would have to share. He eyed the almost empty bottles on the faded Heineken-branded table, clearly having an internal debate as to whether to have one.

"Wa bayi!"

At this, Sunday jumped up, gulped the rest of his beer, and grabbed the cases.

"Let's go."

The little party exited the general arrivals area, with Francis acknowledging the policeman sitting at the door. They were now in open space where touts who could not afford to bribe themselves into the airport building milled. Terry was the obvious target.

"Taxi, taxi!"

"Currency, you want naira?"

"Mr Smith, long time, how is the family?" in a tone that suggested familiarity and was designed to attract a gullible stranger's attention.

Francis parted the mob like Moses and the Red Sea, and they made their way to a slip road with just enough space for vehicles to pull in and collect passengers. A couple of soldiers standing about were meant to stop this. They all waited a few minutes alongside the heavily armed military men who gesticulated aggressively at any of the 4x4 drivers who took too long to load up their passengers.

As soon as what turned out to be their Pajero pulled up, Robert and Terry followed Francis' instructions to get in the rear. Sunday put their bags in the back and slammed the door shut. There was some hesitation as it dawned on them they should tip him.

Robert said, "Keep the change from the beer!"

They were learning Lagos fast.

This did not pass Francis' attention as he clambered in the front.

He nodded at one of the soldiers who waved them on.

"Oya," he said to the driver, who engaged his gears.

The silent occupants of the small convoy headed into the confusion that was Ikeja's early evening traffic.

Chapter 2

Go-Slow Dey

"Every day my people dey inside bus
Every day my people dey inside bus
Forty-nine sitting, ninety-nine standing
Dem go pack themselves in like sardine
Dem dey faint, dem dey wake like cock
Dem go reach house, water no dey
Dem go reach bed, power no dey
Dem go reach road, go-slow go come
Dem go reach road, police go slap
Dem go reach road, army go whip
Dem go look pocket, money no dey
Dem go reach work, query ready
Every day na the same thing
Every day na the same thing
Suffer, suffer for world..."

'Shuffering and Shmiling' by Fela Anikulapo Kuti

Ikeja, where the MMIA is located, is a mainland district of Lagos where several multinational manufacturing companies have factories and offices. The top management of these companies, comprising a mix of expatriates and Nigerians, mostly lived in the wealthier and foreigner-catering island suburbs of Ikoyi and Victoria Island, linked to the mainland by the Carter, Eko, and Third Mainland bridges. Every morning and evening, the entire road network around these bridges would be clogged, like diseased arteries leading to the wheezing heart of the city.

Robert's brewery employer still housed most of their expatriate managers in a compound comprising a block of flats and some bungalows off one of the main commuter roads out of Lagos, the Mobolaji Bank Anthony Way. As leafy as Shonibare

Estate in the small residential area of Maryland may have been, it was but an oasis in the middle of the commuter traffic zone. They exited the airport at the peak of the evening traffic which meant what should have been a twenty-minute journey took an hour. Robert and Terry learnt why Lagos' notorious traffic jams are known as "go-slows".

It did not take long for them to give up trying to have a conversation with Francis. They did get as far as that he had been doing this job for "many" years and had "many" friends who were big men in "many" companies. But his low mumble was hard to decipher, and in any case, half the time, he was on his phone complaining at someone.

They were caught between trying to maintain a dialogue and just staring out at what seemed to be extraordinary scenes outside the SUV, though to the countless number of ordinary Nigerians going about the interminable, soul-destroying routine that is the Lagos commute, nothing was astonishing about it.

The contrasting shadows and glaring headlights picked out scenes of dense crowds of people everywhere; at bus stops, crossing the street, or just milling around. Some, wearing industrial overalls and similar clothing, were workers headed to or from shifts. Others, old ladies with shopping bags, smartly dressed women in office attire, and school kids of all ages in brightly coloured uniforms, all had a similar expression of acceptance and routine.

At every turn were uniforms of another kind: traffic wardens, police in their black shirts and green berets, soldiers. Terry found it odd that so many uniformed military personnel were visible and that they seemed to be accepted by everyone around them.

Insanely packed vehicles of all types and conditions were squeezed into impossibly tight spaces at every junction and roundabout as the 4x4 crawled past the old domestic airport. Motorbike taxis, steered by kamikaze drivers with huddled passengers, often in pairs, clinging to their backs, skidded past. They passed crowds of Lagosians seeking to squeeze themselves into battered yellow buses. The drivers' 'dog' boys banged the sides of the buses and cursed animatedly. Often than not, there would be a policeman or two supervising the melee at makeshift bus stops.

Their driver sought every opportunity to progress, just one car length at a time, amidst the anarchy. Every available space of half a yard would be claimed by an abrupt acceleration. Safely seat-belted in the back, Robert and Terry soon got used to periods of near immobility punctuated by jolts of sudden movement. Occasionally, a motorbike taxi—which they quickly learned were called okadas—would lurch at them only to turn at the last second, missing the Pajero's paintwork by microns.

Terry stared across the streams of traffic but saw less and less of what was in front of his eyes. Did he want to be here? Certainly, his family back in New Cross did not want him to be. His feelings were a mess. Something in him wanted to be away from the dreariness of his southeast London norm. Nigeria was definitely *away*.

Strapped in the back seat, Terry's face reddened at the memory of the epic dust up that followed his decision to leave.

"I can't believe you're fucking doing this, you selfish bastard!"

"Look…"

"Don't give me 'look'! Less than one year you've been back from the army. *'I will get a job locally. I can spend more time with the kids'*. No. Fucking. Job. Any time I ask you to do something with the kids, you just piss off to the pub."

"You know that's not true. Twice a week during the holidays I have taken them all swimming…"

His wife, Rachel, had turned to the cooker, opened the oven door, and flipped what was inside over with a spatula, before confronting him. He still saw glimpses of the person she had been when he'd met and married her.

"Look, Terry. Fish fingers again! Because you're out pissing it up the wall, this is all we get!"

"Rachel, I explained this. Unless I wanna be a security guard, there's no work here! I go down to the pub to ask about jobs. Because nothing has come up, I couldn't afford to turn this one down."

"Fuck off! Coming home after the kids have gone to bed, then falling asleep in front of the telly, is not looking for work! You could have found something local if you tried properly and don't

10

give me that '*Rachel, it's really difficult*' shite! Try bringing up three kids with an absentee father. Now, that's fucking difficult!"

His mother's reaction was similar, predictably.

After storming out of the house, he had headed up New Cross Road towards the pub. Brought up in the area, he had never wandered far until he joined the army, partly just to escape the negativity of his run-down southeast London suburb. The Marquis of Granby was his bolt hole in times of stress. His Millwall drinking buddies were already there when he entered.

"Fucking hell! A bit early for you, Armstrong. You're not normally out of bed this time of the afternoon!"

Just as he placed his order at the bar, he heard the same voice.

"Oi oi Tel, better get another one, trouble's here. Yer Mum's just walked in."

In his head he could see her walking into the pub now; a woman in her fifties, with short dyed-blonde hair, and the kind of dry skin that comes with a lifetime of heavy smoking. Slim, almost skinny, but with a slight tummy hanging over her jeans.

"It is early for you love," Linda said. "You two been arguing? Has she kicked you out? Didn't you go for that interview? I thought that was why you couldn't bring the kids round on Monday."

"I did go for the interview, and I did get the job. They rang me this morning and I accepted it."

"So, what's her fucking problem then?"

He had taken his time before answering, necking a good part of his pint.

"I am going away again. Overseas."

"Oh, Terry!" her tone softened. "Not surprised she's pissed off. You're not going back in the bloody army?"

"No, it's civvie. Engineering in a large company. They want me to run a unit installing and maintaining industrial generators. In Nigeria."

The two others sitting around, who'd been eavesdropping of course, had been quiet to this point. Now they dived in.

"Nigeria! It's dodgy out there, Tel boy. You'll be working with a bunch of fucking darkies. Couldn't you find a place to work with your own people?"

"And them Nigerians, they're all fucking crooks. I've read about 'em."

Terry ignored them and looked at his mother.

She took her time. "You know why I don't like that, Terry. Nigeria. Nigger-land. Look what it did to your granddad." Then, more harshly, "You are a fucking idiot."

"It's good money, loads of perks and that. I know Rachel's pissed off but there'll be money coming in," he said. "And as for all that stuff, it's how many years ago and no one really knows what happened to him out there."

Terry knew that her anger was the result of the sense of dread she inherited from her mother and the memory of her own father who, so long ago, had served in Nigeria; a grim policeman who effectively drank himself to death when Terry was still a kid.

It was past nine o' clock when he got in and Rachel had already gone to bed. He had crept up the stairs and popped his head around the girls' bedroom door. Dolly, the older, slept peacefully on her side while Jade, little more than a toddler, was curled up in a ball, a thumb still firmly in place where she had been sucking it. The memory of them in their matching Pingu pyjamas always made his heart jump a beat.

Along the hall, the light was still on in the boy's room but Josh was already in dreamland. The comics he'd been reading lay open on the floor beside his bed.

Terry had tried to be conciliatory when he undressed and got into bed while Rachel kept reading.

"Look love, I am sorry but it is for the best, believe me. It's really good money and I will arrange for the offshore salary to be paid straight into the joint account. After a couple of months, we can pay off the debts and when I come back on leave, we can afford a proper holiday. I have already asked and they say I can be home for Christmas."

She put her magazine down and looked at him. She had been crying.

With a sense of guilt, he remembered her reaching up and turning out the light.

"Terry, oh Terry," she said. "It's not just about the money!"

Just two weeks later, here he was, stuck in the back of a car with several Black people going nowhere. Although he had expected it something in the reality of their multitude made him sink a bit farther into the car's back seat.

Robert too was lost in thought. At one point, amidst the apparent mayhem, stood a small girl child, no older than eight. She was of a near-olive complexion, with dusty hair loosely tied with a scarf. Spotting possible interest, she reached up and tapped at the window on his side. Her tiny hands opened like birds' wings. She kept pace with the slow crawl of the vehicle, silently pleading with her head cocked to one side. Robert was transfixed. Her face was no further than two or three feet from his.

Emboldened by his attention, she tapped the glass again.

The driver, watching in his mirror, sucked his teeth.

"Please, sir, do not encourage her. They are many. She will bring her friends and they will make wahala."

Terry, who had been watching from the other side of the rear seat, cursed.

"Fucking hell, mate! She's just a kid!"

Without turning round, Francis explained. His mumble was gone now, in its place a world wariness that made his passengers pay attention to the back of his head.

"They work in groups. They are brought down from the north or even from across the border to beg to make money for their masters. You will soon get used to them."

"Christ!" Terry cursed and said no more.

There was a small gap in the traffic just then and the jeep was able to jerk forward a few metres. In the wing mirror, Robert could still see the little traffic girl watching them until she jumped backwards to avoid a homicidal okada. She had already lost interest in them.

Their journey progressed to the flyover past the junction leading to the industrial Oba Akran Avenue, where Robert would be going to work the next day. Then along Mobolaji Bank Anthony Way, where the traffic eventually thinned out enough for them to make steadier progress. Just past the Sheraton Hotel, they turned into Shonibare Estate. A large gate set in a neatly painted wall seemed to open automatically as the jeep pulled into a tree-lined compound. Passing through, they immediately left the Lagos city cacophony behind them into the unexpected peace of a sheltered private housing estate. Even by the low lighting of a swift approaching dusk, it was clear this was suddenly the Lagos of a better-privileged, middle class.

Someone came and met Robert and said he would take him to his apartment. "Fucking hell!" exclaimed Terry, getting out to shake Robert's hand.

By now, Robert had worked out that the phrase could be used universally: the meaning depended solely on Terry's intonation.

"Impressive mate," Terry clarified, nodding towards the smartly maintained gardens. There was a glimpse of a pool and a tennis court amongst palm trees.

Robert smiled and waved at his travelling companion.

"Good luck with your posting Terry."

"Thanks!"

"I know where to come if our generator packs up!"

"Yeah, cheers and all the best."

Terry got back into the jeep.

* * *

It was close to another hour before they arrived at the metal gates of a compound on a gloomy Victoria Island side street just behind a shopping mall. By this time, Francis was asleep in the front and his sole passenger had fallen into an exhausted silence.

The driver horned several times before a side gate opened and a drowsy security guard came out while wiggling his feet into sandals and tucking in a rumpled shirt.

Francis stirred himself awake at the second blast of the car horn.

"GTW. Flat 9," the driver said.

The guard turned sluggishly and disappeared through the side gate. After a few seconds during which the grating sound of sliding bolts could be heard, the gates creaked open.

By the time Terry had unenthusiastically eased himself off the seat that he felt he had become part of, the guard had closed the gate and was standing looking at the latest resident with barely a flicker of interest.

14

Any expectation Terry might have had of a Guinness-style complex with lush vegetation and full amenities was shattered by his first glimpse of the dull compound surrounding a building that emerged out of the semi-darkness like a grey iceberg. A few tatty jeeps and elderly Toyotas were scattered in the car park. A couple of concrete flowerpots contained nothing but dry earth and cigarette butts.

Substantially past its better days, the building had shed patches of its mosaic-tiled covering. Various wires and air conditioner pipes garlanded the façade like macabre cake decoration. The few lights around the car park area were dim and Terry noticed, judging by the coughs and stutters and the smell of diesel fumes, that the generator was due a service.

Terry turned towards his case being unloaded by the driver but Francis beckoned him. They walked to the lobby where there were two lifts. One had its doors propped open by a fire extinguisher; the other at least had a light over the button.

"Any stairs?"

Francis pondered for a moment, shook his head, and muttered, "Fifth floor". Francis pushed the button and the doors croaked open. As they stepped in, the floor lurched downwards six inches before the doors came together with a sudden and disconcerting clunk.

"Fucking hell!"

Terry was relieved to see the lights on the indicator flicker, half holding his breath until it paused on number five. As the door opened, Terry was taken aback. In front of him was a diminutive Nigerian, replete in a starched, pressed white attire, but with a bright, genuine, smile.

"Mister Armstrong, I am Patrick, your steward. Welcome to Roman Gardens!"

Terry was thankful that the apartment itself was significantly better than he feared, given the state of the exterior of the building. The room was sparse but spacious and comfortably furnished. Though it was now dark outside, he could see through the large balcony windows that there seemed to be a view over a waterbody of some sort.

Patrick produced a tray with a plate of ham sandwiches and crisps on it.

"Sir, beer or soft?"

Still somewhat shaken, Terry replied, "Beer, please."

Francis had already ensconced himself on a dining table chair with a bottle of Guinness.

With half a sandwich in one hand and a glass of Star in the other, Terry explored the rest of the flat. The bedroom was roomy, with fitted wardrobes and an en-suite bathroom. The bed looked comfortable and the linen was clean and pressed. Two smaller bedrooms shared a second bathroom. There was a small toilet at the end of the corridor.

For an ex-army, New Cross lad, this all looked very decent and his mood took a significant turn for the better.

'All this room and a bleedin' servant too!' he thought.

Hearing voices behind him, he went back into the living room to find he had a visitor.

"Sir, this is Mr Adebayo," Patrick said. "He has come to greet you."

There stood a tall and impressive gentleman in his mid or late fifties, dressed in a dark office suit and a crisp white shirt open at the neck. He was very dark, with a touch of grey in his goatee.

"Good evening Terry. I am the Executive Director at your new employer, General Trading and Works Limited," he said, pausing slightly, then smiled. "That's the E. D. and G. T. W. for short. I am responsible for Human Resources and like to keep an eye on our expats personally. I heard there was a bit of a cock up with your pick-up and transport so I thought I would pop around with this."

And then he held out a bottle of Johnnie Walker Black Label.

Before Terry could respond, there was a cough.

Francis, somewhat more obsequiously than before, was taking his leave.

"Mister Armstrong, Mister Adebayo sir!"

Adebayo replied without looking, "Thank you, Francis. Please come to the office and see me tomorrow."

"Yes sir. Thank you sir!"

As Francis slunk out of the room, Terry noticed his suitcase had been brought up.

"Thank you Francis," he called out. Then, "Mr Adebayo, please take a seat."

"Tunde to you, old chap."

Tunde Adebayo, as Terry was to learn, was one of those characters as popular in the expatriate community as he was in the local one, with an easy manner that Terry thought was impressively posh.

"Terry, here is your first Nigerian lesson."

He opened the bottle of scotch, stood up and walked to the balcony.

He slid the door open and poured a drop over the railing.

"To the ancestors!"

Tunde came back into the room, lounged into one of the chairs, stretched out his legs and laughed.

"It's libation. We like to pay respects to our ancestors when we crack open a new bottle so the spirits of those folk don't come get us just yet!"

Terry wasn't a whisky drinker. He knew from experience that it affected his mood. But he allowed Tunde to pour him a chaser to go with his Star. Tunde's glass was significantly larger.

"Patrick, bring plenty ice, abeg!" Tunde called over his shoulder. "So, young man, I do like to pop around to meet new expats and have a little drink. Just to get to know them and check on how well they are settling in."

Tunde stood up again, taking off his jacket this time, revealing red clip-on braces which he unclipped and put into the jacket pocket as he hung it over the back of a chair.

Terry was disconcerted. To him, this was too much like fraternising with an officer and a Black one at that. Tunde seemed not to notice. His natural openness was unaffected even though he spoke with the kind of accent that one would expect from a former English boarding school student.

"So, we have been using this as a guest house but as I also look after company properties, I thought it would make do as your place. Your boy, Patrick, is delighted, as he hates looking after the guest house and would much prefer having a regular boss, an oga, as we say here."

"There's no need to rush in tomorrow," he continued. "Take your time and have a chat with Patrick about anything the place needs, make a list. I will send a car round about midday and you can come into the office. We can go through the local terms and sort out some naira and all that stuff."

Terry was realising he had not considered all the implications of his situation. A torrent of questions flooded his mind.

"That's very nice of you, thank you. When will I meet the team? Is there a dress code?"

Tunde leaned forward and dropped more ice into his glass. "I do like a lot of ice. You? Anyway, don't worry about that. Either tomorrow afternoon or more likely Wednesday, as the engineering department is based close to Ikeja. Quite near where you came in from, the airport." He paused. "I have seen your CV. Am I right in saying you haven't been to Africa before?"

"No, sir. I mean, Tunde."

Tunde laughed. "Of course, ex-army right? Royal Engineers? We find you ex-army types are very practical. In any case, you impressed James. That's James Moriarty, our CEO, when he met you after your interview in the London office."

"Really?" Terry was pleased. He only remembered meeting the big boss briefly after his interview.

"Something to do with a tie?" Tunde grinned. "James was impressed with you wearing Bugs Bunny to an interview."

"Yeh, the dog ate my other one," said Terry with a straight face.

Before he could say anything else, there was a loud crash from the kitchen.

Tunde winced. "Patrick is not as young as he once was, but he is honest, and his cooking is pretty good. He makes a particularly impressive prawn curry. He knows the ropes, useful for someone new like you."

He called over his shoulder, "Patrick, you can close."

Patrick came out of the kitchen.

"Sorry sir, I dropped a saucepan. Nothing is broken, please."

He looked at Terry. "Against what time tomorrow, sir? Do you take tea or coffee with your breakfast?"

There was a pause until Terry responded, "Erm, eight o'clock will be fine. Tea, please."

"Yes sir. Goodnight."

"Goodnight Patrick."

Tunde looked at Terry, smiled and called back over his shoulder one last time.

"Patrick, I expect you to look after our new friend well well."

"Of course, oga. Good night, sir. Greet madam for me."

Tunde got up.

Half the bottle of scotch was gone but there was no sign of it in his demeanour.

"Well, it has been quite a day for you I imagine."

Terry walked with him to the door.

"Don't worry about anything. Oh, and here's my card. My mobile is there. You can ring anytime."

Terry was grateful and said so.

"By the way, where does Patrick stay?"

"There's a BQ, a Boys Quarters, on the side of the compound. Anyway, the car will be ready when you want it. Just go downstairs when you are ready. Oh, Tunde looked at the Millwall shirt and said gently, "trousers and a shirt with a collar, even a polo, will be fine. Bolt the door behind me. Patrick has a staff entrance into the kitchen. Goodnight Terry."

As he shut the door, Terry noticed Tunde taking the stairs.

There were three bolts attached to the back of the door. He slid them all in for good measure.

Chapter 3

At Whose Expense?

"Never smile at a crocodile
No, you can't get friendly with a crocodile
Don't be taken in by his welcome grin
He's imagining how well you'd fit within his skin
Never smile at a crocodile
Never tip your hat and stop to talk a while
Never run, walk away, say good-night, not good-day
Clear the aisle but never smile at Mister Crocodile."

Jack Lawrence (as frequently sung by Pat Roberts)

Blessing raised her eyebrows, looked upwards, and then dabbed the edge of her mascara with the corner of a tissue. It was shoulder-to-shoulder around the mirror in the ladies' bathroom as all the girls sought to put on their night-time faces. It was not the most hygienic of places: toilet seats were broken or non-existent, doors swung loose on hinges and if there had ever been locks, they were long gone. All the girls carried toilet rolls in their bags. But there was the clamour of lively chatter: greetings and expressions of mutual admiration, comparisons of make-up and displays of new items of clothing, all punctuated by laughter. There was much hopping about on one leg to pull on a particularly tight skirt and mutual zipping and bra clipping. The humour was bawdy and usually at the expense of some physical aspect of a male of the species.

Occasionally, the harmonious babble would be broken by insults and the abuse that inevitably comes with the competitive nature of their workplace. Actual violence was rare as it would bring in Eric or one of the other bouncers. This would mean one or more of the girls being ejected from the premises and losing the "gate fee" paid to the doormen. Nevertheless, many had a blade discreetly tucked somewhere: less for protection from clients than for seeing off the competition on the rare occasion when things did get serious. This was the world of the girls of Pat's Bar.

Blessing had worn a modest dress on the bus from Ajah but had now slipped on a shorter, tighter number and stuffed her daytime clothes in a small bag she carried with her as she went into the bar.

Pat's had once been a single-room saloon but extensions and alterations had made it a bit of a jumble of semi-open spaces centred around a main bar and the dance area.

That evening, some of the afternoon football and rugby crowd were still jammed around the standing tables in the main bar discussing whichever matches had been on the various televisions high up on the walls. Some of them would drunkenly continue into the later evening, while others would leave and make more room for the regular night-time crowd.

As Blessing squeezed through to one of the back rooms, she caught Pat's eye and he beckoned her over to his usual place at the corner of the bar where his ample buttocks were perched precariously on his usual barstool.

"Hello Blessing. How are you darling? Give Uncle Pat a hug."

Blessing allowed herself to be squeezed onto Pat's massive and always slightly damp chest. He had the look of an overweight pirate but was genuinely affectionate towards many of the regular girls. They were generally safer in his place than many of the other bars in VI as Pat, for all his smiling munificence, very effectively ran a tight ship. Girls and clients were regularly barred for breaching the peace. This meant the girls were willing to pay the doormen a higher entrance fee than most places and put up with Pat's sweaty hugs.

He released her with a pretend jump and a wink at his mates. "Behave yourself!"

She grimaced and made a mock curtsey then slipped into the back room where a couple of her friends had already settled, hiding their bags under a bench. They were not allowed to sit without a drink so most of them ordered a soft drink from one of the waitresses. They would nurse these—a Coke, Fanta, Pepsi, it didn't matter—as they scanned the room and finetuned plans of

21

attack. There was a kind of acceptance between the girls and the staff though little active collaboration.

As the girls waited for the evening to turn into night, they chatted and made small talk, flirting with the DJs as they set up. They also acknowledged other clusters of girls: some with affection and others with suspicion. The real mistrust was saved for the girls who acted as loners. These were the hard girls with blades hidden in their bags, ready to cut any amateur who moved in on one of their targets. Like her, most of Blessing's friends were students or had started as students before the lack of money for school fees pushed them towards other employment.

The outsiders were professionals, the true ashawos adept at milking their clients while building up healthy bank accounts, often from blackmailing or stealing from the more gullible expatriates: the "Please, don't tell my wife" or "I will pay you if you stop texting me" types. After all, ashawo literally meant "those who pick up money".

As the music drew more girls and prospective punters onto the dance floor, Blessing and one of her friends gyrated together, erotically entwining in a way that would attract attention.

Under the coloured lights bouncing off the walls, their revealing costumes caught the notice of several of the men sitting in the bar area. It was still early and there was more drinking to be done. The mademoiselles didn't expect much interest until much later. Some of the bolder girls would walk around and approach tables but Blessing found the constant rejection humiliating. In any case, as one of the younger ones, she had not reached the stage where she felt she had to do that. She had the confidence that she could still attract attention with a properly directed smile.

While dancing, she noticed a face she recognised.

Terry was sitting at a table with a pair of older White guys who were regulars. Judging by their football shirts, they supported different teams. One was sporting a South African rugby shirt while the other wore the all-too-frequent red Arsenal top.

Like many of the girls, Blessing had learned to distinguish between the main teams, even though she had little interest in football. Terry's Millwall top was unsurprisingly not one she recognised, but his large frame and red hair were certainly familiar. She had gone home with him a couple of times and remembered him as one of the nicer ones. The hope was that you would be invited back by someone with good hygiene, who was not violent and would leave a generous wad of naira in your bag. Anything else was a bonus. The jackpot was someone who wanted a relationship of sorts and was willing to pay enough for university fees or to set up a small business. Maybe even a canteen, or a hairdressing salon.

She remembered that Terry didn't talk much but when she had had a shower and remarked about how soft the towel was, he had let her keep it; calling down to security so when she left and they searched her bags, they knew she was allowed to take it.

She flounced over to his table and stood by his side.

"Hello Mister Terry. How are you?"

Terry looked up briefly and half smiled. "Hi."

"You remember me?" He could only just hear her over the music.

"I do, yeh. How are you?"

"I have been missing you, but I know you have not been missing me. Do you remember my name?"

"Err yeh," he grinned. "Comfort."

She puckered her lips.

"I knew you were not missing me. Now you must buy Blessing a drink."

For the first time, Terry looked up at her properly. He did remember her. Her short hair and long earrings set off her round face quite well and there was a hint of a dimple in her chin. She was one of the more attractive girls to be found at Pat's.

She put a smooth, bare arm over his shoulder and let her weight fall against him.

He responded by putting his more solid limb around her waist.

"Can I have a Gordon's Spark, please?"

"Sure, I'll send it over. See you later, right?"

One of the waitresses slid past, carrying glasses.

"A Gordon's Spark for Blessing," Terry said.

". . .and one for my friend?" Blessing said, putting on a girlie voice.

The waitress looked at Terry. He nodded. Blessing skipped back to her table.

The three expats resumed their conversation as if nothing had happened.

The evening wore on. Blessing danced a couple of times, making sure Terry could see her through the undulating mass of bodies. He and his mates had several more beers and the once-animated conversation at their table became slurred and spasmodic. One of the other guys invited a girl to sit on his lap.

Terry eventually beckoned Blessing over to the table.

"Wanna dance, Comfort? Hahaha, Blessing."

She sensed she had hooked her man as she held out her hand for him to lead her onto the floor. Alternating between dancing close so she could rub against his groin and moving away so he could watch her, she made no effort to pull down her dress when it rode up over her thighs. She nestled up to him and on tiptoe whispered into his ear.

"Mister Terry, would you like me to come home with you?"

He swallowed and nodded simultaneously.

"Now? I will get my bag."

She had reeled Terry in, open mouthed like a catfish.

When she got back to his table, he was calling his driver.

"James, I am coming out."

He strode just a touch unsteadily towards the door and she followed.

The bouncers took no notice of him as they left but Eric, the door boss, caught her eye. She knew he would be looking for an extra dash the next time he saw her.

As the car drew up, several car parking touts clustered around Terry, who was just sober enough to let Blessing into the rear seat first and thrust a couple of notes out to keep the boys happy as he climbed in.

* * *

Back in his flat, Terry asked Blessing if she would like a beer and she followed him into the kitchen. While he looked for a bottle opener, she held the fridge door open and saw some leftover chicken on a plate.

"Mister Terry, can I have this chicken, please?"

She had already pulled a whole leg off the carcass and bit into it.

He carried two bottles of beer into the lounge and put on some music. She danced around, eating the chicken and then sucking the bones. He just sat in an armchair and watched her gliding about sucking contentedly until there was nothing left but hard bone pieces, which she dropped onto the coffee table.

Licking her fingers, one by one, slowly, Blessing slid easily onto his lap and took a long swig from his bottle. She looked directly into his face, her lips shiny with beer and chicken. Before he could react, she stuck out her tongue and jumped up laughing.

Terry could not take his eyes off her as she made one more pirouette before leaning forward to grab his hand and pull him towards the bedroom.

Three hours later, Terry awoke with a start. He was coated in a film of sweat. The room was dark and ominously quiet. No buzz from the air conditioner and no distant sound from the generator even though there was "no NEPA", as he had learnt to call the situation when the electricity company frequently delivered Lagos to darkness.

"Bollocks," he thought.

He knew as "the generator guy", that there was an expectation from other residents that he would go down and have a look but not at four o'clock on a Sunday morning or whatever it was. Fuck that!

He got up, pulled the curtain to one side, and slid open the balcony doors.

One of the block's few redeeming features was that it overlooked the stretch of water that came in from the sea and ran into a series of sluggish creeks towards the docks of Apapa and beyond that, as far as the Benin Republic eventually.

From up on the balcony, in the barest hint of light from the early dawn, it was just possible to see over the vegetation behind Tarkwa Bay and out towards the Atlantic. A light breeze was coming in, as it often did, and he let the slightly cooler air dry him off.

He looked inside to where Blessing was sleeping peacefully. She had thrown off the duvet that she had wrapped herself in, not being used to the chill of the AC, and the pale light fell on her smooth, dark buttocks. He felt a slight stirring but his head was throbbing so he stepped back into the still-dark room, grabbed a glass of water by the side of the bed, and took it back out to the balcony. The plastic of the chair felt cool at first but then his bare skin soon stuck to it. He was beyond caring.

The atmosphere was heavy and intense, the gloom penetrated only by distant clusters of light from container ships queuing along the coast before they could sail into the Apapa channel towards the port. They would eventually slide into the docks through the narrow stretch right in front of where he was sitting.

Terry was not naturally a thinker but through the dull ache of his impending hangover, a jumble of thoughts competed for his attention. He had mixed emotions. He did miss the children and felt a pang of regret as images of them fluttered into his inner vision but he knew his home life was a mess and he was happier when away. He had been in Nigeria for the best part of a year and had managed to get back for Christmas, which had been fine, having a bit of money to spend on Rachel and the kids. But he was secretly glad to be absent again.

Work was progressing satisfactorily enough, but he had to admit he was drinking too much. Patrick had refused to work for him after he drunkenly called him "fucking stupid" and Tunde had had to have a serious word with him when the next steward complained about being called a "fucking thief" after food disappeared from the fridge. Tunde had become a kind of mentor and explained that after the leftover food had sat in the fridge for two or three days, the steward had taken it for his neighbours' kids in the BQ but Terry hadn't given him a chance to explain. If another steward complained or quit, Terry would be on his own was Tunde's clear warning.

There had been issues with drivers too. He realised he was building a reputation in the office for being difficult: the way he complained about the state of the department's pick-ups and the shortage of tools was seen as overly aggressive.

Although his team respected his down-to-earth and "sleeves rolled up" approach, they all feared his mood swings.

When Tunde suggested a connection between his fits of temper and his hangovers, Terry had snapped at him, which he later regretted. He had learned to respect the older Nigerian and grown to like him and appreciate their conversations over a beer. It was the first genuine relationship he ever had with a person of a different colour and that gave him pause for thought. Which was not Terry's habitual reaction to anything.

He knew that his forebears, from Glasgow and then London, had been fighting drunks and he was no different. A family tendency. Unfortunately, his only Nigerian mates were hard-drinking, blue-collar expatriates who hung out to watch football and stayed on drinking, playing to his weakness. Not open to him were the more refined circles of the executive class, drinking South African wines and dining in the overpriced and ostentatious Lebanese-run restaurants in VI. His crowd might occasionally go for a curry but usually it was 'pie of the day' at Pat's or chicken and chips at Outsider Inn. He knew that for the sake of his liver, he had to find a different way. But how? He was dimly aware that during moments of lucidity in the self-recriminatory stage of his many hangovers, he had asked himself just that question. There was never any reply.

As his eyes peered out into seeming eternity beyond the bay, he felt that some sort of crisis was looming. In any case, a solution was beyond him in his current state.

He gingerly peeled himself off the chair and stood up, steadying himself against a wave of dizziness. He left the balcony door and curtains open and flopped back onto the bed next to Blessing, but she didn't stir.

When he woke up, the bright light drove a steel pin through his eyes and into his head. He rolled over and groaned. He could hear the splashing of the shower and Blessing singing to herself, eventually coming out wrapped in a towel. She smiled.

"Good morning, Mister Terry. How..."

He interrupted her, "Sorry, Blessing, I'm not feeling great," which was an understatement. "You have to leave. There's some money on the dressing table."

She looked disappointed, then pissed off, at being dismissed. She sucked her teeth loudly and deliberately.

She turned around and scooped up a pile of notes from the dressing table that Terry must have thrown down the night before. She counted it.

"All of it?" she asked with a sudden cheery smile.

"How much is there?"

"Twelve thousand."

He wasn't in the mood. "Oh God! I suppose."

This was substantially more than she expected so she started to dress quickly, so she'd be long gone before he changed his mind. Terry couldn't help watching, even though all he wanted to do was to go back to sleep. She slipped into her day clothes and stuffed her night outfit in her bag.

She pouted. "Mister Terry."

"No Blessing, you can't have another towel," he said. "Pass it over."

He delicately got up, wrapped the towel around himself and walked her towards the lounge and to the apartment door. Though she felt put out by being hurried, he had been generous, and he was not unkind. She turned in the doorway.

"Mister Terry, can I see you soon?"

"No. Err, I dunno. Maybe. I'll see you at Pat's."

He let her kiss him briefly and she turned towards the stairs. He had already shut the door before she got to the first step.

Chapter 4

Isioma

"I am Nigerian because a white man created Nigeria and gave me that identity. I am black because the white man constructed black to be as different as possible from his white. But I was Igbo before the white man came."

'Half of a Yellow Sun' by Chimamanda Ngozi Adichie

Isioma was excited to meet her cousin from the UK, from "the abroad" as her friends wistfully called it. She knew very little about him. Like many Nigerians, she had a large family on both sides, a ring of blood relatives so extensive that it was easier to refer to anyone from the same village as a cousin. This one was a real cousin though. Her mother had rung to say that her aunt who lived in London had been in touch to announce that her son had recently been sent to work in Lagos.

Isioma barely remembered being told that her father had an older sister who had been sent away to the UK when she was barely a teenager. Then again, though that generation spoke very little about what they went through during the period of the Biafran secession, she had noticed that Papa had grown much more willing as he got older.

Isioma had introduced herself by a text message to the number her mother sent her. It had taken a few months to sort things out but at last, Cousin Robert had agreed to meet her at The Yellow Chilli restaurant in Victoria Island.

It seemed her cousin lived in Ikeja and didn't know the island well, so she had chosen this place as a safe option. As it was close to Ajose Adeogun where she worked in a bank, it was very convenient.

Isioma arrived by keke marwa, the ubiquitous Lagos tricycle cab. She had "chartered" it to have some comfort, taking the entire back seat where three people would normally be crammed.

She assumed he had a company car, and probably had a driver as he worked in a multinational.

"He's becoming a full Nigerian though," she mused. African time. Robert was already twenty minutes late.

She sipped the Coke she had ordered while she waited and studied the menu. It was certainly more expensive than the local places where she would usually meet with her friends. But some of her colleagues had recommended it as a place to take someone who did not know Nigerian food too well. She guessed he didn't.

Yellow Chilli was a middle-class "island" restaurant as could be told by the various African prints and artefacts. There was little sign of the plastic tablecloths and chipped mugs that were more common in the places she frequented. It was not that she did not earn enough to afford such venues but her upbringing had taught her to be thrifty. The air conditioning made her shiver a little.

She didn't have to wait much longer as soon enough, she spotted Robert. She presumed it was him as the person clearly didn't know the place. She knew little about him other than his age, so she was pleased that he looked as if he would easily fit in with her friends, given one of her housemates had asked, "What if he's podgy and geeky?"

In those few moments, she had a chance to observe that he looked like he kept himself fit and was quite smart and clean-cut; his shirt and chinos still showing signs of being starched, a sign that he had a steward to do his washing.

He did not see her at first. Isioma stood up and waved, confident she was right.

When he noticed her, he smiled uncertainly.

"Isioma?"

"Robert."

They clumsily shook hands and then shuffled into an awkward hug. Both laughed.

She led him to the table she had been sitting at and Robert plonked himself onto the chair opposite her.

He wasn't sure what to expect as they had only exchanged a few texts. His cousin was probably a few years younger than he was and was dressed in office clothes. She was slim and of medium height in her sensible work shoes. Her open face was framed by a few loose braids that had escaped the band that tied most of them back, exposing small drop earrings that looked as if they were made from coral. She wore glasses that gave her a slightly serious look until she grinned. Her relaxed and confident smile was immediately attractive and put him at ease.

"This looks like a nice place," he said. "A couple of blokes at work said it was where they met on dates." Robert laughed awkwardly. "Not that this is a date, right?"

Isioma laughed. "Abi?"

"So, here you are, son of my father's sister. . .but what we call a full options 'tokunbo'!"

"Not you too!" he raised his hands in mock horror. "Do you know how many times I have heard that? Half the people in the office even call me 'Toks'."

"Is that not better than 'oyibo'?"

"To be honest, I get that sometimes. It is a bit hurtful."

She was a little surprised to hear him admit it as only a few Nigerian men would be so readily open. She liked that about him already. There was a pause in which she gave him a sympathetic smile and then picked up her menu.

"So, what do you know about Nigerian food? Does Auntie Udo cook it at home?"

"Well, Dad's not a massive fan. So, not very often. Also, we tend to use her anglicised name, Peace."

"Oh."

"It's okay."

"So, your father is not Nigerian? Is he. . .?"

"Oyibo? No, he's from the Caribbean. Barbados to be precise. Their food is quite different. He likes pepper but is not keen on the flavour of palm oil. Also, I think Mum was young when she was brought to England, so I guess she hadn't learned that much cooking."

"Hmm."

"They only ever came back once, not long after they married. Dad didn't like it much. So we only ever went back to Holetown, where he comes from, for holidays. So, neither my sister nor I ever came to Nigeria."

Isioma was shocked. "That's terrible."

Robert shrugged. "It's just the way it was, I guess. Oh, and the beaches in Barbados are amazing too."

"But you have family here." She frowned and looked at him. "How long have you been here?"

"Nearly a year."

Now she looked at him, sucked on her teeth and let out a long "mtttsssshew" before holding up the menu and studiously ignoring him for a few minutes.

Robert got the message and allowed the silence to pass while he too considered the menu.

He looked up and put on a local accent: "Isioma, no vex oh, I beg."

There was a slight snort behind the menu so he followed up with: "Can you choose for me, please?"

A waiter, as if he'd heard them, promptly arrived.

Robert said, "Guinness for me, please."

"Large or small?"

"Small. My friend here will order food for both of us."

Isioma's voice came from behind the menu, "Cousin."

Looking up at the waiter, she said, "Two goat meat pepper soup," adding pointedly, "plus plenty of pepper."

Robert looked askance.

Isioma added, "One egusi with shaki and one okro with assorted meat."

She was not going to let him off easily.

When the waiter went off with the order, she looked at Robert with just the hint of a tease in her eye, and said, "At least you didn't order dry white wine."

Twenty minutes later, the sweat was pouring off his forehead and he was already halfway through another Guinness. He could just about handle the pepper and he was used to goat meat. The shaki was another matter. He hadn't realised until he tried to chew the grey leather that was tripe. He also struggled with chewing some of the assorted meats in the okro soup.

"Is this what you call 'draw'?" he asked.

When she nodded, he explained that Caribbean cooking used okra but not in the same way.

She smiled at his clumsiness in moulding the pounded yam to collect his soup but when she noticed one of the waiters staring at him, she could not help but burst out laughing.

"Yeh, yeh," he said, genuinely disgruntled. "I know, I eat like an oyibo!"

"Plenty of White guys come here but I am sure none of them will eat swallow so, Coz, you are trying. The thing is, you look like one of us but eat like one of them!"

By the time they finished the meal, he was on his third Guinness. The sensory heat had dissipated, and he was enjoying the after-pepper sting and the strong flavours that remained in his mouth.

Isioma had drunk a small stout and they were relaxed and enjoying each other's company. She was explaining some of their family background, including the importance of Ngwo, their village. It was now more or less a suburb of Enugu. To many of their generation, it was just somewhere you returned to for family events. For her, it was a home to fall back to. She explained that it had a definable sense of history: how several of the men from the village, including their grandfather, had been killed in the civil war and how survivors made it back to their villages to start again.

"It matters to me Robert, that your mother is my Auntie Udo, and that ties us together as family," she said, shaking her head. "So I just cannot believe she didn't tell you more of this, even if I barely know her!"

"Well. . ." Robert started.

"Or was it you? And maybe your sister as well? Were you not interested in your own family, your history?"

He was shamefaced but he was getting defensive, almost angry. Where was all this coming from?

"You see Isioma, in my school, most of the other kids were White and all the Black ones were born in Britain, just like me. I have always seen myself as British. Of course, I did look up to Black people. But they were mostly, like, footballers, that played for England, or maybe musicians like Omar or Jazzie B."

She shook her head, not understanding.

"At school, I was taught mostly about English history, starting with the Battle of Hastings. Have you heard of it? Henry

33

the Eighth? Empire, and all that. We all had the same education, the same basis for being British. Mum told me Nigerian stuff when I was little, but I guess it didn't mean much to me and never seemed important. She never had any photos and I could never picture it in my head. It wasn't a shared experience with my mates or something they would understand."

"But Robert, of course Auntie Udo told you! Not maybe. You just were not paying attention." There was more than a hint of exasperation in her voice. "It would have meant so much to her but, obviously, you did not understand how much!"

"What makes you say that? How do you know it was that important?"

She was stunned into silence, then quietly, "Your names!"

It was Robert's turn to go quiet. "Robert Agu Afamefuna?"

"Yes. You know what they mean, abi?"

"Well, Agu was my great-grandfather and Afamefuna means something about my name living on."

"Oh, Robert! Agu Ede, our shared great-grandfather is like the patriarch of our family, one we still think of with respect. Your mother wanted to remember him in you, her son!"

* * *

Robert's mouth and ears were still ringing when he got back to the compound from dropping off Isioma. She lived in a shared apartment in a rundown house off Awolowo Road towards Obalende, in the area generally referred to as southwest Ikoyi to differentiate it from the posher Ikoyi neighbourhoods around Bourdillon and Glover roads. He had sat staring out of the window all through the drive to Ikeja. He had noticed the driver stealing glances at him through the rearview over the thirty-minute drive home.

So far in his time in Nigeria, he had been living in a kind of bubble, residing and hanging out with other Guinness expats. In the last few years, there had been several non-White expatriate managers who came in for two- or three-year stints and then left. His Nigerian colleagues treated him as just another one. There was no animosity. On the contrary, the general response was one of detached friendliness. He had been out for a drink with some, on trade visits for example, but there had been little curiosity about his background.

Yet, as far as Isioma was concerned, his coming to Nigeria was inevitable and she was shocked at how blasé he was about that. He had not been able to hide his ambivalence subtly enough and for this, she had given him an earful. It had been as hard to reconcile her certainty as it had been to calm her down after finding out that he really did not care so much about Nigerian history and his Nigerian heritage. She had been incredulous.

His oldest friend and football buddy, Chris, had summed it best several months earlier when Robert informed him of the promotion.

"You are kidding, right? I mean, you never even wanted to go to Nigeria."

They had been walking along Chiswick High Road after football training, having stopped for a couple of pints and takeaway from the local fish and chip shop.

"What are you going to do out there?"

"Head of Reporting and Analysis."

"Er, congratulations?" said Chris, then, tellingly, "Have you told your mum?"

Sitting in his air conditioned apartment with Lynden David Hall pouring from the Bose speaker he had brought out, Robert smiled as he remembered his parents' reaction. His father, ever pragmatic, was delighted at the fact of the promotion itself—a move up the corporate ladder for his son—the *where* was less important. But his mother's excitement was matched only by Isioma's certainty that such excitement was called for. Peace Railsford's major peeve and complaint had always been how "they", meaning him and his sister Cindy, had "forgotten their roots!"

She had called her brother Vitus, Isioma's father, but Robert had made sure he was not home when she did. He and Cindy had always turned their noses up at any attempt to persuade them to eat Nigerian food and Robert continued to spurn her redoubled efforts. Then finally, when she had tried to give him lessons on what she saw as traditional Nigerian behaviour and he had been wilfully less than enthusiastic, she was forced to shake her head and let him be.

Later on, Robert told Cindy: "Mum is already making plans for me to visit the village and marry a nice Nigerian girl. I have had to disabuse her. This is strictly a three-year outing to make some money and then come home. No dilly-dallying out in the bush."

Yet now, here he was in the afterglow of his cousin's cultural effervescence doing what he had never done before: thinking of the tenuous links that connected his family's past to the present and somehow, his own future.

When he went home for Christmas, his mum had seemed disappointed that he hadn't travelled out of Lagos or contacted her family. Thinking about it now, he realised her previous resignation at his lack of interest had been replaced with a forlorn hope that his posting would trigger his curiosity. It dawned on him that he should have met up with Isioma earlier than he had done, considering how his mother must have felt. He had genuinely enjoyed himself and his head was still spinning from all she had told him.

* * *

Over the next few weeks, Robert and Isioma spent more and more time together and became close. While curious, he had remained hesitant about getting into family relationships that he had no intention of following up on, but her openness and enthusiasm had been infectious. He had never met anyone so close to their family, so connected to their heritage. Not only was he intrigued by this, he grew a little embarrassed by his indifference to his family's and his mother's story.

He got to meet Isioma's flatmates and went out with some of her friends and became aware that the expat lifestyle, as superficially attractive as regular tennis and barbeques by the swimming pool could be, was ultimately limited. As much as he had become mates with several of the others who lived in the Shonibare compound, and they did all have a laugh, he began to enjoy the company of Nigerians more. He enjoyed hearing about Isioma's life and how it differed from his: growing up in an extended family close to her kin, having to take responsibility for her younger siblings, fighting to be given the same education as her brothers and finally, the privations required by her family to put her through university at Nsukka.

With an intensity of study that he could never have accomplished, she had achieved a first-class degree in accounting and got into Zenith Bank's graduate scheme. While accountancy wasn't what she would have chosen to study, it was a secure profession and her family was delighted. The pay was adequate for her to send money home to her mother every month and to share a simple apartment, complete with a kitchen and a cramped bathroom, with two colleagues from her bank branch. This avoided the relentless commute from the mainland that so many staff suffered trying to get to work. When Robert complained about some of his staff falling asleep at their desks, she snapped at him and said he should be a little more sympathetic and appreciative of his lot.

He introduced her to the concept of brunch so on Saturdays, he would pick her up in the late morning and after eating somewhere in VI, they would hang out. Robert liked the vibe at the Jazzhole record and bookshop on Awolowo Road particularly. He was soon widening his musical horizon from British neo-soul and American hip-hop and the foray led him to jazz and African music.

Jazzhole was like a throwback: walls lined with dusty CDs and tatty books that all looked like they had been sitting there for years. There were piles of old vinyl records and you could still ask for one to be played. There was a coffee shop at the back. Not the best coffee, Robert thought, but it added to the easy-going feel of the place.

There were also a couple of art galleries nearby. Signature was more formal, but Quintessence had a mix of art and African-style clothes and bags that Isioma liked to browse. She loved the vibrant colours of aso-oke, Okene, and Ghanaian kente cloths. She persuaded Robert to buy himself a traditional-style shirt. A Swedish woman, Aino Oni-Okpako, and her Nigerian husband had set up Quintessence in the mid-70s and when he died, she had stayed on, becoming a pillar of the arts establishment in the city. It was much beloved by expatriate wives, particularly Americans.

Often, he would stay out with them well into the evening, and they would join some of her friends for a drink or go for a meal.

Isioma was not one for clubbing and, in any case, Lagos nightlife didn't start swinging until one o'clock in the morning. In addition, on Sunday mornings, Isioma and one of her flatmates would be up early to attend Mass. There was the impressive Catholic Church of the Assumption by Falomo Roundabout, nearer where they lived, but both had joined St Charles Borromeo across the creek, inside the 1004 Apartment Complex because it was smaller and felt more welcoming. This was one tradition Robert refused to engage in despite Isioma's requests. Anyway, his driver usually had Sundays off, and he still enjoyed his lazy day by the pool. Occasionally he invited Isioma if there was a barbeque, but he realised she didn't feel entirely comfortable in his set.

Transportation was also a problem. He was gradually learning to brave Lagos traffic and Sunday was the best time to do it so occasionally he would drive to pick her up himself after church and then pay for a taxi to take her home.

One effect of the time spent with his cousin and her friends was it seemed to make a major difference in his relationship with his work colleagues. Now, his reply to their inevitable Monday enquiry: "How was your weekend?" was different, more qualitative. He would be excited to describe the Nigerian dishes he had eaten or places he had been with Isioma and her friends. This pleased the Nigerians particularly and they took more of an interest in him. *Have you tried this dish or that restaurant? How do you like our food?* which would be followed by questions about his family.

He could also relate better to some of their conversations. Their lives began to have more context and were less alien to his experience. However, the more he learned, the less he seemed to know. When his workmates started to be curious about his family it became embarrassing how little he could tell them. Nevertheless, his ventures across the city made an appreciable difference in the dynamics of his relationships in the office.

Chapter 5

Agu

"Si kele onye nti chiri; enu anughi, ala anu."
(Salute the deaf; if the heavens don't hear it,
the earth will.)
Igbo proverb

Agu Ede was born into a strong compound in a clan of the Igbo people who called themselves Ngwo-Nwa-Ngwu-Ako—that is, Ngwo, son of Ngwu-Ako. The Ngwo lived in clusters of family compounds amongst the hills around a place they called Ngwu-Enugwu. The men of the clan were mostly hunters while the women farmed yams and other crops near their homesteads. Amongst themselves, the Ngwo believed in ime oyi—doing good to others.

Agu Ede's childhood was a content one spent mostly running chores for his mother. Other times, he could be found playing with the other village boys, practising skills they believed would make them successful. But little Agu Ede also gained a reputation for being withdrawn. He could sometimes be contemplative and take to exploring the hills around their home alone, looking closely at the ground in wonderment at the industry of termites, or trailing a kite sailing leisurely against the canvas of a blue sky.

By fate of geography, the Ngwo settlements were on the very hills that contained massive coal deposits, first discovered at the Udi Ridge in 1909. By 1914, Lord Lugard had amalgamated various colonial territories into a new country—Nigeria—just as the first coal shipment was ready to be transported to support Britain's Great War against the Germans. Rail tracks were quickly built to reach the ever-hungry docks at Port Harcourt. The Ngwo were barely aware that there was a world war going on. Even when the war ended, the appetite for coal did not abate as Europe needed to fuel bigger and bigger machines. Bringing up more of it steadily destroyed the countryside and the Ngwo way of life.

In the period before European priests came, the Igbo had their religion standing on three pillars: the all-powerful divinity Chukwu, the realm of spirits, and the ancestors.

Agu's father and grandfather were respected members of the community. Many years later, he would remember with pride, being allowed to attend village meetings as a young boy and hearing his father speak to nods of approval from their kinsmen. Words were important amongst the Igbo and those who could speak well, with logic and style, were accorded respect.

Inside the Ede compound, Agu's father had two wives who laboured hard so that their stacks of yams never seemed to diminish. When his grandfather died in a hunting accident, his grandmother moved in with them. Ekwutosi seemed old and wise to the young Agu and he was drawn to her. She had been a beauty in her younger days, with skin the colour of light terracotta. She always carried a curved walking stick with a fearsome agbogho mmuo—a maiden spirit—carved into the handle. Ekwutosi sometimes threatened to whack the naughtier children with it but she never did. As often as he could, the young Agu would sit by her side as she grated the cassava for the family's abacha meal, listening to her tales of spirits and masquerades, of their ancestors, and life before the onye ocha.

Unlike most of the compound, she had not been brought up within greater Ngwo but was from further away. Her family were from Arochukwu, the people of the Ibini Ukpabi, a fearful juju shrine, who had a history of resisting attempts to bring Christianity to replace their customary spiritualism. Much later, the role of the Arochukwu as major factors in the slave trade, and their inevitable economic conflict with a Britain determined on more efficient exploitation of the same Africans, would come to light.

"Nothing good will come from the White man and his church," she would say.

The family were traditionalists, mostly siding with Ekwutosi, though there were those in the village already influenced by the new ways. It was clear to everyone that the world was changing

40

beneath their feet, that the onye ocha would be there for a long time, and that there was merit in knowing their habits.

Things came to a head when the Catholics, who had already established a church at Okwojo-Ngwo, opened the St Mary's Primary School. There was a lively and protracted debate in the family before Agu and some of his brothers were allowed to enrol. Their grandmother was of course against it, and came around only when it was clear that this was the consensus. An opinion, however deeply felt, could not override the decision of the clan.

Yet in her heart, Ekwutosi knew that the onye ocha would take and take and take and leave only broken earth in their wake. She worried for her grandsons and could often be found talking about it to the ancestors at the family shrine where she still worshipped the old gods.

At St Mary's, Agu proved himself an intelligent student. He had the mind of a sponge and an inborn desire to expand and feed it. The school only taught up to Standard Six and Agu's family neither had the wherewithal nor the inclination to send him to some distant secondary school. In any case, he was then old enough, at thirteen, to go hunting with the men. He had come of age as far as the norms of Ngwo were concerned.

Even so, the Irish priest who ran the school had a soft spot for Agu and one day a week, his father allowed him to go in and help with the younger pupils. In return, Father Brendan loaned him books and taught him how to use European woodworking tools, for the priest had been a carpenter, and how to ride a bicycle.

In the 1930s, it made for an unusual sight for a young man to be seen sitting and reading in Ngwo. Agu Ede was the forerunner; the one who started it all.

Although the admiration of the community for the obscure knowledge he possessed pleased his mother, others agreed with his resolute grandmother: bringing the words of the White man inside the community boded nothing but ill.

* * *

As Agu grew older, even more coal was discovered in the nearby Iva Valley and gradually the names of the Ngwo villages started to disappear into that of a spreading city—Enugu. Parallel to his young

41

life, Enugu had grown from the idyllic villages of the Ngwo people to become the region's major city as early as 1938.

As the coal mines over at Udi and closer to them in the Iva Valley grew, so did the lives of the local Ngwo people change. The authorities started putting pressure on the elders to encourage more menfolk to work in the mines. The matter was debated heatedly but no agreement was reached. It was left to every compound to make their own choice while an ever-growing number of strangers from farther afield came into the area and more and more pristine bush was cut down. The mines themselves cut into the hills where the Ngwo had hunted for centuries and dirtied the water the communities drank from.

There was an increase in the number of Europeans as well, either working for the mining companies or trading and supplying goods to them. They built their settlement by the new train station which quickly turned into a "Whites only" zone at the heart of what would become Enugu's Government Residential Area. In his youth, Father Brendan, or the occasional priest, were the only White men Agu had ever seen. Now, looking down from the hills above the mines as a young man, he could see dozens of them, reminding him of the termites he studied as a child.

Agu tried to have as little to do with these assorted new Europeans but their influence was hard to escape. He often found himself being asked to interpret letters or documents from the mining officials to members of the community. Inevitably, he would be called to attend meetings with the White men to translate or to explain something to the people, often helping to resolve the inevitable disputes. Occasionally, someone would bring a newspaper to the village, Agu would read it and many would gather round to listen to the news.

While he and his family did their best to continue their traditional ways of living, it became a struggle. The hunters were already being forced to go deeper into the receding forest for scarcer game. Modernity, like the horn blast of the trains that delivered it, had come to the Ngwo and they could not escape it. The indigenous people tried to strike a balance, but it was constantly being adjusted as more ground, metaphorically and literally, was lost. It was ultimately a failing effort at each point, each loss heralded by growing resentment.

When Nnamdi Azikiwe's West Africa Pilot newspaper began to openly question the right of one country to rule another, Agu became aware of the growing nationalist movement. The same papers also brought news that a new conflict in Europe was spreading across a world that, a few years ago, Agu had not even known existed. By 1942, when Zik pronounced how the evil racial policies of Nazism meant that all Nigerians should rally around the Union Jack, Agu volunteered to join the army. He was almost 30 years old.

When Agu joined, his papers said he was a member of The Royal West African Frontier Force but by the time he completed training, he was given a new paybook that stated that he was in the 81st (West Africa) Division of the British Army.

In early 1943, as a member of the 6th Field Company West African Engineers, his brigade was sent to India and then to Burma to support the allies' campaign against the Japanese. Their task was primarily to be pack-carrying porters in the inhospitable terrain of the Burmese jungle but it was expected they would also have to fight.

Many of the volunteers were still teenagers so he was older than most and was naturally respected by his colleagues. This, along with his ability to quickly learn the skills of a mechanic, meant that by the time his unit had completed what was ironically called "jungle training" in India, Agu had been promoted to corporal. For the first time, Agu met and befriended Nigerians from all over the country; other Igbos whose dialects were different from his own, fierce Tivs from the middle of the country, proud men of the old Bini kingdom, and cheerful Yorubas from the west. Many of the brigade's troops were from the Hausa-speaking parts of Nigeria; a martial people, as the British liked to call them. It went without saying that all the officers and senior non-commissioned officers were European.

In Burma, Agu and his colleagues saw immediate action in the second Arakan campaign, operating in the Kaladan valley on the flank of the Indian XV Corps. In late March 1944, Japanese reinforcements outflanked the division and forced it to retreat over a steep range of hills and out of the valley. This was deep bush warfare and the Nigerian troops, often forced to trek in appalling conditions with little food or clean water, under continuous harassment from the enemy, soon gained the respect of their British and Indian colleagues.

Over the next few months, they regrouped and re-tooled and in August, the division re-entered the Kaladan, advancing down the valley once again, as the Japanese gradually retreated, but with countless ambushes and counterattacks, always fighting for every yard.

The advance only reached deep into Burma after attritional, often hand-to-hand, warfare. This experience was a revelation to Agu and many of the others, not just from Nigeria but also from Sierra Leone, Gambia and the Gold Coast as Ghana was then known. This theatre of war saw some of the most hostile and difficult conditions anywhere. The bush was deeper and less penetrable than anything the Indian and West African troops had ever come across. Carrying loads of heavy equipment up steep mountain slopes and down gullies that flooded during the monsoons, they had to hack their way through thick bamboo foliage with cutlasses. Plagued by leeches, diarrhoea, foot rot and disease, including malaria, the African troops coped better than their European officers both physically and mentally.

During short breaks between treks, perhaps while awaiting air supply from RAF Dakotas, British, Indians and Africans would huddle together against the chill of monsoon nights, sharing the same rations. Engineers, porters, and riflemen were all pressed into the same trenches or bivouacs. Agu's platoon sergeant was an affable Yorkshireman who would try to explain the rules of cricket to befuddled soldiers. The "samanja", as the Hausa troops called him, would share his cigarettes or any chocolate he had but he, like many White faces, was easily picked out by Japanese snipers. The last sight Agu had of his affable friend was being carried back to a temporary field hospital with part of his face missing.

* * *

Agu and his colleagues had now seen the White man at close quarters. They had seen he was capable of courage and acts of compassion, yet also capable of fear and even cowardice. Hunkered down together in slit trenches to hide from Japanese bullets, he saw for himself that they bled and felt pain just as he did. They shared

44

the same emotions, laughing for joy at survival and crying the same salt tears for lost comrades. In the fearsome intensity of battle and the tortuous hours of trudging through the monsoon-drenched jungle, mutual respect had been forged and to some extent, the barriers between the African and European soldiers had been lowered.

On achieving its objectives of supporting the taking of the strategically important port of Akyab in January, the division was withdrawn to India in April 1945 and following the surrender of the axis powers, it was returned to West Africa and disbanded on the 21st of August that year.

Eventually, Agu was able to return to Ngwo.

He had endured almost unbelievable hardships during the war. He was not naïve enough to believe life would be different for Black Africans but he expected a modicum of recognition and respect for his contribution towards the war effort. He was to be sadly disappointed. The Burmese exposure convinced Agu that the White men were not special spirit people, nor had they any right to be his colonial masters. As the train brought the demobbed men back to an Enugu they hardly recognised, there seemed to be more onye ocha than ever.

The mines had expanded in the intervening years. There had been visible deforestation to accommodate sprawling shanty towns. It was clear that his dreams while fitfully sleeping on Burma's sodden forest floor, of returning to a simple, traditional life, would never materialise.

There was rejoicing at his reappearance in the village but sadness for the families of those who would never return. One of Agu's cousins had been killed in the conflict and was buried overseas. His wife and children moved into the compound. He had never seen the family's yam stacks so low, or the new yams so small. While Agu had been away, Ekwutosi, had died still warning that the White man's ways would bring nothing but trouble and some believed she had already been proved right.

On his return, Agu, still mourning the loss of his beloved grandmother, had little choice but to accept the colliery company's offer to use his army skills. In 1946, he became a machinist at the Iva Valley mine.

Chapter 6

Down and Dirty

"Life in the ghetto isn't easy
All the youth inna the ghetto they were always busy
If you live in the ghetto you can never be lazy
So the people abeg una hear me again

In the ghetto, sing it o
In the ghetto, tell dem o
In the ghetto oo life isn't easy for we
una hear me

In the ghetto wer me live heyy
And in the ghetto wer me born ooh
Mama tell us heyy to be humble ooh
Papa teach us heyy how to struggle ooh
Every ghetto you know heyy how to hustle ooh
If you come to the ghetto no fumble
If you fumble yes you get trouble
And when you get it you get it double
Hustling and struggling it a run in the ghetto."

'Ghetto Soldier' by Daddy Showkey

From time-to-time, Terry would meet Tunde at a small place called the Havana Bar on Ribadu Road, a side street off Awolowo Road. It was neither particularly smart nor was it close to being a bush bar. It was somewhere in the middle: a comfortable "local" for everyone, whether expats or Nigerians, who lived or worked nearby. It was one of those places—a long narrow bar running down into a small seating area, though it had a separate dining room in the front—that was genuinely mixed.

It served decent European food "with chips" while its local "swallow" was also considered authentic.

On entry, the corner of the bar adjacent to the entrance invariably had a particular group of Brits either perched on high bar stools or standing leaning against the bar itself. Nigerian regulars tended to gather at the farther end. Though the two groups generally kept to themselves, there was always a fair bit of good-natured banter between them and Tunde was utterly comfortable at either end.

Most of these were not of the three-year posting variety expats but contemporary West Coasters. Many had come out to Nigeria on regular posting and just stayed back. Some flitted from job to job while others set up their private businesses ranging from marketing consultancies to import companies, as well as architecture and surveyor practices, all with varying degrees of success. Several had been in Lagos for over twenty years, even thirty or more, and had Nigerian families. They all liked to drink.

Tunde too was not averse to a little drink. While he was a full director in GTW, he had set up his own business on the side like many Nigerians did and had a small private office around the corner. Over the years, he had built up an impressive list of contacts that included many of these localised expatriates and plenty of business was conducted in bars over drinks.

Terry arrived first, acknowledging the regulars with a nod before finding himself a table at the back. After a few minutes, Tunde came in.

"Good evening gentlemen! Are we all well?"

"Uncle Tunde," greeted one of the bar-proppers. "Drink?"

Tunde looked at the bar. It was a standing joke wherever he went that he could never make his mind up, and he never failed to enact this piece of drama.

"What's everyone having?"

There were three or four of them gathered around him and they all waved their tipples at him. "Our usuals," someone said.

"I think I will have . . ." he paused.

There were mock frozen expressions on the expats' faces as they waited. The waitress behind the bar looked at him expectantly. "A Jack and coke, please."

47

She turned to pour the drink when a different voice called, "Don't forget. . . 'with plenty of ice'."

There was laughter. Tunde was popular. Not just because of his easy charm but because he was someone many of these guys had turned to in times of need for advice and help. Over the years, his being a natural networker had earned him a wide circle of friends. He had links into the police and military and had been able to use these to do people favours when they needed them. Nigeria was, and still is, all about who you knew. Tunde knew people. He wore all this easily and didn't make a fuss about it; he acted without shakara.

He engaged in a few minutes of bar-room banter and cheerfully caught some local gossip until his drink was brought. Only then did he look towards Terry, sitting at a table.

"Actually chaps, I came here to meet someone."

"Invite him over to join us!"

Tunde explained they had a little business to discuss but he would bring him over to be introduced. He beckoned to Terry: introductions were made, cards swapped, and hands shook. Several recognised Terry from various places already. Generator guy was a popular occupation in a country where you could not rely on mains electricity.

"Those are good people for you to get to know, Terry," Tunde said when they got back to the table, having barely touched his drink. "The wider your network the better, both in a business sense and in terms of security as well. You never know when you might need a hand in this place and those blokes have all been 'round the block."

Terry nodded. He had already done a couple of one-off favours for friends of Tunde but was not quite clear what the arrangements were.

"Checking or servicing someone's generator for them could make you a friend who will help you out or bring some business your way," Tunde added, winking, "Talking of business. . ."

Over the years, his responsibilities in GTW covered a wide range of functions. Tunde soon came to see it as an opportunity and had set up a company a few years earlier. Apart from some opportunistic importing, a little trading, and a dabble into property, he regularly brought in generating sets for people. This

48

was at odds with his role with GTW but as he confirmed, the company was not in great shape and he needed to build a little pension pot of his own. There was an opportunity for Terry to do some earning on the side by managing the installation of the gen sets Tunde brought in privately.

Terry was delighted to earn a few extra dollars or even naira. Tunde had certainly looked after him in GTW and provided what could be called fatherly advice. And he had long since overcome his initial discomfort with Black people who were in a position of authority. The proposition was a no-brainer as far as he was concerned. They sealed their arrangement with a call for another round of drinks.

"So," asked Tunde, "how long is it since we shared that Johnnie Walker on your first night?"

"Well over a year now," said Terry. "I should thank you for all the support you have given me Tunde."

Tunde smiled appreciatively. "I was a bit worried when we had that spell of complaints. You seem to have established yourself better now. I hear your team genuinely respects you. They love the fact that you get stuck in, properly greased up to your elbows! Fighting for them to have better tools has made a difference, especially since you've been taking them out for the occasional beer and peppersoup."

Terry was shocked. "Jesus, Tunde! How did you know that?"

Tunde just smiled. "I have my ways. Anyway, where did you learn those tricks?"

"When I was in the Royal Engineers, I was a corporal," he wavered. "I was a sergeant for a couple of years actually, but I lost a stripe for D and D."

"Drunk and disorderly?"

"Yeh." Terry looked down for a moment. "But I was a team leader. If you wanted the guys to get behind you, that's what you had to do. I just found doing the same thing here, treating them just like a bunch of squaddies, works a treat. They take the piss at my red face when I eat that bloody soup but when you get to know them, they're all good lads."

"Well, it seems to work."

"Mind you, they'll still thief anything that isn't bolted down. I've stopped giving out work boots. They just disappear. I've started fining them two hundred naira if they turn up in flip-flops."

Tunde chuckled at the odd Nigerianism—*thief*— but he could see Terry was getting the hang of it, though he still had to explain that those work boots would be saved up to be worn as Sunday best in church.

"Outside of work, apart from watching football at Pat's Bar, what have you been doing with yourself?"

"Oh, you know. Not much really."

Terry was still not one for opening up but in the last few weeks, he had been thinking about the drinking routine he had fallen into.

"But I don't know. It's hard, isn't it?" he continued. "All the blokes I have met are like me, ex-army or technical working blokes. What do we do except go down to the pub? The only other Brits in GTW are the MD and Michael in accounts but he's a bit of a wanker, you know. Looks down on me like he has shit under his nose. Anyway, he's married. What else is there to do?"

"Well, you have a club membership as part of your package. If you top it up, you could join Ikoyi Club. You know, golf and tennis and that kind of thing."

"Can you see me there? In whites?"

Tunde shrugged and then nodded towards the far end of the bar. "Those guys over there. They would be good to spend some time with. Yes, they like a drink but they go to different places, not just Pat's Bar. They mostly have families, and you could meet more people through them. Because Terry, the thing that really makes a difference is escaping the trap of only going to places full of expats. Try to get to know more Nigerians better. Some of the managers at work or. . ." he laughed, ". . .you won't like this, but even joining a church."

Terry saw the joke. "Fucking hell, Tunde! Now you're pushing it."

As they laughed, they realised someone had approached their table.

"Sorry to disturb you. It is Terry, isn't it?"

Terry jumped up. "Fucking hell! It's Robert! Rob, how you doing?"

He turned to Tunde. "Remember when I arrived there was a bit of a logistics cock up and Francis put me and someone else in the same car and we dropped him in Maryland? Well, this is him."

"Come and join us," Terry said, pulling out a chair.

Robert shook hands with Tunde, took the proffered chair and sat down.

"I can't stay long as I'm meeting someone. Saw you and thought to say hello."

Terry was genuinely pleased to see him.

"All good mate. And how's it going with you? Are you a Nigerian yet?"

Robert was taken aback for a second and then laughed. "You are crazy, you know that? But you know what? That's a very good question."

Tunde looked a bit confused, and Robert had to explain.

They shared a few of their experiences as the older man listened with interest and they exchanged numbers. Just then, Robert's phone beeped.

He stood up. "Sorry guys, that's my cousin. She lives round the corner on Keffi Street and she's ready for me to pick her up."

As leave-taking handshakes were exchanged, Robert paused and added, almost as an afterthought, "You know what? If you really fancy doing something different, I am going on a trade visit tomorrow. Visiting local bars to check on sales and stuff. Somewhere on the mainland. Your office is in Oregun, right? It's not far from us so I will text you with the details."

After Robert had gone, Tunde said, "Well, I would take up the offer if I were you. Sounds like what we were talking about; a chance to do something different. He seems like a decent bloke too."

* * *

Twenty-four hours after the Havana conversation, Terry's GTW pick-up rolled to a stop at the Guinness office car park on Oba Akran Avenue in Ikeja. Robert was already waiting with two salesmen in their branded cars. After introducing the salesmen—

51

Ade and Martins—he handed Terry a Guinness branded polo shirt with a grin.

"It took the guys a while to find extra-extra-large!"

Robert suggested Terry's driver follow them and they got into one of the cars.

As they drove through traffic, he explained the evening's strategy.

The Guinness CEO was keen on office-based managers accompanying the sales team on visits to what they termed "trade", as a means of keeping them close to the core business. Robert had taken to doing this every few weeks. It was a change from being stuck at his accountant's desk and helped him understand the sharp end of the business. Above all, he found it to be a window into the Lagos he would not otherwise see.

This evening, they were due to visit some bars in Apapa. On the way there, they were to call on a place in Ajegunle where a proprietor had made a product quality complaint.

Like many ghettos, Ajegunle started off as a pure slum and the worst areas were still like that: narrow streets which flooded regularly, smelling of sewage and the human detritus that piled up on corners within a few feet of stalls selling roasted corn or fried akara. There was always a face peering out of a kerosene-lamp-lit shop, from a broken-mirrored barber shop, or a pot-stirring bukka owner.

Countless children stared from behind a mother's skirt or on an older sibling's lap, at any strangers driving nervously through their area. Certainly, the ghetto was never still. There was constant, 24/7 commercial activity of every conceivable kind, legitimate or not, and a plethora of bars from the humblest couple of boxes to the more aspirational and sophisticated. How many people lived there? No one knew for sure. Five hundred thousand, six, three-quarters of a million? Squeezed into a place not much bigger than Hyde Park. Most lived in self-built breeze block, single-storey, two-room buildings with rusty cast-iron roofs. Others lived in hovel-like shacks and lean-tos or even slept under any shelter they could find. Yet beside these modest shacks were two or three-storey houses, often ostentatious and shouting 'look at me, I made it!', with tough-looking security guards and polished Mercedes' squeezed behind huge wrought iron gates.

Ajegunle, or AJ City, meant many things to those who whispered its name. So much depended on whether you were an ajebota or an ajepako. As an ajebota, someone who "ate butter", in other words born in luxury and living on the island, the name Ajegunle was a byword for criminality. To be an ajepako, pako meaning "wood", was therefore to be a hustler or street person. Ajegunle was somewhere you made some bread or at least learned the tricks of the trade: a bolt hole for the dispossessed, the desperate, and those seeking to avoid the eyes and hands of the law. The name, Ajegunle, loosely translated means "where riches dwell". It was a place where stolen goods were to be found or where you learned to how create money from nothing.

Local heroes who had grown out of Ajegunle included a legion of footballers, musicians, and very many pastors. The dreadlocked crooner, Daddy Showkey, was the Prince of Ajegunle. A product of the ghetto who made his living by singing songs of the ghetto in the words of the ghetto and who still lived there.

It was still just light as the two branded vehicles, with the GTW pick-up truck in tow, came to and parked near a large bar on one of the better-paved streets.

The salesmen suggested Terry and Robert sit at a table outside while they went in to talk with the bar owner. Ajegunle was always a hive of activity and though they were only actually on the fringes, it was fascinating for the visitors to watch everyday life unfold in this most remarkable of cities within a city. It was all very relaxed until what appeared to be a minor traffic incident occurred.

An okada was parked outside the bar, some twenty feet from where the guys were seated. A few moments later, a smart four-wheel drive pulled up to park and clipped the handlebar of the motorbike which then toppled over. Someone, obviously the owner, walked out of the bar and remonstrated with the driver who, obviously feeling himself above a mere okada rider, slapped him hard across the face.

Suddenly two MOPOLs ran out from the beer parlour and smashed the driver with the butts of their weapons. It all happened in a blur of action within which both Terry and Robert were suspended in shock until the reality of what had happened hit them like a bucket of cold water.

It turned out the rider was an off-duty policeman. The two mobile policemen were his colleagues with whom he was having drinks. Such was the reputation of the area that police took their weapons with them when drinking in the pub.

The driver had collapsed to the ground as they continued to "beat am propa".

Robert made to stand up but Terry, more experienced at watching bar fights from his army days said, "Sit the fuck down!"

Robert obeyed.

"We must do something."

"Like what?" asked Terry cooly.

The usual rent-a-crowd turned up and there was some jostling as people argued for the MOPOLs to let the man go. Others joined in saying he deserved it. As Fela would say in his lyrics: propa katakata was kicking off.

Concerned for their guests, one of the sales guys, Martins, who was the older of the duo, went in and told the barman to serve the MOPOLs some beers. The barman walked casually over to the melee, interrupted the policemen's continued kicking of the driver and told them they had beer on their table. They looked over, shrugged as if nothing had happened, and walked back to enjoy their freebies. Behind them, the victim squirmed as the more helpful of the rabble helped him to his car. In three minutes, it was as if nothing had happened and Ajegunle just carried on with its nightlife. It was as if a pebble had been thrown into a puddle.

The two sales guys returned and joined them at the table with the bar owner in tow. A bar boy followed, carrying four small bottles of Guinness.

"Good evening my ogas," he said and apologised for the fracas.

They then had a short conversation about how his business was doing and how well his two friends, as he slapped the salesmen on their backs, supported him. He enthusiastically invited the visitors in to see his place.

The outside area where they had been sitting was mostly furnished with fading branded tables and chairs: Star, Gulder,

Guinness, and all the other popular beers were represented. Inside was considerably smarter, with rows of neat square tables with clean plastic tablecloths and upright wooden chairs where a few customers were seated, some hunched over steaming bowls of pepper soup.

There was only mild curiosity as the oyibos walked in and were shown the array of sponsored fridges, each stocked only with that company's products as was the custom.

Out in the back, a woman was sitting on a low stool, her wrapper pulled up over strong knees so she could sit astride a metal bowl cleaning fish, probably tilapia.

Another was stirring a massive bowl from which came a steamy mist of aromatic vapours. It rested on a metal tripod under which a distinctly dodgy-looking gas canister fuelled a floor-level stove. There was a sense of well-practised routine and that preparations were well in hand for a busy evening.

The proprietor, Ofortokun, "call me Otokun", was clearly proud of his establishment and happy to be showing the visitors around.

Paradoxically, it was Terry who felt more at home due to his now weekly excursion with his team to local pepper soup joints. Robert still very much came in the ajebota category, more like the typical Ikoyi dweller who would never see or be seen in a place such as this. Even so, this was far from bush. It was a respectable place and the guys were impressed at the cleanliness of the surroundings despite the lack of piped water in the area. Like most places in AJ City, water was collected from a standpipe, or from a communal borehole, or else they relied on "pure" water sold in bags of twenty 60ml sachets.

They politely declined the offer of a bowl of gbagba fofo, a signature Delta soup as Otokun was an Itsekeri man. They had a busy evening before them and Terry for one, was thinking they would be a long way from a decent toilet for some time.

They ate at a local place later on. Ade and Martins, the two salesmen, explained as they walked into Kingstine Jo, a massive fast-food restaurant and bar in Apapa, that this would be their last place and they thought they could stop and get a bite.

They sat and chatted over the noise of several dozen other customers in a lively and popular joint, full of workers from the nearby port. All four opted for fried chicken, dodo, and jollof rice, having sent food out to Terry's driver who was watching over the vehicles. The reps were quite used to taking visitors around bars in their territory and were quite at ease with their companions. As always, they were interested in Robert's background. Terry noticed that Robert seemed better informed than the first day they arrived and he felt, a lot happier talking about it.

The conversation got round to the inevitable: the banter that four blokes of different circumstances could engage in anywhere in the world. Both salesmen were big Arsenal fans but had to admit it was already certain that Man U were unstoppable on their path to the premiership title, with Ronaldo and Rooney scoring goals at will. There was some pride in an African, Didier Drogba, being the league's leading goal-scorer so far, but the one thing all of them could agree on was that they all hoped Chelsea would not win the title.

Terry thought Robert was being unnecessarily smug and was a little pissed that neither Ade nor Martins had even heard of Millwall but as he was driven home later, he thought it was one of the best evenings he'd had since arriving in Lagos.

Chapter 7

An Unexpected Song

"To the place of my birth
Back down to earth
Ain't talkin' 'bout no roots in the land
Talkin' 'bout the roots in the man
I feel my spirit gettin' old
It's time to recharge my soul
I'm zippin' up my boots
Goin' back to my roots
Yeah

To the place of my birth
Back down to earth."

'Going Back To My Roots', originally written by
Orlando Julius Ekemode but attributed to Lamont Dozier

Isioma had been strongly suggesting that Robert have a birthday party or at least a get-together of some sort. Her friends liked her British cousin, finding him amusing and quirky. Not that he thought of himself as quirky, but he was an accountant after all. He was just struggling to fully embrace a culture he had been thrown into; one that previously had no resonance nor held any interest for him. The girls liked him of course, because in his Britishness he appeared quiet and gentle to them. The boys were slightly more ambivalent. It was really only the football that was a shared interest. Either way, he had the money to pay for drinks and small chops, so they all encouraged her to persuade him to have a birthday party.

Some of her friends teased her: that she had to be careful if she secretly fancied him, as marrying your cousin could mean bad things for your children. Mostly, her girlfriends just took her word for it that she liked Robert as a member of her family and not romantically. So that could encourage her to put in a word for them to arrange a date with him. Imagine that: a British-Nigerian husband with a full British passport and a job in London! Isioma could also see that her cousin seemed to enjoy himself with her mates. Even if he was a little quiet, he was relaxed and socialised easily. But she also noticed that he ignored their coquetry and less than subtle come-ons. Any male Nigerian she knew would have jumped at their enthusiastic flirting.

After their early conversation when she made it clear theirs was a family thing only, she started to feel a genuine affection for him. Almost like a protective older sister, except she was the younger one. Having recovered from that initial shock at finding out how little he knew about his own culture, she enjoyed being his guide to all things Nigerian and for her part, learning about life in "jand", as many young Nigerians called the UK.

Now that he had allowed himself to be persuaded to host a party, the next question was the venue. Although it would have been easy to have it around the pool at the Guinness compound, it was more convenient for Isioma's crowd to have it on the island. In the end, they plumped for a bar at the small Bogobiri Hotel just off Awolowo Road. It was new and had gained for itself a reputation as somewhere for the artsy, as the décor was African as opposed to the sterile uniform of the larger hotels. It had an art gallery and often had live music in a second bar to the side.

Robert's birthday was on a Thursday so they booked an area in one of the bars for the Friday after.

Isioma and her flatmates spent the evening before the party baking a chocolate cake, and then took it down to the hotel before any other guests arrived. Robert had given them a budget for drinks and small chops, so the three girls ordered cocktails and chatted excitedly about the impending evening.

Isioma and her friends were generally modest in their alcohol consumption, so they soon felt the impact of the vodka and schnapps in the cocktails they had chosen. Two of the girls, Isioma and Ezzy, which was short for Ezinwanyi, were Igbo. The other, Florence, was from southern Kaduna. They had all met while working at Zenith Bank and having a shared hatred for the long commute, had agreed to pool their resources to find somewhere closer to the office, hence the apartment on Keffi Street.

As junior managers who had come out of the bank's graduate scheme, they were relatively well remunerated but by the time they had paid their rent and sent some money home to their mothers, as all three did, they didn't have much disposable cash. Sitting and drinking fashionable cocktails was a treat.

At work, they had to wear sensible skirts and their normal weekend wear was variations of a jeans theme. All three had splashed out this evening with new dresses and two of them had spent long hours at the hairdresser's earlier in the week. Isioma had stuck to her habitual braids, but Ezzy and Florence had put themselves through several hours of tugging and sewing, not to mention the best part of a week's wages, for good quality weaves.

Florence was particularly excited about who Robert might be bringing. She was a year or two older than the others and was already being asked by her family that, as happy as they were that she was making a career, shouldn't she be thinking of marrying soon?

"Really?" asked Ezzy at Florence's hope that he brought some oyibos. "I mean, what would your folks say if you turned up with a White boyfriend?"

Florence chuckled. "It's all about the money. If he has a good job and is ready to look after me, they wouldn't mind."

"*If she marry taxi driver, I don't care*," sang Isioma, from a popular old-school song. They all laughed and joined in, "*Plenty husband is too much! If she must go, don't you worry! Let her go, nobody cares!*"

"No, seriously," Ezzy said when she stopped singing. "Even today, it can be a problem. When I was at LASU, one girl had a White businessman as a boyfriend and there was graffiti in all the toilets 'Halima S fucks White men'. It was a problem for her."

"Nah! Things have changed. This is 2006, not 1906."

"Not that much, Isi. That was only four years ago," Ezzy replied. "Anyway, it doesn't matter to me. I will be satisfied with a good Igbo boy that knows how to make money and loves his mother."

59

"But those oyibo boys are always so fresh and clean. They smell so nice!"

Florence was sniggering.

The other two were shocked.

"Oh, Florence!" they both screamed in horror. "You haven't?"

"Hahahah!" Florence thought it was hilarious. "No, I am only joking . . . but that's what I have heard from someone who knows."

"Yeh right!" chortled Ezzy. "You are a naughty girl, Florence Maigari and a very bad influence on us sweet Catholic girls."

The girls were about halfway through their cocktails when Robert walked in with a couple of his colleagues.

"Hi girls," he waved cheerfully. "Meet my colleagues. Nigeria's finest. Afolabi and Danjuma. Guys, this is my cousin, Isioma, and her roommates."

The tallest and darker complexioned of his friends, Danjuma, smiled at Isioma.

"Hello. I can tell you we are so pleased to meet you! He's hidden his family from us for way too long."

"All good things are worth waiting for," she responded cheerfully, grinning. "This is Ezzy and Florence," she said, then walked over to the bar where Robert was ordering drinks as her friends introduced themselves.

"I thought you would be bringing more people."

"Some more will come along later," he said. Then catching her expression, he laughed and added, "And maybe some oyibos. There was a sales conference in Abeokuta and a few had to go to, so I hope they will come when they get back. Now, another drink?"

By ten o'clock, there were a good dozen to fifteen young people scattered around the bar, drinking and eating the usual small chops. Apart from his two colleagues, all the others were friends of Isioma's.

One of her friends in a garish red dress whispered to Florence, "Na wa o. Shebi I thought there would be some fresh something. You know what I am saying? But see oyibo, eh? They don't want to come down and mix with proper Naija?"

Florence shrugged. "This one no be proper Naija?"

60

"Not at all," was the firm response. At which point, Red Dress suddenly preened, which made Florence turn round to see the tall, somewhat overweight, and now turning reddish, Terry, walk into the poolside.

Robert was chatting to someone with his back to the door and it took Terry a few moments to spot him and walk over.

"Hi Robert, sorry I'm a bit late."

Robert was delighted to see Terry.

"Hello mate!" he said. "Pleased to see you! What can I get you to drink? Star, I suppose?"

"No, Robert. Let me get you one."

They walked to the bar and chatted while the waiter got round to their order.

"I was beginning to think you were not coming. I was getting a feeling that people. . ." his eyes indicating Isioma's friends, "were starting to think I don't have any British friends, if you know what I mean."

Terry nodded. "Sorry o. I had a tricky installation that went on late."

"No problem. Come and meet Isioma's friends. They're dying to meet you."

Within a few minutes, Terry was comfortably ensconced at a table with several of the girls. Red Dress was sitting particularly close to him on a bench seat, hanging on his every word.

Isioma was standing with Robert. "Who is that girl?" he asked.

"That's Mimi."

"Is that her real name?"

"It's short for Oghenemine or something. She's from Warri. Why, are you interested?"

Robert turned and looked at her. "Are you kidding? She's a bit full-on, isn't she?"

"She's a runs-girl."

"A what?" Robert looked bemused.

"A runs-girl. She does runs."

Isioma shook her head as if to signify that she could not believe how little he knew about life.

"Runs. They go out with big boys for money. It's not like they're ashawo o," she paused, looked at him and shook her head,

61

again. "If you are poor and hang out in a club or one of those bars like Pat's or Ynot then you are classed as an ashawo or prostitute. If you come from a well-off family and just go home with rich guys you pick up at a party and expect an envelope to say thank you, you are a 'runs-girl'. You do 'runs'."

"Really?"

"Yes. Some of these guys pay ridiculously big money. Of course, the real deal is if a girl becomes some old big man's side chick and then she might get herself an apartment, car, and everything."

She looked at Robert's expression. It amused her.

"Mimi's not in that league but your friend better watch out."

"Oh, I am sure he knows how to take care of himself," Robert said, though he was not entirely convinced how true this was.

Robert's birthday evening was panning out nicely. A few of the guests started dancing around the tables to music being played in the bar: D'banj, Lagbaja, Styl-Plus, and TuFace's "African Queen" which all the girls loved so much. Robert had learnt the hits of the day and was happy to join in. The girls teased him about his dancing style.

Isioma was happy to see her cousin enjoying himself.

Suddenly, she wondered where his friend, Terry, was. It dawned on her that she hadn't seen him for quite a while. He was not outside the immediate pool area. Perhaps he had gone into the other bar where they had live music?

She wandered through, telling the ticket sellers at the door she was looking for someone. Once in, she found there was a historic name from Nigeria's music scene playing. Orlando Julius was in his sixties. He was still popular, though probably more so overseas than in his own country, as was so often the case with Nigerian musicians.

She was surprised someone like him would be playing in such a small venue but there he was, large as life with a small band, playing some of his dance-orientated high life music. There were maybe twenty people sitting and listening. And there, standing at the back, drinking his beer, was Terry.

"Hello Terry," she said. "Is everything alright?"

"Oh yes, thanks," he replied, then looked down at her. There was quite a height difference. "It's Isioma, right? I am sorry, I didn't really get to say hello properly."

"Yes, Isioma. No problem," she replied, smiling. "I just noticed you weren't next door so I thought I'd check on you."

"Oh, I am sorry. I didn't mean to be rude. I just went out for a breath of air and heard this music and came to investigate. He's brilliant. Don't you like it?"

"Well, it's a bit too old school for me but, yes, he's a classic really. Somebody my parents would enjoy."

Terry looked at her and laughed. "Thanks!"

Isioma put her hand to her mouth. "Oh, I am sorry, I didn't mean. . ."

Terry laughed again. "No, I know. Don't worry."

He held up his empty glass.

"I am going to get myself another beer. Would you like a drink? You have to now after that."

"I've had two cocktails and I don't usually. . ." she paused. "Oh, go on then. Can I have a Gordon's Spark?"

While Terry was at the bar, she realised she knew the song Orlando Julius was playing. By the time he got back, she was swaying happily in time with the music.

He handed her the drink and said, "You seem to be enjoying this song."

"I remember it from home. It was always played at family parties. I think it's called something like 'Going back to my roots' or something."

"Yeh," Terry agreed. "It sounds like something I know. Maybe our parents were listening to the same music?" He emphasised the word "parents".

She laughed. "Who knows? Why not?"

For a few minutes, they alternated between listening and chatting until they were disturbed by a panting Ezzy.

"This is where you two are. Come quick!"

"What happened?" asked Isioma, fearing a catastrophe.

"Nothing. We just forgot the cake, that's all, and some people are ready to go home. Florence is getting the staff to bring it out now."

"Oh my God," squealed Isioma. "How could we have forgotten? Come on, Terry, we must help Robert cut the cake."

Pulling Terry's hand to follow her, they got to the other bar just as Florence was lighting the candles and Robert's friends were gathering around.

Ezzy smiled. "We were wondering where you were."

She and Florence exchanged glances, which Isioma noticed and pulled a face at.

Robert endured the full Nigerian Happy Birthday rendition that included the extra "How old are you now?" chorus, successfully blew out his candles and helped the girls distribute the cake.

The cake was blissfully consumed by all present, except Terry who said it would spoil the taste of his beer. He was given a piece to take away for later.

"It's for Ron," he stated. Everyone looked confused.

"Yeh, 'Late-R-on'."

Terry enjoyed his joke while everyone looked on bemused.

"Even I don't find that funny," said Robert.

It was getting on to one o'clock and Robert's colleagues wanted to convoy onto the mainland for safety, so Terry offered to give the girls a lift to their place.

Isioma explained a couple of the other girls were crashing at theirs too.

"That's okay," said Terry. "It's a double cabin so we can all squeeze in. It's not that far anyway."

Everyone went out to the street. There was much calling out to drivers and general leave-taking and "Happy Birthday Robert!" shout-outs.

Terry's latest driver, Saturday, pulled up.

Four of the girls squeezed into the rear seat while Isioma sat in front with Terry and the driver. The girls were all singing along to the song on the radio as they drove up Awolowo Road, still busy at peak clubbing time, as they turned into Keffi. When they arrived, Terry got out and received quick kisses from each of the girls.

When Isioma reached up, Terry asked quietly, "Can I have your number?"

On tiptoes, she held his face in her hands and gave him a peck on the end of his nose.

"You're sweet oyibo," she said, and added laughingly, over her shoulder as she caught up with the others, "But not that sweet."

The street door closed and Terry stood there for a second. There was a faint glow from the occasional window and up the road the harsh lights outside Dodan Barracks scattered the darkness, but otherwise, it was just the glare from the pick-up that lit up the road. For a moment, Terry considered his options. He thought about going to a late-night bar. Instead, he turned on his heels and got back into the front seat.

"Saturday, home please," he said.

The gates at Roman Gardens were still as rusty as the night he arrived and the guards as dozy as ever.

"Fucks sake!" he muttered, with little conviction, as they waited while the guards went through their side-gate, trouser-tug, and creaky-main-gate routine.

As the pick-up stopped at the front of the block, Terry opened the door and then turned back.

"Work tomorrow, Saturday. But not until ten o'clock."

He handed over a couple of five hundred naira notes.

"Get some breakfast. See you in the morning."

"Goodnight sah," said Saturday, cheerful, unaccustomed to the sudden largesse.

Up in the flat, Terry couldn't settle.

He wandered about aimlessly with a glass of water in his hand. He checked the fridge out. There was nothing in it he fancied. He remembered he had left his piece of cake in the pick-up. He grabbed a packet of crisps and took his glass out onto the balcony.

Far, far in the distance, there was the faint glow of an electric storm. This time of year, storms would likely stay way out at sea and there would be little chance of rain.

When there was NEPA and no generators, it could truly be quite peaceful.

At times like this, he wished he still smoked.

As he sat on one of the plastic chairs, there was a ping from his phone which was inside the house. He finished the last of the crisps. Cheese and onion, not his favourite.

He had a message. It was from Isioma: '*This my no got urs frm rob*'.

He thought hard but couldn't think of a reply that expressed his feelings, so he just sent '*tanx XXXX*'.

In fact, he did not really know what he was feeling.

The evening was an unusual one for him. He had downed a few beers but not as many as his usual Friday night out. It had been strange talking to girls who, though they flirted, were not available in the same way as the bar girls. The conversations had been, he struggled to articulate it—normal. The Nigerian guys had generally kept their distance but had been perfectly friendly. The few minutes he had spent in the other room listening to the band, then chatting to Isioma, had felt unlike anything he had experienced before. At least not in Nigeria. It just felt natural, like he was at home somehow. There had been several White people in the small crowd, but it was mostly Nigerian. It seemed as if everyone felt as if they were at home too. A certain, inexplicable ease.

"I must buy myself an Orlando Julius CD tomorrow," he thought, just before he fell asleep.

Chapter 8

Strike!

"For many years have they ruled us.
We are not an unreasonable people,
and like a good house servant,
it is only fair that we should give our masters notice
of our intention to quit, so that they can effect
arrangements either to employ new servants
or to serve themselves."

Anthony Enaharo
'Motion for Self Government',
Constitutional Assembly 1953

Agu Ede was too busy working each day at the mine's workshop and doing what hunting he could in the evenings and weekends to be active in Zik and Herbert Macaulay's nationalist party, the NCNC. In addition to his work, he had married a girl from nearby Ozalla, Chimbuchi, a year after his return from Burma. They quickly started a family with a daughter, Ngozi, born within a year of their marriage, followed by a son, Okafor.

Despite his responsibilities, Agu kept up with the news and firmly believed that all Nigerians should see themselves as brothers in the fight for independence just as they had been while fighting in Burma and elsewhere. Hausa, Yoruba and Igbo bled and died the same, like all men everywhere.

When the underground workers sought better conditions, they argued that the war had ended and they had sacrificed all they could for the war effort while it lasted. It was now time for the authorities to pay a living wage and make good their promises of new boots and safety gear. As they organised, Agu would help translate letters from the authorities or write letters on behalf of his colleagues. He could not help but be appalled at the way they were treated or the conditions in which some of the newcomers had to live.

Things had not been going well for the miners of Iva Valley. There had been a rush to have the new mines operational for the first world war so there had been no time to build a formal settlement for them. The workings expanded and production increased during the interwar years but workers had been forced to still live in informal encampments with no facilities. Despite promises, nothing was done.

By the second world war, with its further escalation in production and consequent increase in labourers, living conditions were squalid.

In November 1949, things were coming to a head and there was agitation for industrial action. The relationship between the miners' representatives and the colliery management broke down and several incidents started to make the colonial authorities jumpy. The British correctly saw Enugu as a hotbed of Zikist nationalism and any threat to mining output as sedition. Yet, for all this, the miners' three-point demands were modest: an increase in allowances, particularly for those working underground, better living conditions, and new boots.

Conditions down in the pits were dangerous. Certainly, no Europeans worked underground, which was telling. The groups known as hewers and tubmen were particularly aggrieved. These were the lowliest of workers, toiling underground to cut the coal, shore up the mines with wooden props, and then shovel the coal into "tubs" that were manually pushed above ground along tracks, up steep and arduous slopes, until they reached the surface. These men had the most dangerous work in the suffocating and stifling darkness, yet were denied commensurate allowances. Most worked without boots. Many had been forced into the mines by chiefs pressured by the British to supply labour to meet production targets and quotas set by the colonial government. Desperate to improve their conditions, the workers unionised and began to take collective action.

Eventually, all this agitation culminated in a subversion campaign called "welu nwayo" or go-slow which started on the 4th of November, 1949. All the miners refused to work for longer than the minimum required hours and operated strictly to the minimum of their contracts. Productivity fell dramatically. The tension between the miners and the panicking authorities reached breaking point. Agu Ede, as one of the natural leaders of his community and the chief machinist at the Iva Valley mine, was at the centre of all the drama.

After three days of the work-to-rule, the colliery management's nerve broke and on the 14th of November, they attempted to dismiss two hundred hewers and employ new workers to replace them. The hewers' response, fearful of losing their jobs and incomes, was to occupy the pitheads, staying underground where management had no control. To support their husbands, women came to bring food and to demonstrate outside the mines. There were several scuffles with the police that culminated in some damaged equipment and broken office windows.

The mining company, supported by the colonial administration, refused to engage into dialogue with the miners who the system had decided were part of a wider nationalist plot. Fearful that independence activists would get hold of the explosives stored near the mine head, managers ordered the over-ground workers to hand them over to the authorities. On their part, fearful that this meant the government was closing the mines, the miners refused this order and brought the hewers and tubmen back to the pithead to protect them.

At an impasse, nine hundred police and military reinforcements from outside the area were brought in. These men were predominantly Hausas from the north of the country who spoke little English and no Igbo at all.

Late in the morning of 18th November, Captain F. S. Phillips—a Senior Superintendent—marched an armed unit of police, newly equipped with protective gear and tin helmets, to the mine head office to forcibly remove the explosives. They were met by demonstrating miners and over-ground workers, dancing and singing in solidarity. They sang hymns and traditional songs and chanted in unison: "We no go gree oh, we no go gree! Bekee nye anyi ihe ruru anyi! We no go gree!"

F. S. Phillips and his two officers, Assistant Superintendents Browne and Ormiston, were inexperienced in Africa. They could not speak Igbo and were completely out of their depth. Instead of songs of comradeship and of a community seeking basic rights, all they could see, as Phillips later testified at the Fitzgerald Commission, were "natives singing tribal war songs" and becoming "more and more menacing."

When hewer, Sunday Anyasade, danced too close, "dancing up and down and his eyes popping out of his head", Phillips lost his nerve.

* * *

It is a matter of public record that the British colonial police captain, F. S. Phillips, fired the first shot. The bullet went through Sunday Anyasade's mouth and out the back of his head.

Sunday had come to Enugu's coalmines from his village near Owerri to earn money as he had recently gotten married. On the day he died, he was demonstrating for the boots he had been promised. Boots and a little dignity.

Livinus Okechukwuma, who had been standing next to him, had screamed in horror. Captain Phillips shot Livinus while he simultaneously called "open fire!" to the line of uniformed policemen recently arrived to reinforce the local troops.

It was at that moment that Agu, who could speak Hausa, from his time serving with northern Nigerian soldiers in Burma, stepped forward and shouted.

"Mu yan'uwanku ne! Kada ku harbe mu!"

We are your brothers! Do not shoot us!

For a second, the intensity of his belief in Nigerian unity and the sound of their own tongue coming from the mouth of one of the demonstrators caused the Hausa soldiers to hesitate.

Assistant Superintendent R. A. Browne, who understood not a single word of any local language, simply pointed his revolver at this closest of the miners who had stepped resolutely out of the panicking and scattering crowd and, at the same time as he repeated the order "fire!", shot Agu Ede straight through the neck.

Instantaneously, a volley of rifle fire echoed down the valley.

Agu was already fatally wounded when another twenty of his brother miners were massacred. Countless others were wounded. Though the colonial records of the time were sketchy, as many as eleven of these later died of their wounds.

* * *

The Iva Valley shootings certainly catalysed many Nigerians into believing the time had come to end British colonial rule. In the immediate aftermath, there were riots across the country to the extent that on the 28th of November 1949, "disturbances" in Aba, Port Harcourt, and Onitsha, were discussed in the House of Commons at Westminster.

The Governor General, John Macpherson, was forced to institute a state of emergency and to forestall more problems, he announced that a commission of enquiry would be constituted. On the 12th of December 1949, the commission began sitting in Enugu under the chairmanship of Sir William Fitzgerald, a British judge with a brief to examine the direct and remote causes of the shootings.

The eminent Nigerian lawyer and nationalist, H. O. Davies, led the team representing the miners and their families. He insisted that they be given the right to put the British police officers and the colliery management on the witness stand and Fitzgerald agreed. Under Davies' cross-examination, the feebleness and poor judgement of the officer in charge, Captain Phillips, was revealed. It transpired that the police had been at the mine with the demonstrating miners for more than an hour and a half, under the command of Assistant Superintendent Ormiston, with no problems whatsoever.

When Phillips and his second-in-charge, Assistant Superintendent Browne, arrived with additional police, they had taken up more aggressive positions resulting in a confrontational situation. Despite their protestations, Davies soon exposed flaws in their narrative and it became clear that in their ignorance and inexperience, they had utterly misread the situation and panicked unnecessarily.

In his closing remarks to the Commission on the 6th of January 1950, H. O. Davies stated, concerning Phillips, that he "was not a witness of truth" and that he and the others responsible should be held accountable and punished. As such, he insisted that none of the officers be allowed to return home until the commission's findings were made public. The reality was, within a few days of the end of the commission, Phillips and Browne escaped to the United Kingdom and joined the ranks of thousands of obscure colonial officers whose acts of violence would become whitewashed into the conventional history of the glorious Empire.

The commission, for its part, condemned poor colliery management for allowing the incident happen in the first place, as well as the behaviour of the police officers for causing unnecessary fatalities. It blamed the government for confusing a purely industrial dispute with a political confrontation. Condemning the colonial authorities' trade union policy, it went on to criticise the government for its response to calls for independence.

The commission concluded: "Tragic as the events at Enugu were, there is a lesson to be learnt which, if learnt. . . will not leave that tragedy as a mere waste of life or bitter memory."

* * *

The hollow closing statements of colonial politicians and the commission judges were no comfort to the families of the deceased. Agu Ede was buried according to tradition, in his compound, in front of his obi. Offerings were made to the spirits and to his ancestors to keep his name alive. It was believed that a man is not dead while his name is still spoken. Given the number of people that came to the compound to pay their respects, his was a name to be remembered.

Yet, there was another incident that stayed on the lips of the Ngwo people for many years. A question that many feared to know the answer to.

On the last day of the enquiry, just as Fitzgerald was about to make those concluding remarks, something extraordinary happened.

Without warning, a commotion started when an old woman, dressed in a wrapper with her shoulders bare, strode out of the public area towards the front where the witnesses sat. The court sergeant called for attendants to stop her. The Nigerians were transfixed. Time seemed to slow down. The woman pointed a finely carved walking stick at Phillips and Browne, who were sitting with the European witnesses, shook her head and spat on the floor. For a split second, a halo of silence and inaction formed around her, and her voice could be heard clearly.

"*Unu wụ ndị ọcha, ndi efuruefu, ndị kitikpa ga-agbagbu,*" she said. "*Etu a unu siri ghopu ofu anya'm nji a fu uzo, ọbụbụ ọnụ'm ga na-eso unu. Unu ga-eji ọbara unu wee kwụọ ugwọ ọbara nwa m. Mu umu gị ga-eburu kwa ya!*" You white people, you lost souls, those whom smallpox shall afflict. How you have plucked out the one eye I see with, you shall carry my curse. You shall pay the debt of my son's spilled blood with yours. Your children and your children's children will carry my curse!"

The bench and lawyers were either British or non-Igbo speakers and would have assumed it was just the ramblings of a senile old woman had they not been able to tell by the shock that had descended over the court that something disturbing had happened. After she was led out of the building, she just seemed to melt into thin air. She had not come with any of the bereaved families. No one knew who she was or where she had come from.

For a long time afterwards, local people spoke of the incident, embellishing it at will. But it was solely in the compound of the Ede family that the woman was recognised, had a name and a history of sacral strangeness. To them the truth was inescapable; it was none other than Ekwutosi. Grandma Ekwutosi, who had died nearly ten years earlier, before Agu Ede returned from Burma.

73

Chapter 9

Desperate Measures

"His hair is long, his feet are hard and gritty
He spends his life walking the streets of New York City
He's almost dead from breathing in air pollution
He tried to vote but to him there's no solution
Living just enough, just enough for the city...
yeah, yeah, yeah!"

'Living in the City' by Stevie Wonder

Early the same afternoon as Terry was undertaking his first trade visit with Robert, another football conversation was happening between four young men around a bar table not far from Ajegunle. It was at a simple bar just across the everlasting roadworks known as the Badagry Express. It was much closer to being a "bush" bar than Otokun's. Tucked into a side road off Baale Street in Orile, this shebeen was informally named after the moniker the owner went by—Hope. There was no branded signage above the door. There was no door. Hope's was at the lower rungs of the Lagos hostelry gene pool. It was not a fully formed structure: part-demolished brick building, part shack and part lean-to. It certainly offered al fresco dining, though not of the kind that normally springs to mind.

Having said that, it had the basics. There was an old chest freezer that when there was electricity, still cooled a pond of brackish water down to a level that made the few bottles in it drinkable. There were a few bits of the ubiquitous plastic furniture that had seen better days, supplemented by the odd upturned beer crate or box. There was even a television, powered by a small I-beta-pass-my-neighbour 5 kva generator, just strong enough to power the one TV and a couple of dull lamps at night. The television was bolted high on the wall, enclosed in a cage with an opening large enough to watch the screen, but too small for the device to be taken out—stolen—without a long-lost key to the dull gold padlock behind it.

To one side, half in and half out of the bar area, was a small bukka also owned and run by the eponymous Hope. The name Hope, was just the English translation of her true native Efik name, Idoreyin. Hers was an ethnicity whose women had a reputation for being fine cooks. The beer bar was a sideline to her prowess as a cook. Her edikaikong soup was popular throughout Orile-Iganmu and customers came from farther afield to eat it.

Today, as always, she was bent over the two or three pots that she constantly stirred and tasted. So frequently did she taste her soup that the bravely foolish had been known to ask her if she was fattening herself up for marriage, as was the custom in Calabar where she came from. Her right arm, as pudgy as it was, spent all day stirring her soup or the poundo, which meant it could also deliver a dirty slap that reputedly caused hard men to cry.

Towards the back of the bar, the animated football conversation between four young men was dying down and the topic moved to whether they had enough money between them for more beer. After pooling their last five and ten naira notes, they had just enough for two large bottles of Legend Extra Stout, which was a cheaper rival to Guinness. Besides, Legend was made by Nigerian Breweries at a massive factory just a few blocks away, in Iganmu. They beckoned to the barmaid who soon brought the beer, barely looking at them as she set the bottles on the table and collected their money before opening the drinks. After these were studiously shared into four chipped glasses, the discussion got more serious.

"So cousin, what is it that you so desperately wanted to talk about today?"

The youth, all in their early twenties, wore a selection of tatty jeans and tee shirts. One had on a Patrick Vieira Arsenal shirt that had seen better days.

They were indistinguishable from the hundreds of thousands, nay millions, of young men in a city with a youth unemployment rate of over fifty percent. These four were all originally from the same suburb of Enugu. Maybe they were first-generation born in

Lagos, or maybe brought there as children by a father desperate for work or equally, they might have been some of those who had left the village to catch a night bus to find a future on the streets of the nation's commercial capital. It did not matter. With so little employment available, despite possibly good intentions, they, like so many others, gravitated to the slum area of Orile where family members offered them a roof and a floor. They occasionally ran errands or did some labouring for relatives but usually relied on petty trading, petty crime, or both, for food and the odd beer on a good day.

Ndu, who seemed to be the oldest, brought a plastic bag from the floor between his feet and put it on the table. "Yesterday, my auntie asked me to get something from her box. I found this in it." He looked around surreptitiously before opening the bag and brought out a weighty package of brown paper. As he unfolded it, there was a gasp around the table.

"For the love of God, where did you get that?"

"Chidi, keep your voice down," said Ndu.

He folded the paper and returned the package to the plastic bag.

There was a clamour of voices. "What was that?" "Was that what I thought it was?" "Where did you get that?"

"It is my grandfather's revolver from the war. He must have brought it to Lagos with him," Ndu explained.

"What, from the Biafran war?" asked Chidi who got an *are-you-stupid?* look in return.

One of the others, Ama in the Arsenal shirt, had more doubts. "So how did he get it? Does it work?"

"Well," said Ndu. "Papa was in the Nigerian Army before the war and deserted to join our side. I guess he just kept it somehow. It's a Webley, which the British used and then probably left for the Nigerian Army at independence. I guess when he died, Aunt Chika just kept it hidden away as something of her father's.""Yes, but does it work? I mean, it's old, abi? Have you tried it?"

"Of course, it works. I haven't tried it because there are only five bullets and that would waste one. Why wouldn't it work?"

Ndu was getting touchy with all the questions.

76

"So, what are you going to do with it?" asked Ikem, the fourth around the table.

"Are you going to kill someone?" asked Chidi excitedly.

"Yes, you," said Ndu, giving him another *are-you-stupid?* stare. "Especially if you don't keep your voice down!"

He leaned forward and spoke quietly.

"So, I have a plan. We can use this to rob a bank."

He paused to let the protestations die down.

"Okay. I know everyone is shocked, but do you all want to keep living the way we do? There is no dignity in spending our days doing little hustles to feed ourselves. My auntie is always complaining that I have nothing to contribute and I avoid my mother's calls from the village. We can do this, just once. Then we go back to Enugu to hide and when the noise dies down, we can repay our debts, help our families and we will have money left for ourselves. Just once, that's all."

This time there were no noisy protestations, just the sound of sighs and thoughtful tooth-sucking. Chidi, of course, was up for it. Young and brash, he was always in trouble, rarely considering the consequences of his actions. Ikem and Ama were more studied. They were desperate to alleviate their poverty, but they had practical questions, primarily: "What are our chances of getting away with it?"

Having virtually no money, every spending decision for youths such as these had to be carefully weighed and once taken, the "enjoyment" had to be maximised. The discussions would only continue up to the last drop of beer. Ndu, Ikem, and Ama, sipped their Legend for a good twenty minutes as they deliberated Ndu's idea. Chidi, congenitally incapable of doing anything slowly, had already drained his glass and was visibly over-excited.

"Can we wear stockings over our faces? You know, as a disguise."

"Jesus, Chidi! We haven't even decided if we are going to do it yet."

Ndu looked around. It was getting to evening and more customers had come in.

"And I told you to keep your voice down!"

The more they talked about it, the more Ndu's determination won over. First Ikem and then gradually, Ama. The three "grown-ups" decided to do some more thinking. They would look at a couple of possible targets and consider the logistics."What about me?" Chidi said. "I have a friend who has a Dane gun. I can ask him to borrow me."

"No Chidi!"

The other three were quite clear.

"Do not do anything without asking us first."

It was about this time that Madam Hope made it clear that they were about to incur her displeasure. She loomed over them in the dusky gloom of her badly lit bar the way a stealth battleship emerges from a sea fog.

"You," she said, as she lifted Chidi from his seat by his ear, "have had an empty glass for too long. I know you have no money and I have paying customers who need a seat."

"Madam Hope abeg," pleaded Ndu. "Two minutes."

Chidi's nyash was hovering about a foot above the plastic chair and came down with a thud as Hope released him. "Two minutes," she said and wiped her hands on her apron as if it was Chidi and not that voluminous smock that was covered in grease and fish scales.

"Okay, so we meet back here in a week. Someone better come with enough money for some beer," Ndu said, looking at Chidi.

"Shouldn't we meet somewhere secret, like. . ." said Chidi, his face showing the strain of thinking, ". . .a cemetery?"

Ikem put his arm around Chidi's shoulder.

"Chidi, we come in here whenever we have money to chop. When do we ever go to the cemetery? Where is more secret or obvious?"

Ndu rolled his eyes and walked off with Ama. Ama raised his eyebrows.

"Oh, he'll be alright. He does what he's told."

A week later, when the four plotters met again at Hope's, as usual sharing large bottles of Legend, they seemed to be closer to a strategy. They had identified their target as a branch of Union Bank in nearby Festac Town. The one they had chosen was at

321 B Road, down a cul-de-sac where they hoped there would fewer people.

Festac had the benefit of multiple options for the getaway and being reasonably close to Ajegunle and Orile, they felt confident they could quickly melt into the dense urban areas where there was little authority, and disappear.

The plan was to steal a pick-up to approach the bank. Disguised as workmen, they would take the single, armed policeman by surprise and disarm him. Then, holding the gun to a security guard's head, they would have him take two of them through the security doors and into the branch itself. The other two would wait outside, holding the policeman hostage. Once the two inside had a bag each filled with cash, they would exit the bank and all four would escape a few blocks away in the pick-up truck. They would then dump the truck at some point, split up, and walk into the nearest one of the two densely populated areas.

"It would have been good to have two guns but once we have disarmed the policeman, you two," Ndu said, nodding at Ikem and Chidi, "can have machetes to keep the guards quiet."

"I can still borrow my friend's Dane gun," said Chidi.

Dane guns were originally flintlocks, imported it is said, by the Danish, hence the name. However, virtually any homemade rifle, of which Nigeria had many, usually for hunting, was colloquially called a "dane" gun.

"Chidi, how many more times!" Ndu said, his voice on edge. "They are unreliable and dangerous."

Chidi shrugged.

After Ndu went through their less-than-meticulous scheme, he leaned forward.

"So, any more questions?"

Ama too leaned forward.

"I have one. Who is going to drive the pick-up?" No one spoke as the sound of the caged television drifted across the mostly empty bar. "Can anyone actually drive?"

"I. . ." said Chidi before Ndu silenced him with a stare.

Three pairs of eyes looked at Ndu. "Cousin Kachi worked for an oyibo family before they sacked him. He learned to drive with them. I wanted to keep it to four but. . . .all is well. I will speak to him."

Just then, there was a commotion by the bukka. Madam Hope was standing, her formidable arms on her mighty hips, making her views known to whoever was within earshot. A few feet in front of her were five or six men with mostly bare chests and juju-style skirts, attended by two hyenas and a large and evil-looking baboon.

Walking across Nigeria, never stopping in one place for more than two or three days, this small ensemble of performing minstrels and showmen lived in the tradition to be found in almost every culture on the planet. These, however, had a unique proposition. They were the hyena men of Nigeria. Reputedly originally from Kano, this band of eight men and a couple of children wandered around the country selling traditional medicines and putting on shows with their hyenas, baboons, and pythons. The hyenas were held by strong metal chains and had woven leather muzzles but as terrifying as the scavengers' canines first appeared, they were more passive and therefore less destructive than the baboons that screeched and lurched away from their keeper at every opportunity.

Despite the growing fundamentalism, both Islamic and Christian, many devout Nigerians retained a healthy respect, if not an atavistic fear, of the darker side of traditional religions and their rituals.

The men had traditional medicine or juju artefacts hanging from skin belts tied around their waists or looped around their shoulders. Small skin pouches that contained bones and other fetish items dangled alongside strange-shaped bottles, large canine or primate teeth, and even the odd, indeterminate, dried animal part, all swinging menacingly as they moved, putting fear into the superstitious.

Now and again, the group would stop and put on a kind of show. Muzzles were taken off and the adults displayed their dominance over the animals by putting their hands and faces in the mouths of the hyenas. The children also took part: sometimes clambering on the backs of the beasts and showing an absolute lack of fear, other times circulating onlookers with a collection tin. The troupe members were as feared as much for their "medicine" as they were for their animals.

Madam Hope thought it was a bad idea having such creatures in her vicinity, however strong the chains may be. Having said that, she was not going to turn away custom. After being shown that they did indeed possess naira, she agreed that they could eat but out, in front of her place.

They settled down, squatting on their haunches until one of her small girls bravely took out some boxes for them to sit on. Eventually, they were all making suitable noises of satisfaction as they hungrily ate from bowls of soup accompanied by swallow.

A few local children stood at a safe distance and stared at the animals.

The troupe ate in silence though one of their number occasionally looked up and barked something at the kids who, although not understanding Hausa, knew from the tone that they were to "back off".

As Ndu and the Orile Gangstas, as Chidi now dubbed them, tried to leave, one of the hyenas thought they had gotten too close and rose, snarling through its muzzle.

Though they all instinctively jumped back, Chidi, as always, had to be the one to make a fuss and made a face and pretended to bark. The nearest troupe member took offence at this and leapt up.

"*Za ku zama abinci ga kare na,*" he said in Hausa, indicating that for his effrontery, the offending Chidi would be his hyena's next meal.

Ama pulled Chidi away before he could do anything more foolish.

As he did so, the troupe member reached to the hip of his fetish skirt and pulled a knife out of a dangling scabbard. He pointed it at the pair.

"*Zan yanke makogwaro idan kun kusanci,*" he threatened, his other hand simulating the slitting of a throat.

None of the four could speak Hausa but the intonation and the gesture were crystal clear. For a split second, the youth stood stock-still. Not wanting any disruption to her business, Hope promptly stepped in and waved them away. Madam Hope's ire being as formidable as any wild animal, the four quickly turned and strode off into the Orile evening.

The hyena men settled back, faces over their soup as if nothing had happened, looking for all intents like a family sitting down contentedly for supper.

Chapter 10

Who Pulls the Trigger?

"If not dem go shoot am well
Dem go shoot am for armed robbery
On top of the road
On the side
People dey waka
Office workers, labourer workers, workers' workers...
To try to make ends meet
Oh yes dem go dey try
Dem go dey hustle
Authority people dem go dey steal
Public contribute plenty money
Na authority people dey steal
Authority man no dey pick pocket
Na petty cash him go dey pick
Armed robber him need gun
Authority man him need pen
Authority man in charge of money
Him no need gun, him need pen
Pen get power gun no get
If gun steal eighty thousand naira
Pen go steal two billion naira."

'Authority Stealing' by Fela Anikulapo Kuti

The robbery did not go according to plan. It started to fall apart at the onset when at their meeting point, Ndu had to tell the others that Ama had chickened out.

In the two nights since their last meeting, Ama had nightmares in which the hyena man kept pointing at him. He was sure that some bad medicine had been directed at him. Nothing

Ndu said to change his mind worked. Ama was so spooked he attended Mass for the first time since he was a child.

On a positive note, their cousin, Kachi, had confirmed he could drive and was willing to join them.

"Orile Gangstas," yelled Chidi.

"Shut up!"

A pick-up truck regularly parked overnight not far from them, within Surulere, had also been identified. Presumably, the driver worked for a company that allowed him to take it home. When the unsuspecting man opened the vehicle door in the morning to clamber in, Ndu walked up to him, showed him the pistol and said with a resolve he did not feel, "Get in. I will show you where to drive."

Twenty minutes later, they pulled up behind a derelict warehouse.

Ndu again pointed the pistol at the terrified driver.

"Remember, I know where you and your family live. Do not report the car stolen until tonight, nor give out any details, or else your family will suffer. You understand?"

As the driver ran off, Ikem, Kachi, and Chidi, emerged from their hideout.

Ikem looked at Ndu and said, "I thought we would get a double cabin. This is only a single cabin."

"I couldn't find one. Three of us can sit inside and Chidi will be okay at the back."

Ndu noticed Chidi was carrying something enclosed in an old wrapper.

"What is that?"

"I just thought it would be useful," he said, unfurling the cloth to expose a Dane gun. It had what looked like a shotgun mechanism with a hand-carved wooden stock and two tubes welded together as the "double barrel".

"It's my friend's hunting gun. He loaned it to me to go hunting."

Ndu could hardly contain himself. Rather than shout the abuse he wanted to, he restricted himself to a long glower.

"You," he said, "will sit in the back. Do not say another word. Stick to the plan and do not say anything."

Chidi gave his usual shrug.

Kachi said, "Ndu, this is a manual gearbox. I only learned to drive automatic."

"You didn't tell me that."

"Well, I just assumed you knew. Most pick-ups in Lagos are automatic."

"How was I to know?"

Ikem shook his head. "Na wa o. I think we should give up. First one thing, then another. If only Ama was here."

Ndu ignored him and looked at Kachi, "Can't you drive it at all?"

"Well, I can give it a go."

"Then I think we should go ahead. Who is ready?"

Kachi nodded weakly. Ndu looked at Chidi.

"Well, Chidi?" he paused. "And. . .?"

"You told me not to say anything."

"For the love of Jesus. Yes, or no?"

"Yes."

Ndu held his hands open as if questioning Ikem.

"Your Ama is not here but three out of four of us are good to go."

Under pressure, Ikem nodded assent. Ndu suggested that Kachi drive a couple of practice circuits around the warehouse yard. Kachi climbed in and switched on the ignition and the truck lurched forward. It was still lurching by the third circuit but he was getting the hang of the stick shift.

"Okay."

Ndu tried to appear calmer than his racing pulse sounded in his head.

"You all remember the plan? Ikem, now that Ama has left, you come inside with me. Chidi, bring the bags, get in the back and when we get there, leave that stupid thing in the truck. You understand? Everyone ready?"

"Can we at least say a prayer?" asked Ikem.

They gathered around him as he mumbled a few words about God protecting them as they tried to feed their families and forgive them for doing wrong but they meant no harm as life was not easy and. . . until Chidi impatiently broke off to clamber onto the truck. The others squeezed in the front.

84

Ndu took the Webley out of a plastic bag. He checked it was loaded and jiggled with the safety catch.

They set off and as they progressed through Amuwo Odofin, Kachi's use of the gears improved but there was still enough jerking and stuttering to make it an uncomfortable ride for Chidi. No words were spoken in the cabin until they reached Festac. Ndu thought his heart was going to explode out of his ears even as he struggled to breathe. Ikem wondered why he needed to ease himself when he had already pissed twice back at the warehouse. Kachi was focused on his driving.

Specifically built for the 1977 Festival of Black Arts and Culture, Festac was laid out as a grid, so they bounced across 3rd Avenue and stuttered down 32nd Road eventually turning towards their target.

As they pulled closer, Ndu spotted an empty parking space immediately in front of the bank. His voice constricted by the tension, croaked at Kachi, "Quickly, into that space!"

Ndu readied himself to jump out quickly, holding the Webley in his left hand so his right was free to open the truck door.

In the back, lying on the metal floor, Chidi took the wrapper off the Dane gun and primed himself. As soon as they pulled in, Ndu pushed the door open, Ikem right behind him. He was about halfway out when Kachi took his foot off the clutch while he was still in gear and the pick-up suddenly lurched forward with a hard jolt. Ndu, the revolver still in his left hand, fell out of the door, right side first. As he went down, he fell onto a parked car and his left hand smacked into the car's wing mirror so hard that his finger pressed the trigger. With an ear-shattering bang, the gun went off, sending a .38 calibre bullet a few short feet to where a woman was just turning from an ATM towards the noise. The bullet went straight through her nose and distributed the entire back of her head across the wall of the bank.

At the same time, as Ikem was following Ndu out of the door, the sudden jolt threw his head against the frame, knocking him momentarily unconscious.

Chidi too was thrown against the bulkhead of the cabin, disorientating him.

One moment, the solitary armed policeman was seated, dozing in a plastic chair next to the door of the bank, the next, a pick-up truck had swung in, almost driving straight at him, and all hell had let loose. He dropped his weapon, an AK47, in shock, but had time to pick it up as Ndu scrambled under the open door to retrieve the Webley that had jumped out of his hand with the kick of the shot.

Grabbing his semi-automatic, the policeman had all the time in the world to stand, walk around to the front of the pick-up and point it at Ndu. He pulled the trigger. As the safety was on, there was no response and Ndu had a split moment to shout "Chidi!"

Chidi, who had recovered, stood up in the back of the vehicle, his Dane gun pointed at the policeman. He fired.

There was a massive eruption of flame as two cartridges exploded in Chidi's face, tearing it apart and sending him hurtling backwards over the side of the truck.

By this point, the policeman had flicked the safety and put several rounds into Ndu's body. Kachi, realising he was in trouble, put the pick-up into reverse. Except it wasn't. He'd stabbed his foot on the accelerator and smashed forward into the policeman, crushing him against the wall.

Ikem rolled out heavily and was just coming around as Kachi found the reverse gear and shot straight out into a car that belonged to another customer who, seeing what was happening, had leapt out and run away, leaving his car in the middle of the road where he had been waiting to park.

The sudden movement meant Ikem was thrown on top of a dying Ndu while, at the same time, the crushed legs of the policeman gave way and he collapsed forward where his AK47 spilled. As it hit the ground, the catch on the automatic released, and the rifle let off a burst of several rounds. Some of them ripped into Ikem while others ricocheted off the ground and out across the road where one hit a newspaper vendor in the leg.

Just at that very moment, a black Nigerian Police Special Anti-Robbery Squad Hilux pick-up turned into the road and three officers, fully kitted with helmets, body armour and more AK47s jumped out.

The first of the Orile Gangstas they saw was Kachi, in the pick-up, unable to select a gear in his panic. Two of the policemen immediately fired several bursts.

From only a few metres away, the bullets easily went straight through the door hitting Kachi multiple times. Those that didn't hit him, carried on until they crashed through the windows of a nearby nail parlour where, fortunately, all the girls had long since been lying on the floor.

One officer carried on towards Kachi to make sure he was dead and the other two walked over to Ikem and Ndu. By now Ndu was lifeless but Ikem was struggling to stand.

The first policeman put several bullets into Ikem's body and it slumped, still jerking, face down on top of his cousin.

The policeman turned him over onto his back with his foot. He saw the dark patch where Ikem had involuntarily urinated and sucked his teeth in disgust.

The blood of the two young men pooled onto the street. The officer spotted the Webley. He picked it up gingerly, to not get blood on his hands, and noticed the safety catch was broken.

He turned to the other policeman who was tending to the bank guard whose legs were broken. Everyone ignored Chidi, who was rolling in agony, his hands flailing as he couldn't bear to touch the shattered mess of his face.

The third officer walked over from where he had been checking Kachi and, seeing the boy's pain, looked at his colleagues as if to say, "Why haven't you done anything?"

Without any perceptible emotion, he put two bullets into what remained of Chidi's head. Chidi's body shuddered and lay still.

Gradually, as it became clear that the shooting was over, a crowd started to gather. Shocked employees and customers tentatively came out of the bank. Someone asked where the security guards were. Long gone. People from along the street, traders, workers from nearby shops and offices, teachers and kids from a local school, gathered around.

There was no taping off or securing the crime scene. There were no ambulances. The police ordered the bank manager to drive their injured colleague to a hospital.

Friends and family gathered around the wounded newspaper vendor and tried to organise someone to carry him for treatment. The mob was free to stand within touching distance of the bodies. There was much jostling to get close and a mini-commotion started when someone stepped in the blood.

No one knew who the woman from the ATM was. Someone tried to open her phone, still clutched in her stiffening hands. Eventually, a bystander had the bright idea of getting the card from the ATM and taking it into the bank to check who she was and contact her family.

It took over an hour for a van to come from the Lagos State morgue to scoop up the bodies and unceremoniously dump them in the back. The crowd had already started to drift away. Pity is short-lived in Nigeria.

Over at Iganmu, at St Pio Catholic Church, Ama sat in a pew, rocking slightly as he tried to remember his catechism lessons. It would be a few hours before he would learn of his narrow escape from the massacre.

Unable to cope with the news of the loss of his friends and feeling he could not return to his aunt's place where he had been staying, he became one of the many homeless on Lagos streets. There was nowhere for him to turn. He could not confess to the priest what he had done and as his mental and physical state declined in the weeks that followed, he joined the ranks of the wide-eyed insane that wandered amongst the traffic, matted hair and barely clothed, until several months later, he was hit by a truck on the expressway and died instantly.

Meanwhile, in Benin City, the hyena men were preparing to entertain shoppers at the busy New Market. They had collected good money in their couple of weeks in Lagos and had chartered a danfo to carry them and the animals to Benin. The hyenas were always happy to visit this place.

There was a large butchery section to the market and a distinct lack of sanitation around the management of it. What would be considered a disgusting stench to the average human was a sweet aroma to the four-legged scavengers. The handlers made sure all the animals had their fill before they put on their show. Domesticated to some extent, a hungry hyena with the smell of carrion in its nostrils was not something easily controlled.

Even before the boys' own families learned of the tragedy, Hope was in the know. She had a formidable network and a customer who had witnessed the aftermath came in to share the news. As the messenger described the scene, hardly needing to add her embellishments, Madam Hope put her hands on her knees and pushed herself straight to stand over her pots. She wasn't getting any younger. Half listening to the story, she called out to one of the girls to bring out a bucket of fish. She was still listening as she prepared the fish for that night's peppersoup.

"May their gods have mercy on their souls," said Hope, as she chopped a particularly large catfish into four pieces and threw it in the pot. "They were not bad boys. This is what poverty does. I pray that their mothers have more children."

She wiped her hands on her ever-greasy apron.

"Amen," said the customer, nodding.

Chapter 11

Who is to Judge?

"Sections 3(d) and 3(e) of Police Force Order 237
permit police officers to shoot suspects and detainees
who attempt to escape or avoid arrest.
Under section 3(e) of Police Force Order 237,
the police are allowed to use firearms to 'arrest a person
who takes to flight in order to avoid arrest,'

"... in July 2004 police authorities told the NGO
Human Rights Watch that the police had killed 7,198
'armed robbers' in shoot-outs between January 2000
and February 2004. The IGP showed Human Rights
Watch a chart, which indicated that 3,100
'armed robbers' were killed in 2003 alone.
The NPF's official figure for that year was 545 deaths."

'Killing At Will: Extrajudicial Executions and Other
Unlawful Killings in Nigeria'
Amnesty International, 2009

"What were they thinking? They did not stand a chance!"

Isioma was slumped in the seat next to Robert. She had rung him on that Thursday to tell him the news but he was not able to get to the island until Saturday.

"I can't help thinking about it."

He had his arm around her and though he wanted to say something along the lines of "They were robbing a bank, what did they expect?" he knew that that was not the time.

Instead, he asked, gently, "Tell me about them."

"They were my cousins. Our cousins."

"Yes, I know. What I mean is, did you know them that well?"

They were driving along Western Avenue on their way to Orile as Isioma wanted to pay her respects to the boys' families. Robert was not particularly enthusiastic about it and did his best to dissuade her but when she insisted, he felt he should swallow his reticence to support her.

Isioma took a deep breath. "Okay. So, you know there were four or five boys?"

"Yes."

"Four were killed but another seems to have been involved but has gone missing. I knew Ndu best because he was about my age, just a year or two older. I had not seen him for a while. Just family functions like weddings and . . . you know."

She paused to re-gather her thoughts. She sat back in her seat and spoke in a calmer tone.

"So, the boys' grandfather fought in the civil war with ours. Grandpa Okafor didn't make it through the war, but the boys' grandpa did, and it turns out he kept an old army pistol he had. He had a large family. There were two daughters, one of whom, Auntie Chidi, is Ndu's mum. The other, Auntie Chika, did not have any children. She was the youngest and stayed in the village to look after her parents but when they passed on, she moved to Lagos and lives in Orile. That's where the family is gathering today. So, when Ndu came to Lagos to find work. . ."

"Which he didn't?" interrupted Robert.

"Yes." Isioma gave him a look. "It's not easy, you know. They all tried."

"Yes, sorry."

"When Ndu came to Lagos, he stayed at her place. I knew he hung out with Chidi and Ikem; they're cousins. Their fathers were Auntie Chidi and Chika's brothers. I didn't know the other one. Anyway, from what I heard, Ndu must have found the pistol in Auntie Chika's box where she kept a few family things. Now she is distraught and blames it on herself."

Robert had several questions but waited for a few minutes as they drove in silence. Isioma was deep in her thoughts as she looked out of the car window. As they passed the National Theatre, she muttered more to herself than anyone else, "It's just not fair."

Eventually, Robert asked, "So, Isioma, were theirs, and our grandpa, brothers?"

"Well, not really. So, our great-grandfather, Agu Ede, is sort of our family patriarch. He and his brother fought in the second world war for the British. His brother died in the war, so Papa Agu took his wife and children into his compound, and they became like his wife and children too. All those boys are descended from that branch of the family."

"Wow," said Robert. "I did not know Nigerian troops fought in the war."

"To be honest, I am not too sure of the details. I know there was a West African regiment, and the Nigerian Army still has an 81st Division in recognition of that. I know because it is in Enugu. They fought in North Africa and the Far East but that's about all I know."

Robert was impressed. "Did you learn that at school?"

Isioma shook her head. "There is virtually no serious history taught in schools. Much of what there is seems to have come more from some irrelevant curriculum left over by the British. You know how they say, 'History is written by the victors'? Our colonisers, if you remember, even though you call yourself that—were British."

Robert was taken aback.

"Isioma, I had no idea that you were so passionate about our colonial history. I must admit to being a bit shocked. It also sounds like you are having a dig at me?"

"No Robert, sorry. I am just angry at the injustice of what has happened." She looked at him. "But think about it, my, our, family come from an area blighted by an industry built to serve the British, then they fought in their war in some far-off country where some died. Years later, the British supported the federal side in our civil war. A war in which more of our family were killed. Don't you think we should feel strongly about it?"

"Well, yes. The way you put it, we should."

"I am sorry, Robert. I did not mean to rant."

She took a deep breath and looked at him.

"As a child, my father would talk about our family. If I am honest, being a girl more interested in helping my mother, it did not always sink in but as I get older, I understand why he wanted me to know." Isioma's voice trailed off before she resumed more quietly, almost as a whisper. "And now, to know my family have perpetrated more violence and innocent people have been killed. I. . ."

She stopped mid-sentence and lapsed into silence, not bearing to think about the unfortunate woman who had been shot dead just going about her daily business.

As they made their way through the traffic, Robert too became engrossed in his thoughts.

All he had done was accept a three-year contract as an accountant in a brewery. He had not realised it would trigger so much soul searching. He was not even sure he wanted to be here, right now, doing this, not knowing what he was about to find out. There would be yet more to come that day as they drove into a garage on Eric Moore Road in Surulere.

Aunt Chika lived in a part of Orile that was difficult to access so the family had sent someone to meet them at the petrol station and act as their guide. He got in the front and directed Mathew, Robert's driver, and they soon turned off into the heart of the township.

Robert watched as the paved road turned into what was little more than a narrow track. Even in the dry season, it was difficult terrain, rutted and hard but now in the rains, it had become slippery and treacherous. The community was trying to persuade the Lagos State government to improve the drainage. There were a few metal signs by piles of material to say there was a project to build new gutters but, judging by the weeds and heaps of litter, nothing was happening.

On the side of the road, stalls had been built on old wooden planks, almost like rafts, where everything from eggs and cigarettes to batteries and sachets of milk and chocolate powder were piled up or hung for sale.

Houses and small concrete apartment buildings with various styles of metal gates ran the length of the street, interspersed with the odd space where a building had either been demolished or collapsed. Some of these had been partially cleared while the debris of others lay where they'd fallen. They passed a lot of old cars, though Robert could not decide whether they were wrecked or just badly parked.

93

Eventually, they came to a block where the rusty gates were propped open. The small area in front of the building was already full of vehicles but their guide said he would stay with Mathew and watch over the car.

As they got out, Isioma turned to Robert. "Have you got any money on you? I forgot to ask."

"Some. Why?"

"We should make some contribution," she said.

"I have about twenty-five thousand on me. I have a couple of cases of Guinness, Harp, and Malta, in the boot. My monthly allowance. I can give those?"

"Perfect."

They had to squeeze round the parked cars and go down a narrow path to the side of the block. They followed a woman, who had come to meet them, up narrow and dingy stairs into an apartment. They were ushered into the main room, set up with a couple of settees where several weeping women were sitting. Other hard-back chairs and armchairs were arranged around the sides of the room. Younger women and girls scuttled around offering drinks and snacks to visitors.

Isioma went straight to two of the grieving women who were both wearing traditional wrappers. She hugged them.

They responded, "Nnoo nne, deeje."

She knelt in front of them, still holding their hands and offered her condolences. "Aawu, ndo nu ndi nnem. Obi gbowaram nke ukwu. Onwu, onwu!"

Robert stood there, trying to look sympathetic until Isioma turned to pull him in.

"Aunties, this is Cousin Robert. Auntie Peace's son from the UK."

One of the women held out her hand.

"Eeyi, nnoo nna. Ibiarute ofuma? Oyiri nnaya! Kedu ka nne gi Peace nwanne anyi mere? Ahu adikwa ya mma?"

"He doesn't hear Igbo, Auntie Chika. He has come here to work from London."

The woman pulled him down with her hand and hugged him.

"It doesn't matter. You are here and we appreciate it. How is your mother?"

Robert was focusing on the ungainly hug, trying not to fall over onto the grieving sisters.

"She is fine, Auntie. I am so sorry for your loss."

The other aunt, Chidi, looked up at him smiling sadly. She reached over and stroked his face.

"Nwa nwanne nwanyị anyị ahụtụbeghị."

"Yes," said Chika. "The son of the sister we have never seen. Perhaps we did meet your mother as children in the village but those were confusing times before the family moved to Lagos and war came and she was carried off."

She gestured to some empty chairs. "You are welcome. What can we offer you?"

"Auntie, Robert has brought some drinks as a contribution. Perhaps someone can pick them up from the car?"

One of the older boys was sent downstairs to collect the drinks.

Robert sat on a hard chair and one of the girls brought him a side table with a malt drink and a saucer with some small chops on it. Isioma was still with her aunties. *Their* aunties, he had to remind himself. She was on her haunches talking to them in Igbo.

There were several outbursts of tears and exclamations of pain. This was real, unadulterated, grief, to a degree that he had never before witnessed. It was almost infectious, and he could feel the emotion in his throat as he swallowed his drink.

Every few minutes, new people would come in. As women arrived, they would invariably hug the family and sit or squat near them, talking and sharing the pain. The men would express their formalities before nodding to Robert and the other men, sitting, lining the walls, not speaking apart from token greetings. There were fewer men than women. Often the men would stay just a few minutes and leave.

As Robert sat, he looked around. Despite the squalor outside, this was a tidy living room, or it would have been before the furniture was shifted to make room for mourners. There were lace curtains at the windows and framed pictures around the walls, mostly photographs or badly painted family portraits, though he did notice an incongruous print of Constable's 'The Hay Wain'.

All the women, except for Isioma, were wearing traditional dress, wrappers with white embroidered blouses, and seemed supportive and sympathetic, whereas the men all seemed to be dressed in work clothes or trousers and shirts and were less engaged.

As he was to find out later, the incident caused so much pain and embarrassment that there was almost a major split in the family. There were those, particularly the women, who showed understanding and compassion to the boys' mothers while others, particularly the men, viewed them as parents to criminals.

While these conversations were happening in Igbo, Robert could feel the tension between those who wanted to sympathise with mothers who had lost children and those who believed that, as said children had been killed while robbing a bank, sympathy was misplaced. To them, the cousins' behaviour had disgraced them all, to the extent that their immediate families should be shunned.

Just as his mind started to wander to whether he could get to a television in time for the United game, someone sat on the chair next to him and slapped his knee.

"So, young Robert. Welcome to Lagos. Is this what you expected to find?"

Robert looked round to see a trim, smartly dressed man in a well-pressed, eastern-style, gabardine suit, smiling at him. A touch of grey at his temples suggested him to be in his fifties but his smile was more youthful.

"My name is Onyeka. My father was your grandfather's brother. I remember your mother because we went to the same primary school in Ngwo-Enugu. Except she was called Udo then."

Robert was taken aback at meeting a relative he was unaware of.

"Hi Onyeka, sorry, Uncle. No, this is certainly not what I hoped I would be finding but it is nice to meet you." He gestured to where the women were. "Well, sort of. Also, I find it hard to remember my mother's name was originally Udo."

"Yes, short for Udodirim, which means 'Peace be unto me'. I don't know whether it was at school or later when she met your father, but she anglicised it to 'Peace'."

"I don't mean to be rude but today is all a bit of a stunner. First, this whole emotional scene and now about my Mum. I was never clear about the details."

Onyeka laughed. "No wahala, young man. How is your mum, by the way? I did visit her and your dad in London once when I was travelling for work. You were just a toddler then, so I don't expect you to remember. But, you know, your father was not a huge fan of her Nigerian family so I backed off."

"I had no idea. Well, I knew Dad didn't enjoy his one visit here and never took to Nigerian food, but I have never felt he was anti-Nigerian," Robert said, coming to his father's defence. "I just don't know really."

"I don't think your dad was 'anti-' per se, but I think he just didn't want to be dragged into the family thing."

He gestured towards the settee groaning under the weight of several women either sitting on it or perched on the arms.

"He might have been right, you know?" Onyeka said, slapping Robert's knee. His lightness was certainly in contrast to the general gloom. "That's probably why she gave you Afamefuna as your middle name."

"Right, sure," said Robert, though he wasn't.

"Uncle Onyeka!" exclaimed Isioma, who had just come over, and hugged him.

"Robert, this is one of my favourite uncles, but I warn you: my father said I should never trust him!"

Onyeka laughed again and then realised they were being a bit loud.

"Ssh Isioma! Don't give away my secrets. What are you? Your cousin's minder?"

He winked at Robert and whispered theatrically, "We should meet up for a drink one evening, and I can tell you about all the skeletons in the family closets."

"That sounds like a plan but before we do that, Uncle Onyeka, is there anything that can be done about the bodies?" Isioma spoke in a more hushed tone now.

"No, Isioma."

Onyeka was quiet now, but his tone was suddenly and unmistakably serious. "I am sorry. There is nothing that can be done without a great deal of money. Look, I know they were not bad boys but this matter. . ." His voice trailed off and he shook his head.

He and Isioma looked at each other until he said, more brightly, "Well, this cousin of yours is having a tough lesson on Igbo family life. I think you should take him away to that comfortable island where you people live, and leave us villagers and slum dwellers to our own wahala."

Isioma play-slapped him on the arm still speaking quietly, "Uncle, see you eh? Na wa for you o. Robert lives on the mainland, in Ikeja. It is just me that hides from my family on the island."

"Well daughter, I can't say that I blame you." Onyeka turned to Robert. "Good luck, young man. I would love to have that beer at some point but really, I think you should carry this young lady home. As much as she wants to support her aunties, this is not a place for you two to be."

It took some time to finally take their leave as Isioma was once more engulfed in more intense conversations. Eventually, they were able to make their way to the car and Mathew retraced their route out of Orile. Little was said for some time.

Eventually, Robert turned in his seat. "Are you okay?"

She nodded and sighed. "It is such a mess, Robert."

"Onyeka seemed very sure that we should not have been there," he said.

"I suppose he is right, really. Maybe I should not have taken you and, certainly, you should not mention it to anyone at work. I knew there was some risk, and I certainly cannot let the bank have any inkling about it. But I believe in family and I wanted to, at least, comfort my aunties. It was not their fault but now they will suffer."

"I don't even know what to say. There is so much to process that I am still taking it in."

He hesitated, then asked, "What was that about the bodies?"

Isioma sighed again. As she was explaining it, Robert could see the tears welling up in her eyes behind her glasses.

Exactly as Isioma said, it was all a terrible mess. Her aunts had told her that after the family heard what had happened, some of them went to find the bodies.

After trying several places, they found that they had been taken to Isolo General Hospital. The corpse of the woman who had been shot was still there, but the police had taken the boys' bodies away. After yet more calls and visits, they tracked them to the Isolo mortuary. The police were deliberately unhelpful, and it was not until the next day that they admitted that they had indeed taken the bodies, and they would be held in the mortuary as they were required for "processing".

The mothers' protestations eventually got them to meet the station commander, the DPO, who was blunt. To retrieve the bodies the family would have to pay substantial amounts of what were, effectively, bribes. These were dressed up as "processing fees", "expenses", "compensation for the injured policeman", and other inflated charges. They were told that without a substantial down payment, they could not even see the bodies.

The police knew they were on strong grounds. There was no disputing that the boys were indeed "shot in the act", which was compounded by the shooting of a bystander and the injuring of a police officer. Any complaints about the police extorting money from them would get no traction. There was also a possibility that the woman's family would come after them for some kind of blood money.

Later, Robert came to learn from Isioma that only a few members of the family were sympathetic enough to contribute to any collection to raise funds. The most common advice was that both aunts and other close family members should leave Lagos and move to the village. Even the parish priest was unresponsive. The boys had violated God's law and he refused a service for them. If the bodies were recovered, he told the women, then he would not allow a funeral mass in the church. No one ever did see the boys' bodies. They would stay decomposing with a dozen other criminal cadavers at the back of the morgue until it was clear the family could not afford to recover them. Then they would be thrown into communal unmarked graves.

Robert later asked Nigerian colleagues at work, without explaining why he was asking, what happens to bodies in Nigerian Police custody when they are no longer of use to extract money? The response was inevitably shrugged shoulders and stories of late-night body dumping in the lagoon or of secret shallow graves behind certain notorious police stations. He realised just how deep public cynicism towards the police really was. Had he known that the Webley was never officially recovered or that the revolver was responsible for fatalities in at least two other armed robberies, and everything that implied, he would have become even more contemptuous of the Nigerian justice system.

As Isioma said just before Robert dropped her off: they were just another Nigerian family to suffer the brutality that is poverty and the cruelty of a corrupt and indifferent establishment.

To which Robert added that nothing seemed to have changed since colonial times.

"In fact," he concluded, "maybe it has even gotten worse."

"Maybe, maybe not," said Isioma thoughtfully. "Who is to judge? Either way, in times like this, there appears to be little hope for ordinary people."

Chapter 12

The Family Endures

*"Time by itself means nothing, no matter how fast it
moves, unless we give it something to carry for us;
something we value."*

Ama Ata Aidoo. "Our Sister Killjoy"

After the turmoil of 1949, things were never the same for the
families of the murdered miners. The killings of that year was the
turning point, a moment when it was recognised that all things
past had fallen apart and the future, frightening in its starkness,
was upon them.

The peaceful valleys where game had been plentiful were
replaced by running gullies of effluent from the mines. The green
hillsides seemed suddenly denuded of vegetation as all the trees
had disappeared to meet the limitless need for pit props and
firewood. The scars of mechanisation benefitted only a distant
government, and now the compounds of the Ngwo people were
surrounded by businessmen and industrialists. There was
employment for men ready to work underground, but the
customary living of small-scale farming and hunting was gone.

Many of the men, disenchanted with the poor conditions of
the mines, drifted towards the cities, looking for other
livelihoods. Agu Ede's oldest son was no different. By the early
1960s, Okafor had married and taken his young family to the
capital of newly independent Nigeria: Lagos. There he found a
sense of optimism, swept in with fervent hope for the young
republic. While it was not all plain sailing, Okafor soon found
work as a driver on the project to extend the new University of
Lagos. While still caring for their two young children, Vitus and
Udo, Okafor's wife, Abigail, made good money running a small
canteen for the many Igbo workers. Between them, they could
afford two rooms in a house in Surulere.

One day in late 1963, Abigail saw an advertisement in *The Daily Times* for domestic staff, placed by the High Commission of Trinidad and Tobago, itself newly independent.

Within a few weeks of applying, the whole family moved to the staff quarters of the Deputy High Commissioner's residence in Ikoyi: Okafor maintained the premises and drove while Abigail worked in the house. Winston and Simone Duke were newly arrived, as were so many of the diplomats from the newly independent Commonwealth countries. Unpractised in the usually hierarchical and elitist world of old-school colonial-era diplomats, they became friendly with this young Nigerian family and with their grown-up children back in the Caribbean, they practically adopted Vitus and Udo, who had the run of the house and garden.

For three years, the Ede family developed happily. They were able to save a little money, the children grew healthily and attended a nearby school and on Sundays, they all went to Mass where they met many other families from the Enugu area and caught up with local news. In their frequent letters back home, they were able to describe a life of some contentment and even enclose a little money for the family. It was not to last forever.

The Ede family's tranquillity was disturbed by the failed officers' coup attempt in January 1966, followed by the counter-coup in July of the same year, which saw Colonel Yakubu Gowon become Head of State. Things became worse as news started circulating of anti-Igbo sentiment culminating in widespread violence and slaughter across the north of the country. With his diplomatic contacts, Winston Duke had access to inside information about tensions within the hierarchy of the military government and early warning of the Eastern Region governor, Chukwuemeka Odumegwu Ojukwu's plans for secession.

News was also coming in of the mass exodus of Igbo people from Kano and the bigger cities in the north back to their ethnic heartland in eastern Nigeria. The Ndi Igbo grapevine was soon calling able-bodied men to return home, to prepare to take up arms to protect their fellow countrymen as the name "Biafra" became more and more prominent.

Okafor was loath to give up the stability that life with the Dukes presented but felt honour bound to take his family back to his homeland. There was increasing tension in Lagos and several incidents of harassment against Igbos had appeared in the papers. They prayed that it might blow over but by early 1967, Winston was reporting that conflict appeared inevitable. Okafor was more and more determined to return to the East and defend Ngwo.

The Dukes suggested he leave Abigail and the children with them, where they would be safe in a diplomatic compound. But Abigail refused to leave her husband's side.

Simone suggested, "So, perhaps it would be better to leave the children with us?"

Despite their deep-seated reluctance, the dramatically worsening situation forced Okafor and Abigail to decide it would be safer to leave the children with their willing employer-friends in Lagos. The children themselves were becoming more and more aware that their idyllic life was under threat. Several times, teachers had had to break up fights between the older Igbo boys and other children in the playground.

When Ojukwu announced the creation of the Republic of Biafra and her secession from Nigeria on the 30th of May 1967, the political situation speedily began to unravel. Prejudice against anyone from the other side of the Niger began to be more prevalent, to the extent that riots broke out in several places on the mainland and the federal army and police started rounding up Igbo men and even women in Lagos. While Ikoyi was relatively safe, it would not last. Several of Okafor's friends hastily put together a plan to gather a small fleet of cars to leave Lagos in a convoy and drive to the east.

They would need to move by night and avoid the main roads.

By then, Vitus and Udo were no longer attending school. At fourteen and twelve, they were old enough to attract the attention of those who wished their people ill. They knew something was about to happen but were unprepared when Okafor and Abigail sat their children down to explain that on that very night, they would be collected by friends to rendezvous with other families for the drive to the newly christened Biafra.

Nothing the children could say, no volume of tears and pleas would persuade their parents to change their minds. War was inevitable and it would be safer for Vitus and Udo to stay in Ikoyi. The Dukes joined the family, promising the distraught children that they would look after them and that in a few weeks, months at the most, the mess would be over and everything would be normal again.

Around 10 o' clock that night, a battered old Austin pulled up outside the gates and flashed its lights. As it drove in, two men got out and helped Okafor and Abigail put their bundles in the boot. They were travelling as light as they could. As the Dukes came out with the children, Vitus, carrying a small and unseen bag of his own, twisted away from the grip of Simone and somehow slipped into the back seat of the car. When the adults attempted to persuade him and pull him out, he clung on.

"I am nearly a man Dad," he cried. "I am not staying. I am coming with you."

As his parents remonstrated, the other men became impatient. "We must meet the others. He is nearly grown. Let him come. Quickly."

There were tears, harsh words, and a sense of panic. Before Udodirim Ede grasped what was happening, her mother, father and older brother were gone, leaving her sobbing in the arms of Auntie Simone. It was to be fourteen years until she next saw her brother, but it was the last time she ever saw her parents.

* * *

The details about exactly what happened on the road east are not clear. It seems there were about a dozen vehicles in their small convoy but there were many thousands of refugees in other convoys or travelling on foot, desperate to get to Igboland before the conflict started.

It was possible to avoid the federal roadblocks around Lagos by travelling out via Epe but eventually, the streams of refugees converged on the Benin road around Ore. It seemed half of humanity was stretched out along the road, hemmed in by the bush. Lines and lines of vehicles: buses and mini-buses, the odd small truck or mammy wagon, but mostly cars; Peugeots, Morrises, and Volkswagens, of varying ages, all with cases and bundles bursting out of trunks or tied, inelegantly, onto roofs.

Looking ahead along the line of refugees, the sun seemed to rise from the very place they were heading towards. Increasing traffic at every junction meant bottlenecks formed and progress became slower and slower. It was impossible to avoid the federal troops. Okafor and other men of military age were at particular risk of arrest, or worse. At every checkpoint there were incidents. Some men disguised themselves as women, but Okafor and his colleagues opted for the strategy of getting out of the cars with women or elderly men taking the wheel just short of the roadblocks. They would trek through the bush and rejoin the convoy further up the road after the roadblock had been passed.

This had been successful on the first few occasions but at some point, near Benin, where the army was particularly jumpy, the men were seen coming out of the foliage where they had been hiding, waiting for their families. Whether there were scuffles or resistance or whether the soldiers were just trigger-happy, no one knew. Maybe one of the men had a weapon. In the aftermath, what was clear was a one-sided firefight in which several of the men were killed or wounded, with the rest fleeing back into the forest.

Abigail was one of those never to find out what happened to her husband, the father of her children.

* * *

Abigail did not see Okafor's body but the wife of one of the survivors later told her that he was wounded as he fled into the bush. She lived in the hope that he had escaped and would one day return to Ngwo. She and Vitus had no choice but to continue in convoy with the other women and children and one or two survivors who managed to catch up with them.

After painfully slow progress in the long stream of what were effectively refugees, they made it as far as Asaba where federal troops confiscated all the vehicles before they were allowed anywhere near the bridge.

When they eventually made it across, they had nothing of value left. Everything had been taken from them by Nigerian soldiers guarding the bridge itself. From Onitsha to Ngwo was barely a hundred kilometres but it still took them over a week: walking, grabbing the odd lift, sleeping in the bush, and begging for food from mobilising Biafran soldiers.

For the first few weeks, they were able to recuperate with the family, but any hope Okafor would join them or that they would have any respite was destroyed when federal troops began shelling Enugu. By the beginning of October, they joined other civilians fleeing the occupying army. To make matters even worse, as young as he was, Vitus was seen on the road by recruiting officers and was forcibly conscripted into the youth corps. He was taken away as Abigail stood with other families in utter wretchedness, in the middle of a road strewn with misery, as their young sons were driven to an unknowably bleak future.

Despite a harrowing time and several desperately traumatic experiences, Vitus was one of those fortunate enough to survive the war. Abigail was not so lucky. In February 1969, she was living in a makeshift camp in the bush just outside of Owerri with several other women from their extended family. One morning, hearing some foreign aid had arrived, they made their way to the market at Afor-Umuohiagu to barter the last of their collective valuables for any food or supplies they could find.

At one in the afternoon, a federal bomber appeared overhead. It made one pass over the market only to return to bomb and strafe the crowded space filled with women and children, many of whom were there for the daily Red Cross ration. Abigail Ede and her kinfolk were buried close to where they fell.

Chapter 13

An Innocent Question

"But who made the law that we should not hope in our daughters? We women subscribe to that law more than anyone. Until we change all this, it is still a man's world, which women will always help to build."

Buchi Emecheta. "The Joys of Motherhood."

"You know he has asked me out?"

Robert and Isioma were sitting in a pizza restaurant in VI. It had taken Isioma a while to understand Robert's fixation with anything with cheese on or in it. In her opinion, cooked cheese was up there with runny eggs and rare steak as far as unpalatable European cooking was concerned. Robert loved his pizzas and there was a new place run by an Italian woman that was very popular, and it became one of his preferred destinations.

Eventually, under duress, she did find a pizza that had plenty of pepper on it that at least provided more flavour than the usual bland oyibo food. They did make decent suya too, so she occasionally agreed to meet there.

Normally he would not come to VI mid-week but he wanted to check on Isioma after the weekend and share a conversation he had had with his mother.

Then she dropped the bombshell and Robert was genuinely taken aback.

"You're not going to accept though, right?"

"I might. I haven't decided yet," she said, laughing. "What is wrong with you? You should see your face. I thought he was your friend."

Robert was defensive. "Nothing. He is. Well, kind of."

"How can someone be 'kind of' a friend?" she asked. "He either is, or is not."

"Terry is a funny bloke. I mean, when I first met him at the airport, he looked like a thug. He was wearing a Millwall shirt. You know about Millwall? They are the worst football fans in England: racist, violent, homophobic. But we were stuck in a go-slow for ages and once we started chatting, I thought he was quite human, even funny. The next time I bumped into him, he seemed a bit lost. So, I invited him out."

"Why do you say he seemed 'lost'?"

"I don't know really," Robert replied, pondering for a moment. The restaurant was quite empty at this time of the day, with more activity happening at the bar island and the kitchen behind it than in the seating area.

"I know when he first got here, he hung out at Pat's Bar all the time with a heavy bunch of expats at that. But when we went out that time, he told me how tired he was of that scene. He knows the drinking brings out the worst in him but that does not mean he will stop doing it. Where he comes from is one of the most violent areas in London, or, used to be anyway.

"In the early eighties, there was a terrible fire where a load of Black kids were burnt to death at a party. There were a lot of stories that it was arson, that some local had firebombed the place. I don't know the details, but it still stirs up strong feelings. It is a very divided community and that is where he was brought up. Poverty does terrible things to people, I guess."

He continued, "Yet, I suppose, in a way, though his background is so different from mine, there are weird similarities. We are both out of our comfort zones and thrown together somewhere where neither of us knows anyone. It can be difficult to break away from socialising with just a few work colleagues all the time. Especially if you live in the same compound. Until you and I started hanging out, my experience of Nigeria was very different to what it has become."

Isioma smiled. "At your party, when he went out to watch Orlando Julius, he and I struck up a conversation. I just thought there was something sad about him. I thought he was quite sweet really."

"But you know he's married right?"

"Robert!" she exclaimed. "Don't be such a prude. All I am doing is maybe thinking of meeting him for a drink. I am not going to jump into bed with him. He just messaged me, and I said I'd think about it."

Robert held up his hands. "Okay, okay. Don't get your knickers in a twist."

"What?"

"Oh, it's just an expression. You know, like, don't get upset about something."

She shook her head. "You people say some weird things."

Robert ignored her for a minute.

"Anyway, how are you doing? And how are your aunts and the family coping?"

Isioma explained about the continuing saga about the bodies and admitted she had decided not to get involved. She had spoken to her father about it in a long phone conversation and he had insisted she stay out of it. Despite her affection for her aunts, the possible ramifications of her getting caught up in it were just too serious. If her workplace got to know that her family were associated with an attempt to rob a bank, especially with firearms, it would damage, if not end, her career. She told Robert that for once, her father agreed with Uncle Onyeka: that she should stay on the island and avoid spending any time with the family on the mainland.

"Talking of Uncle Onyeka," said Robert, "I too had a long call with home and I asked my mum about what he told me."

"That's interesting. What did she say?"

"It turns out that Onyeka did visit them a couple of times, maybe twenty-five years ago, but he started asking for money for a project. Apparently, my dad lent him nearly a thousand quid and never got it back. Eventually, on another visit, Dad confronted him about it, and it all got heated and nasty. I think he might have got some of the money back, but it left Dad genuinely angry. It also made it a little harder for Mum to keep in contact with her family. It kind of helps me understand why there was so little talk of them at home."

Robert had finished his pizza and was eyeing Isioma's unfinished one.

"Are you going to eat that?"

"No, you can have it."

"And, of course, Dad did not really want to come out here again."

Now Robert started picking bits of the hot red chilli off Isioma's pizza.

"Robert, for the sake of God, just eat it. It's not that hot."

Isioma wanted to hear more but was frustrated at Robert's reaction to the pepper.

"You know you can be really annoying sometimes? So, what else did your mum say?"

Robert described the phone call with his mother to an intently listening Isioma. How she had not spoken that much previously about the family but when he told her about going to offer condolences to Aunt Chika and Aunt Chidi, meeting Onyeka and the whole story, she had become emotional. He could tell she was crying over the phone and that upset him. At that point, Robert's voice choked a little and, not for the first time, Isioma was surprised to see a man of his age show his emotion so openly. None of her Nigerian male friends and colleagues would have done so and she had thought Robert seemed so typically British in his reserved manner.

He went on to explain that he felt he owed his mother an apology for never having shown any interest in her history and his Nigerian heritage.

It was only now, after meeting some of her family, that he realised how lonely she must have been when she first arrived in London and how estranged from her home she must have become. He had promised her that on his next leave, he would spend more time with her and hear more about her memories instead of going out all the time to catch up with his mates or play football.

Isioma studied his face attentively, her expression sympathetic.

"Why don't you bring Auntie Peace back out with you next time you go on leave? You should bring your sister too."

Robert nodded. "I thought about that. I think Cindy would be up for it, particularly if Mum came. She has always been a bit closer to Mum than me."

"We daughters are more sensitive to our mothers' needs, you know," said Isioma, in a matter-of-fact tone. "Anyway, I think that was an important conversation. You know I have never understood how you could be a complete person if you were somehow separated from your roots. I suppose you never knew anything different, but your mum must have felt like half a person for most of her life."

"I am only really discovering that now. I feel kind of ashamed."

"Well, I was going to say you should, but I realise that's unfair," Isioma said, smiling. "I know we are products of our environment to some extent, but in my Igbo worldview, even though I am a Christian, I could never refuse to acknowledge what I owe to my ancestors."

Robert was not so sure. "But if I never knew who my ancestors were, how could I acknowledge them? I mean, okay, now I am physically closer to them in Nigeria but what bearing could they possibly have on me in London?"

"I believe they influence you in ways you would not necessarily recognise. I am sure, just as an example, they had something to do with you coming out here."

"No, Isioma," he almost snorted. "I came out here because my employers made me a job offer that I could not refuse. It was just about the money and my career."

"You *could* have refused. You believe in free will and self-determination, right? I just happen to believe that your conscious decision-making is influenced by something deeper."

"Maybe," Robert paused. The conversation was getting a bit too philosophical for him. "But our ancestors cannot get me to eat this pepper, it's bloody ridiculous. Even though I have taken it off the pizza, the flavour is still making my mouth sting. I need another beer."

Not for the first time, Isioma shook her head as if to say *'I give up'*.

Robert ordered his beer.

"So, you avoided the question. Are you going to accept Terry's invitation?"

"I think I probably will. I am curious."

"Curious? About what?"

Isioma pulled a face as if to say she was not clear about it herself. "I don't know really, but something in me thinks I should."

Robert waved his fingers in the air and made a mock ghost sound.

"Maybe it is the ancestors influencing your decision. Or . . ." now she gave him a look. ". . . it is his ancestors making him ask you out."

"Robert Railsford, I am going to come to that side of the table and give you a dirty slap!"

He laughed. "But seriously. Do White people have ancestors telling them what to do?"

"Obviously!"

She was beginning to get irritated at the trend of the conversation. She suspected he was making fun of her.

"Yeh, but what I mean is, seriously, are Europeans, say, unconsciously influenced by their ancestors even though they do not realise it?"

Isioma still wasn't sure where this exchange was going. "Well, they used to be, didn't they?"

"How do you mean?"

"As you still claim to be British, you should be more aware of your history and culture."

"Go on." Robert was not quite sure what was coming next.

"'There are more things in heaven and earth, Horatio, than are dreamt of in your philosophy'. Ghosts are ancestors, you understand?"

Robert was impressed. "Clever clogs. Hamlet? We studied it at school."

"Yes, so did we. We read more Shakespeare than we did our own writers. Apart from a couple of Achebe books or the occasional play by Soyinka, we did not study any African, let alone Nigerian writers."

"Like? I cannot say I have heard of many."

Isioma was indignant. "Oh Robert, there are plenty. For example, there are loads of great Nigerian writers, in fact, women writers. Flora Nwapa's *Efuru* is a favourite of mine or anything by Buchi Emecheta. *Everything Good Will Come* by Sefi Atta came out a year or so ago. I enjoyed that; it's about growing up

112

in Lagos. Another new writer is Chimamanda Adichie. Her *Purple Hibiscus* is brilliant. I would recommend that to you. She has another book about the civil war just come out, but I haven't read it yet."

"I did not realise you were such a reader," said Robert.

"We can't afford DSTV so that's what we do in the house. It's only when my rich cousin comes from abroad that I get to go out," she grinned. "Seriously, thanks for taking me out. I do appreciate it."

"Well, now you have a new White boyfriend to take you places." Before she could respond, he added, "I am sure he is a decent bloke, but he is still married. As I said, he drinks heavily and hangs out with some not-particularly-nice people. I cannot honestly say that I think it is a good idea for you to go out with him. However, knowing how stubborn you are, you probably will. So, be careful."

As they got up to go, she patted him on the arm. "Thanks, I know I have my big uncle Robert to call on if there's a problem."

He stood waiting as she looked in her handbag for something and straightened her work skirt. Eventually, he impatiently sucked his teeth. "Oya now!"

She laughed as they headed for the car. "Ooh, who's getting all proper Naija?"

Chapter 14

Food for Thought

"E get this fine lady
Her body na die nwa baby
We suppose to live like family 'ey, I no dey lie (no dey lie)
There's nothing stopping me
She dey feel my swag and I get money
I dey try my best, I be somebody
'Cause I'm living life
This girl dey make me high, high
I dey feel this baby
You no go believe
This girl na die, die
If you see this baby, tell am say
She must chop my money, chop my money
Chop my money, 'cause I don't care."

'Chop My Money (I Don't Care)' by P-Square

The girls were excited.

Ezzy and Florence were helping Isioma choose what outfit to wear on her date with Terry.

"You know, it's no big deal. I don't know why you are making so much fuss."

Isioma was laughing as they were pulling tops out of her box.

"I think you should wear something nicer than trousers on a first date," said Florence, holding up a loose shoulder-less top, "but if you insist, then this will go well with it, especially if you wear the red bra."

"I think this one is better. It clings and shows off your shape."

Ezzy was on the case too.

"I give up with you two!" Isioma flopped on the bed. "It's not a proper date and there probably will not be another."

Florence turned up the small boom box they used for music and the two girls pantomime serenaded her along with Boys II Men: *"I'll make love to you like you want me to. And I'll hold you tight, baby, all through the night."* They both got down on their knees and opened their arms in mock supplication. *'I'll make love to you when you want me to! And I will not let go 'til you tell me to!!"*

Isioma rolled over and put her head under a pillow.

"Help! Someone save me from these mad women!"

She jumped up, whacked the nearest crooner with the pillow and turned the music down. "Seriously though. It is not a proper date. I really cannot imagine having an oyibo as a proper boyfriend."

There were two single beds in one room of the small apartment and a fold-out settee bed in the other that they used as a sitting room. Along one wall there was a small built-in kitchen. They shared a lavatory and a bathroom with another flat carved out of the first floor of the old house. There was just one shared wardrobe and each girl had a chest, or box as they called it, full of neatly folded clothes and personal belongings. There was a fold-out clothes-horse that invariably had towels and various items of underwear hanging on it. There was no television. The girls had done what they could to make the place presentable with available resources and, given there was little room, it was homely. A safe place in a city where women had to be on their guard every minute they were outside their front door, and often behind it too.

None of the girls had regular boyfriends, despite pressure, particularly in Florence's case, from families worried that though still only in their late twenties they were getting old for the marriage stakes. Isioma had suitors during her university days but did not date anyone seriously. There was a shared feeling that the boys matured at a slower pace than they did. On the other hand, too many older men were married and just wanted "something on the side". Florence was under more pressure because there was increasing ethnic and religious conflict where her parents still lived in southern Kaduna. As a member of a minority, largely Christian group, the family was concerned about security in an increasingly polarised future. They saw a good marriage as the best hope for their daughter even though she had the potential for a decent career at the bank.

As yet, both Isioma and Ezzy's families had made the odd comment but there was no real push. Isioma's father, Vitus, in particular, wanted his daughter to focus on her career. Hence his agreement with Onyeka that she should not get caught up in the family's problems in Orile.

"What do you think your folks would say if you took Terry home?" asked Ezzy.

"I don't think they would mind, as long as he behaved decently. But that is irrelevant as it is not going to happen," Isioma replied.

"Yes, but supposing you get a taste for . . .?" interjected Florence.

"For what?" asked Isioma, her voice betraying her suspicion that her roommate was about to be controversial.

"You know," laughed Florence, and then whispered as if someone could overhear them. "White dick!"

Ezzy threw herself on the bed in hysterics. "Florence!" she screamed.

Isioma could not prevent herself from laughing but tried to put on her serious face while standing with her hands on her hips in a double-handled teapot. "Miss Maigari, go to your room at once!"

Florence danced around her chanting, "Isioma, admit it!" Isioma grabbed her and they fell on top of Ezzy on the bed, all of them in stitches.

Eventually, Isioma tried to get up, but the other two girls kept pulling her down.

"Look at the time," she said. "I will be late!"

"Who cares?" screamed the others. "He's a man! Make him wait."

* * *

Terry could not understand it.

He paced around the apartment like a manic guardsman. He could feel his heart racing. *"Why should I be feeling like this?"* he asked himself. The other side of his brain reminded him. *"You*

116

haven't been on a proper date in years." Other questions flashed through his mind. *"What will we have in common?", "What can I talk about?"* and even, *"What the fuck am I doing?"*

Terry was in unfamiliar territory. He would readily admit that he was not the most faithful husband. In the army, years after he and Rachel had been married, he had gone out with the lads in Germany and other postings to girlie bars and brothels. Here in Nigeria, he had been more than an occasional frequenter of the girls of Pat's, Ynot, and Outside Inn. Yet, somehow, this felt different. It felt more of a betrayal.

But why should that be?

He had only met Isioma once, although they had exchanged frequent texts. Nothing was likely to come of it. Certainly, he had to ask her several times before she agreed to go on a date, making it clear nothing physical was going to happen.

He also really liked Robert and did not want to upset him.

Why did Isioma haunt him so? Sure, she was not unattractive but she was nothing like the girls he usually found appealing. He tried not to think of her in sexual terms. Something in him thought that was disrespectful but, at night, alone in his bed, he could not help but wonder. *"Don't even go there,"* he thought. Then again, he had almost no experience of socialising with Nigerians. Apart from the odd drink with Tunde and Robert's birthday, he had very little social contact with locals outside of work. Certainly, beer and peppersoup with his engineering crew did not prepare him.

They would make an odd couple as well. Apart from the colour difference, there was the matter of him being a foot taller. *Why didn't Isioma want him to pick her up?* He had met her friends when he gave them a lift back from Robert's bash. Then, there was the venue. She had chosen a very posh restaurant on VI.

It wasn't the cost that was the real issue but more that those kinds of places were out of his comfort zone. He had never even heard of it but when he asked Tunde about it, Tunde had laughed and told him to start saving up. Tunde also said to mention his name to the proprietor as they had known each other for years and warned him to wear smart trousers and a proper shirt, no jeans or tee shirt!

He was still consumed by these thoughts when he realised it was time to set off.

When he got in the pick-up, Saturday almost did a double take at the sight of his boss in such smart clothes. Terry himself thought he might have overdone the aftershave when Saturday started coughing and surreptitiously opened his window.

When they entered the restaurant parking area, he could not help but notice the other vehicles all seemed to be Mercedes or Land Cruisers. He walked in and was immediately struck by the surroundings. There was a water feature by the door that he thought was particularly poncy and over the top but just as he subdued his natural inclination to say *"Fuck this, I'm off down the pub",* a voice broke into his thoughts.

"Good evening. You must be Terry. Tunde Adebayo let me know you were coming."

A tall, elegant Lebanese gentleman held out his hand.

"Welcome to Villa Medici. Would you like to go to the table or have a drink at the bar while you wait for your guest?"

At the magical word "bar", Terry immediately felt better. He smiled wanly, stammered "Thank you", and allowed himself to be led to a cocktail-style bar.

He perched one bum cheek on a stool and, suddenly wondering if they served beer or only cocktails, was relieved when the white-jacketed barman said, "We have small Heineken sir."

He did his best to sip rather than gulp his beer and pick at the bowl of nuts, before he took a surreptitious look around. It was still quite early, and the place was far from full but there was a hum of conversation and the clink of crockery.

Terry was relieved that no one seemed to be staring at this out-of-place interloper.

He did notice there was a mix of Nigerian and White faces in the restaurant and at several tables, which helped put him at ease.

"So Terry, Tunde told me you are colleagues."

The tall Lebanese gentleman was now standing beside him.

"Well, he is my boss. It's nice of him to tell you I was coming."

"I have known Tunde for years. He often pops in for a drink. A man of great charm and discretion."

Terry was not quite sure but thought there was just a hint of a wink. *"What the hell has Tunde told him?'* he thought, but he heard himself say, "Nice place you have here, Mr . . . I'm sorry, I didn't catch your name."

"Mouin. Thanks. My wife, Pat, is the boss. I just do what I am told." He laughed easily, then suddenly stiffened. "O God, I hate this bloke! Completely odious fucker! Enjoy your meal, Terry," Mouin said, as he walked towards the door where Terry could hear him say "Mr Odummuh, how are you, sir? So lovely to see you!"

Terry looked at his watch. Isioma was fifteen minutes late. His first reaction was to think *"Oh for fuck's sake, she has sent me here to take the piss and stand me up"*. The other side of his brain told him to *"Calm down, she wouldn't do that"*. Then he thought, *"Oh fuck, I need a piss. Supposing she comes while I am in the bog?"* He decided he would have time to go, and quickly walked to the bathroom. But in his haste, splashed urine on his trousers. *"Fuck. Fuck!"* He stood on tiptoe in front of the vanity unit to catch the reflection of his leg in the mirror. *"Thank fuck!"* It wasn't visible without really looking. Someone came in through the door just as he went out. *"Jesus, that was close!"*.

Back on his exposed and awkward perch he gave up sipping, downed his Heineken and ordered another. The stress was killing him. *"What is the fucking point? Nothing's gonna happen. She won't like me and this is going to cost a bleeding fortune. Oh shit, did I bring enough money?"*

Just at that moment, Isioma walked in. She was dressed in dark trousers and a loose, cream top that exposed her smooth shoulders. She was wearing heels, so she looked taller and more chic than Terry remembered. She saw him immediately and strode easily to the bar. As he clumsily eased himself off the stool, she put a hand on his arm and allowed herself to be kissed on both cheeks.

Mouin was busy with his recent arrival's party. A diminutive but elderly Nigerian headwaiter scuttled over and asked if he could escort them to their table.

Terry turned to grab his beer, but the waiter quickly said, "Don't worry sir. I will bring it."

At the table, another waiter held Isioma's chair and tucked it in as she sat down. He took her starched white serviette, flicked it with a practised wrist, and placed it on her lap, saying, "I will be back in a moment to take your drinks order, ma'am."

They were left alone, and it was the first chance Terry had to speak. "You look lovely," he said.

He spoke as if he meant it. He did.

"Oh, Terry. First, I am sorry for being late but, oh my god, this place is so over the top, I had no idea. It was just recommended to me. It is going to cost a fortune. I feel so bad."

Terry did not care. He was just so happy she had arrived, and they were sitting down so she could not see he had sprinkled on his trousers.

"Oh my God!" she exclaimed in an excited whisper. "Don't look now but that noisy guy over there is always seen in the newspapers with my oga pata pata, Jim Ovia, who owns the bank I work for. It's crazy being here with people like that. Supposing Mr Ovia comes in? Do you think we should leave?"

Before Terry could say anything, Mouin appeared at their table. "Good evening, madam." He smiled warmly. "Would you like a drink or would you like to go straight to wine with your meal? Actually, while sir is enjoying his beer, I would like to offer you a glass of champagne with my compliments."

Isioma looked at Terry who made a face that seemed to say, "*Don't ask me, I haven't a fucking clue what's going on but you may as well*".

"Thank you, that would be perfect," she said and smiled back at Mouin.

"Thank you. Someone will bring over your menus."

"Well, too late to do a runner now."

Terry just shrugged his shoulders and grinned at his own comment, "We better get stuck in then."

The meal was a success. They had to guess some of the items on the menu but anytime they seemed to need something, Mouin appeared like a genie out of a bottle.

Terry was a bit disappointed that nothing seemed to come with chips, but they were both impressed with the giant piri-piri prawns. After her glass of champagne, Isioma allowed herself to be persuaded to have a glass of wine and Terry managed to restrict himself to just two more beers. By the time he dripped chocolate ice cream down the front of his shirt, he was too relaxed to care. His army stories and descriptions of his team's antics seemed to entertain her, and he enjoyed her description of living with her flatmates. She talked about getting to know Robert and what that meant for the family.

The only awkward moment was when she asked him about Rachel and the children. When he hesitated, she touched him lightly on the arm and told him this was just dinner and she did want to hear about Josh, Dolly, and Jade. She loved their names and asked if they took after their mother or their father.

They were still there when the big oga's party left, with plenty hand-shaking and repeated "What a pleasure to have yous" from Mouin. When he came over to ask if they had enjoyed their meal, Isioma confided in him that she was one of the lowly employees of his client's good friend.

"I love his money," Mouin said graciously, "but I much prefer to have people like you enjoy my food." Then mouthed "fucker" to Terry, which made them both laugh.

When he brought the bill, he also told Terry that all his good customers were allowed to sign the bill and pay later, which was just as well because Terry was not sure he had enough cash on him. He made a mental note that he owed Tunde "a good little drinkie" but did wonder exactly what story his friend had told Mouin.

When they left, Isioma reminded Terry to tip the waiters. "Why?" he asked. "I can't afford to come back here again." She gave him a look, so he doled out a few notes.

"Those guys rely on tips for a decent living. Never forget that Terry," she said as she slipped her arm through his.

"We could go somewhere for a nightcap?" he suggested, more in hope than expectation.

"No," she said gently. "But you can give me a lift home, please."

As the car drew up outside her place and he got out to say goodbye, she laughed.

"You do know I am about to get a full interrogation, don't you?"

He could swear he saw a first-floor curtain twitch.

She reached up and kissed him on the cheek. "I had a lovely evening, Terry. Thank you." He watched her until she went in the door.

He went straight home, did not say "For fuck's sake" when it took ten minutes for the security guards to wake up and open the gate, gave Saturday two one thousand naira notes for the weekend, and almost skipped up the stairs when both lifts were out of order yet again.

As soon as Isioma walked into the living room, she found two dressing-gowned wraiths with hair in nets waiting for her.

"Oya!" they demanded.

"Make me a cup of Milo while I get these tight trousers off. Then I will tell you all about it."

Chapter 15

A Frank Exchange

"A tortoise's shell is a house of the poverty
and if the tortoise is taken to the wealthy town,
it will still be living in its house of poverty."

'Ajaiyi And His Inherited Poverty' by Amos Tutuola

Mathew managed to find a spot in The Bungalow's tricky car park. Robert told him he would be a couple of hours and would send out a malt drink, nodding to the Darth Vader impersonator at the door as he walked in. The Bungalow was more of a proper sports bar and eatery, with none of the more dubious nighttime activities usually attached to such places in Lagos. For bigger football matches, you had to book a table in advance because it was always busy. Terry had suggested to Robert that as he had something he wanted to talk about, they could grab a bite to eat and just watch whatever match was on that Sunday.

Robert was there a bit early but as Terry had reserved a table, he sat down and half-watched the TV. There were so many televisions that wherever you sat you could comfortably see a screen without twisting around. The place was so much cleaner than Pat's and it popped into his mind that the clientele looked cleaner too, less like they had been there all weekend. Many were wearing football shirts and XL was still the predominant size but it was a different crowd. There were also plenty of Black faces and several mixed tables. The tribal undercurrent was of the football variety with goals and near misses celebrated with the usual atavistic roar or groan, though the atmosphere was more collegiate and less overtly aggressive than many similar places.

The big match had started by the time Terry came in wearing a polo shirt and reasonably smart shorts. As it involved neither of their teams, they half chatted casually and tucked into burgers and fries to soak up Robert's Guinness and Terry's Star without watching seriously. Robert was aware that the conversation was slightly stilted on Terry's part. He too was a little tense as he suspected he knew what Terry wanted to talk about.

Soon after the main game had finished and the general volume in the room came down to a more conversational level, Terry started to talk about Isioma: how she was easy to talk to, how she made him feel relaxed, how she teased him and so on. Robert knew they had been out together once or twice and was surprised to hear it was, in fact, several more times. He could not quite understand his cousin's attraction, which was probably why Isioma had not mentioned it. He could sense where the conversation was going, and he was bracing himself for it.

"So Rob, I just thought it was fair to let you know, her being family and us meeting because of you and stuff. I really like her and want to take her out properly, like a girlfriend, you know and all that."

The whole subject was awkward and Robert was already feeling that he didn't want to be having this conversation. He looked down at the table and sighed, but did not say anything.

Terry was uncomfortable with the silence. Trying to lighten the mood he half-joked, "It's not like you're her dad and I am asking for your approval to marry or anything, but I just thought it decent to let you know."

Robert looked up. "Actually, Terry, I do disapprove." His face was set hard. "I mean, I appreciate you letting me know but I do think it is wrong and I am going to tell her so. Sorry."

Terry was taken aback. "Why?"

"Why? Are you serious? Why?" Robert was incredulous. "Terry, it is just wrong."

"No, tell me. Why?"

"Well, for a start you have such completely different backgrounds. She is making a career and her family wants her to focus on that. They certainly wouldn't approve and even if she did agree to go out with you in that kind of relationship, which I doubt, they would make it hard for her."

"What, you mean because I am White?" Terry said, agitated.

"No Terry. It is because you have such different backgrounds with such different aspirations. It is not what the family would want for her."

"Oh, so that's what it's about. You just don't want me mixing with your family. I am some rough Millwall fan from a dodgy part of London and you're from arsey posh Chiswick with all those wanky little shops and nice schools that got you to university and all that! You may be Black but because you had all them advantages, you can talk properly and work in some fancy office with the bosses while I am just a mechanic by any other name. In fact, these days it is easier being coloured than being proper British. In the old days, it was 'upstairs and downstairs', you know, class war and snobbery and all that but now it's even worse. It is harder for White working-class people to get decent jobs because of all the immigrants, job quotas for coloured people, best council housing and all that shit. So, I'm alright for a beer but not good enough for your innocent cousin. I get it!"

The anger and bitterness flowing across the table was physical in its intensity. Robert leaned back a little and watched the frustration ripple across Terry's face. Instead of being triggered to respond in kind, Robert felt surprisingly calm, almost detached. Terry was still leaning forward, erect, challenging, almost ready to start swinging. Robert refused to allow himself to be intimidated. He paused before responding, breathing in and keeping his voice soft to avoid ramping up the confrontation, but firm.

"Terry. Really?"

He left the question hanging in the air for a moment as Terry stared at him.

"You don't think it could be the small matter of you having a wife, not to mention three kids who, by the way, I know you adore? You know better than I do what would happen to your chances of seeing them if you left Rachel for a Nigerian girl."

Terry appeared to expand slightly, his jaw working, his fists clenched on the table in front of him. Some kind of inner conflict was evident in his expression and was physically represented in his unnatural stance. He was partly standing and for several seconds he kind of hung in mid-air, struggling to speak until he slowly exhaled and seemed to shrink in size.

Terry slumped back in his chair, not saying anything. He was still looking at Robert but he was not glaring. There was no longer any aggression in his eyes.

Robert waited, then carried on. His voice was calm but certain. "Only one part of what you said was true. The first time I saw you wearing that stupid football kit I did put you down as a typical Millwall racist thug. But when we chatted, stuck in that go-slow, I thought you were a decent bloke. I still think so, just about. Also, just for your information, my father was a mechanic too. A bus mechanic in Shepherd's Bush. But he and my mother went to night school to improve themselves to get better jobs. They earned everything they possess. They saved up and struggled so they could move out of the council flat and into their own little house, so don't give me that racist shit about immigrants and council housing and quotas. And by the way, I went to a comprehensive school too, so bollocks."

By now it was Terry looking down, staring intently at his empty glass. Robert maintained a steady gaze at Terry's face. The sound of voices and glasses clinking filled the space between them. Somewhere, on some distant planet, someone scored a goal but the celebratory singing barely registered in their consciousness.

Robert's words hung in the air until, eventually, Terry, still looking down, just said, "Yeh." After another pause, he sighed and stood up. "I need a wazz." Then, "Want another drink?"

Robert looked up. "You go for a piss, I'll get them."

A waitress walked past the table and Robert called her to order two more beers. The drinks had arrived by the time Terry was back from the toilets. There were small but visible splashes of urine or water down his trousers. As he sat down, Robert said, "And you can't even piss straight."

Terry shrugged. "I know. I dunno what's up with me. I keep doing it."

"It's because you've got a tiny White boy winkie."

Terry smiled at the putdown, then looked at Robert directly.

"Mate, I was bang out of order. I am sorry."

Robert shook his head. "I know, Tel, but it is not that easy. Do you know how many times I have heard racist crap followed by 'Oh sorry, I don't mean you Rob' or 'Oh sorry, I didn't know that was racist'? You can't just spout shit like that and then say, 'Oh sorry'. Then what? You expect me to say 'Thank you, sah' and carry on as if nothing happened? You just spouted the British National Party's racist manifesto at me that basically wants me and my parents rounded up and deported and then it's 'Oh sorry mate'. People with that view beat the shit out of a good friend of mine just because he walked into the wrong pub wearing an old 'Rock Against Racism' tee shirt. Or the charming views of the fans from your football club, yeh the one you were wearing the shirt from that day I first met you. Not to mention other teams around the country where they still throw fucking bananas at Black football players. You want me to go on?" He paused to let it sink in, then: "'Oh sorry, I didn't mean anything by it, mate', I mean, do you even know what comes out of your mouth?" Now Robert allowed himself to get worked up. He pointed his finger, then jabbed it on the table. "Not proper British! What the actual fuck!" He put on a mock Terry voice, "'Oh sorry mate for being out of order'. Eh? Really? It is not that fucking simple."

Even in the noisy bar, people heard the raised voice and a few turned and looked. Robert did not notice. He just leaned forward on his elbows.

He shook his head, leaned back in his chair then suddenly rocked forward again, talking directly but back to his calmer voice. "Anyway, if that is what you really think, then why do you want to go out with Isioma? She is Black, in case you failed to notice."

Terry's expression was contrite but Robert, his voice still with an edge, continued, "If you just want a shag before you go back home to your missus then what's wrong with the hookers from Ynot and Pat's? They seem to have kept you satisfied for the last year or so."

Now Terry was more animated. "No, mate. That's not fair. I know I can be a twat but that's not it. I really like Isioma. I know she's not like that and I would never do anything to hurt her. It's different."

Robert raised his eyebrows. "Really?"

It took a few long seconds before Terry spoke.

"Robert," he was struggling to articulate his thoughts. "Look, you are the clever one."

127

He looked up to see Robert frown. "No, really, yes. I know what you're thinking. I did go to a decent school too but, well, I bunked off most of the time. My parents weren't like yours. I got the odd thick ear when the school got in touch with them, but they didn't really give much of a shit."

Robert's face was impassive.

"I went out with Rachel a bit before I went in the army and got her banged up, so we got married when I was back on leave. Don't get me wrong: she is a nice person. She deserves better than me. She's a great mum and I do love the kids." He stopped as he was gathering his thoughts. "But I just feel kind of suffocated when I spend too much time there. I mean, the army was great, apart from all the usual discipline shite of course, and there were some great blokes, and I learnt a trade too. But the family was always nagging me to come and get a job at home so I bought myself out. The six months I spent at home was a disaster. I couldn't find a job for love or money and ended up on social. I was pissing most of it up the wall at the boozer then I bottled it by getting this job and running away from it all."

He swallowed a good slug of his Star. Robert watched him with a look of detached indifference.

"Yeh, it took me a while to settle down here. It was too easy to get into the drinking habit with other working blokes down Pat's. Yeh, I know, and the girls too. But I was already thinking I got to do something to break the bad habits. I even spoke to Tunde, you know, that bloke from GTW you met in Havana. He has been really decent, to be honest, and gave me some sound advice. He had already given me a bit of a bollocking for my behaviour. Then, seriously Rob, going out with you that night round all those bars with your blokes was another bit of an eye-opener. It was the first time I really thought that African blokes could be just like me. You know, family issues, money trouble, laughs, and all that. I mean I still get pissed but it's only occasionally. No whoring, and I have been working on getting better acquainted with my team. You know, having the odd beer and pepper soup with them after work, having a chat and this and that. Just one or two beers then I just go home. They're good lads, just like a bunch of squaddies really and it makes me think about what their lives are like compared to mine and what they have to put up with and all that stuff. So, I have calmed down quite a bit."

"And then you met Isioma."

"Yeh, and then I met Isioma. What more can I say?" Terry finished the last of his Star and gaped into the bottom of the glass then up at Robert. "One more and that's that. Home."

Robert nodded resignedly and watched as Terry called over the waitress and ordered.

"I know you're not happy about it, Rob, but please give us some time."

"Time to do what?" Robert would have said more but the waitress leaned between them with the drinks and wiped spilled beer from the table.

"Honestly, I don't know," said Terry before Robert could continue. "I just feel different about her somehow. I have been straight with her about everything, and she asks me about Rachel and Josh and the others. We have been out several times and I have only ever kissed her goodnight, but I think she likes me."

"So, what about the racist stuff? Am I supposed to pretend I never had to sit here and have that spat in my face?"

Terry was genuinely shamefaced. "Look Rob, I don't even know what to say. I . . ." he paused. "I know it's not an excuse but where I come from, it's just what comes out of the frustration and anger at having a shite life. And seeing other people doing better and having a nicer life. It's just easy to have someone else to blame even if you know in your heart it's not true."

He was looking down when he spoke but suddenly looked up at Robert.

"You think people can change? If I don't, I will end up the same way as too many of my family. Everybody ends up getting permanently pissed and permanently angry and I just can't do it anymore."

Robert noticed Terry's eyes had tears in them. Part of him felt some connection but a greater part of him felt something else. That part of him wanted to be dismissive: tell Terry he was just being pathetic. He wanted to tell him that his parents did not have the luxury of that self-indulgence. There was no one ready to listen to the Windrush generation, to Biafran escapees, or other immigrants, including the Irish for that matter. If they whined, no one heard, so they just got on and did what they had to do. In the same way, his father never allowed him to forget that truth so when he complained that his White mates were all down at the park, his dad would stand over him until he finished his homework. Failure at school was just not an option and as for bunking off. . .

Just for a moment, he was going to tell Terry exactly what he thought but finally, though not without some tension in his voice, he allowed his more considerate nature to speak.

"Mate, people can change but, frankly, it is rare. It is not easy and it does not happen overnight. And, I have to tell you, good intentions mean diddly-squat. I mean, fuck all. And," he spoke more pointedly, "my cousin is not your crutch or experiment or dalliance. You understand me?"

Terry nodded. They lapsed into silence, each locked in his thoughts, absorbing the conversation.

Eventually, Terry said in a strangely subdued voice, "You're probably the first bloke I have been able to talk to, you know, like that."

Robert pulled a not-unsympathetic face, then swallowed the last of his Guinness and stood up, just a touch unsteadily. Four small Guinness was more than his usual.

"Okay," he said. "Fair enough." His eyes lingered on Terry's face until, with a half-smile, he continued, "Anyway, I probably don't have to worry because if you keep pissing down your trousers you won't get a moment's consideration."

"Yeh, fair point," replied Terry, as they paid the waitress and headed for the door.

Just as he got into his pick-up, Terry could not help but take a quick peek down the front of his trousers, then, looking up, saw Robert was watching from the back of his car and shaking his head.

"You're fucked mate!" he called over, laughing, as Mathew drove them out of the car park.

Chapter 16

The Kola is Shared

"A man who calls his kinsmen to a feast does not do so
to save them from starving. They all have food in their
own homes. When we gather together in the moonlit
village ground it is not because of the moon.
Every man can see it in his own compound.
We come together because it is good
for kinsmen to do so."

'Things Fall Apart' by Chinua Achebe

It was nearly a week after the meeting with Terry and Robert was waiting for Isioma at the lobby area of the domestic terminal of the Lagos airport. He was still unsure what he thought about the conversation with Terry, and about what he ought to say to Isioma.

She had finally persuaded him to take a long weekend and come and visit the family home in Enugu. She had suggested her usual night bus route but there was no way Robert was going to put himself through that experience, so he coughed up for tickets on Changchangi Airlines. He had made a couple of work-related trips by air so he knew the ropes and the mayhem to expect. He had rung up Francis the Fixer to get the tickets and help them check in. Checking-in could be a truly daunting experience for the uninitiated.

More people wanted to travel to some destinations than there were flights, and with obliging airline officials willing to ignore the rules, standing patiently at the back of a queue often meant you would never get a seat. On some flights, there was no seat allocation at all. This was known as "free seating", akin to a public bus.

Check-in desks were like a seething bowl of catfish in a point-and-kill fish pepper soup joint. Unless you had five hands—two to hold your luggage, two to protect your valuables, and one to wave your ticket aggressively in the face of the check-in clerk— it could be tough. Inevitably, just about all expats and the better-off Nigerians would use a tout. A would-be flyer would pay a few hundred naira extra, more if the guy smelled you were desperate, to be able to stand behind the mob while he dived in on your behalf. Eventually, with luck and after considerable trepidation, he would emerge with your often handwritten, no-seat-number, boarding pass. However, there was no guarantee. There was a reasonable possibility that he, always a "he", would just disappear into the morass, sell your ticket to someone else, and escape. The trick was to keep an eye on him as he wormed his way to the desk, and then in the luggage area behind as he carried your checked-in bag, hopefully to be tagged and thrown onto the correct trolley.

A couple of years earlier, Robert would have been a target for these keen-eyed predators, but now his body language had changed. In some imperceptible way, his very stance and outward confidence no longer signalled hesitation or weakness. Any tout that approached him now was immediately put off by a head shake or a visible tooth suck. After speaking a few words, it may still have been clear that he was a Tokunbo but it was no longer apparent from his demeanour.

Robert smiled to himself as he looked up at the official FAAN signs outlining the penalty for using an "unauthorised person" and then again at the touts waving tickets at harassed airline staff. As calm as he appeared outwardly, his stomach was knotted with tension, particularly as Isioma was late.

Fortunately, just as he saw her climb out of a yellow taxi, Francis turned up with their boarding passes. As a long-timer with a track record of dash and Christmas presents, courtesy of his corporate clients, Francis indeed considered himself a "protocol officer" as opposed to a garden variety airport tout. Their functions were the same essentially, but perception was everything.

After hurried greetings, Francis went through security with them. Having overcome the check-in process and the less-than-secure security, the next experience was the waiting area. It could barely be described as a lounge. There were rows of hard, curved metal benches that had been in service in airports across the country for at least fifty years. To be fair, they were surprisingly comfortable, which was important because flights were rarely on time. As often as not, they would be more than a couple of hours late. There were rarely any announcements and those that were made, crackled out of such bad speakers that they were unintelligible. Passengers just dozed or milled around until the incoming flight had landed, which was a sign that their flight might board within the next twenty minutes to an hour.

Francis' boys kept a lookout, so he was able to give them a warning to get ready for the next scramble: getting on the right bus to take them to the right aircraft amongst the several parked haphazardly all around the apron. That was about as far as his duties extended, so as they elbowed their way onto the bus, he was already speed-shuffling his way to the next assignment. They made it to their seats without undue fuss.

The flight itself was uneventful for anyone used to internal Nigerian flights. To the unaccustomed, such pleasures as the dry cake and small carton of warm juice delivered with a hint of malice by a miserable-looking attendant, the barely operating air conditioning and consequent runnels of sweat, and finally the round of applause from relieved passengers as the landing plane bounced down a rutted runway, might constitute mini events worthy of comment. To regular users of Nigeria's airspace, these were routine.

Enugu's Akanu Ibiam International Airport was smaller than its name might suggest. Robert and Isioma walked down the wheeled steps with some trepidation as they were distinctly shaky, and then followed other passengers across the tarmac to the arrivals area.

Though Isioma wanted to bring a suitcase full of gifts for her family, they had confined themselves to carry-on luggage at Robert's insistence. She smiled as they sidestepped the crush around the baggage collection area and exited into what, compared to Lagos, was relative calm.

Robert felt a tug. A diminutive, elderly man took his wheelie and Isioma's bag.

"Ndeewo sir. Nnoo."

Isioma was beaming.

133

"Mr Emanuel, how are you? This is Robert. . . Robert, Emanuel has been with our family since long before I was born."

Robert held out his hand, and Emanuel shook it with a firm grip that belied his size and appearance. "You are welcome once again, sir." To Isioma, "Your parents are expecting you, young madam." There was a tone of affection and even pride in his voice.

They followed him to the car park opposite the small terminal, to an old Mercedes 230 that Robert guessed was at least twenty-five years old. Emanuel placed their bags carefully in the footwell of the front seat, and they settled into the roomy rear.

"The boot has fuel containers in it and stinks of petrol," whispered Isioma.

The airport was on the other side of the city from the suburb of Ngwo where many of the Ede family still lived, so their route took them through the centre of Enugu. The streets were wide and straight, as befitted a colonial regional capital, and as mixed as Governor Nnamani's legacy would be, he had improved many of the roads around the city. Though it no longer had the regional importance it once had, it was still one of eastern Nigeria's major centres.

The recent opening of Nigerian Breweries' Ama brewery nearby, ironically just by the Iva Valley at 9th Mile Corner, had brought fresh commercial activity and employment with it. This new investment could not disguise the truth: that the old coal and colonial civil service affluence was a thing of the past. Despite some signs of regeneration in the town centre and along the main road, the surface became potholed and the surroundings became less well-to-do as they drove through the city and into the Ngwo neighbourhoods. Gradually, the houses on either side of the Old Enugu-Onitsha road thinned out and signs of the bush taking back its own space were more evident. As they turned into their part of the suburb, Okwojo-Ngwo, past St Mary's Catholic Church, it was clear that this had once been a rural area and there were many patches of ground still under a kind of informal cultivation. Occasional patches of cassava or corn grew in clearings or rough spaces between buildings, many of which had been unoccupied for years.

A street or two past the church, they arrived at a long drive into a cul-de-sac at the head of which was a compound ensconced in trees, quite different from the poorer dwellings on both sides of the narrow road. The gate was already open and Emanuel drove straight in, horning as he did. The main residence was a two-storey house with a high-sloping roof and a balcony. In addition to the main house, there were smaller buildings around the edge of the compound that left enough space for four or five cars in the middle. Leafy trees gave a shady, cool ambience.

By the time Emanuel parked, Isioma's parents had come out of the front door. Isioma jumped out of the car and ran to them. They stood together, the mother in traditional, tied Ogodo the father in an open-necked shirt and trousers, the starch and creases giving the sense of a man who though no longer young, was still mindful of his appearance. Standing as they were side by side, they gave a sense of being one, joined by years of adversity and shared experiences. They were, in some way, visibly where they were meant to be. After a dutiful bend of the knee, Isioma gave her mother a mutually joyful squeeze. Her father smiled as he watched his wife and daughter greet each other until Isioma turned to him and after a slightly more deferential dip, they too hugged. Then her father turned to face Robert.

"Robert," he said simply but tenderly, "You are very welcome to your family compound."

Robert took his proffered hand respectfully. "Uncle Vitus. What can I say, sir?"

Dorothy Ede was less formal. She pulled Robert into her ample bosom and hugged him so tight he could feel the buttons of her lace blouse through his shirt. He struggled to understand her jumble of accented English and Igbo, but the warmth of her greeting was unmistakable. Then she held him out at arms-length and surveyed him seriously before turning to her husband.

"A fine young man. Your sister will be proud of him and happy he is here."

* * *

It was just one short weekend. But when he thought about it in the comfort of his apartment in Maryland, it was a mental

135

jumble of fast-forward and time-lapse clips. In the days after he returned to Lagos, Robert tried to absorb what he had experienced. It was both about what he had learnt and more importantly, how it made him feel.

Although the house was clean and comfortable, it had the feeling that time had somehow passed it by. The front door opened into a living room with a mish-mash of armchairs and sofas. Multifarious curtains hung around the walls and covered the internal doors and windows. This kept the room cool but it also had the effect of giving it an atmospheric duskiness. It smelled a little musty. There was a ceiling fan and several standing fans but Isioma had already warned him that there was seldom electricity and their small generator was only enough to power a few lights and kitchen appliances. The large compound generator was rarely turned on as it guzzled diesel.

His guest room had a single bed and though there was an old square window air conditioning unit, the plug was hanging down signifying it was not in use. He didn't bother plugging it in. The sheets were worn but clean, as were the hard and scratchy towels folded neatly on the bed. The shared bathroom had the ubiquitous plastic bowls in the bathtub; so much more efficient as a form of bathing than a shower that had no pressure.

Isioma took him around the compound and explained where some of their ancestors had been buried, including their great-grandfather who had fought for the British in the second world war. Robert had no idea that it was the Ngwo custom to bury the deceased within the confines of their compound. She also took him to one of the smaller houses to the side of the main house. It was where his grandfather and grandmother had lived when they were first married. His uncle Vitus and his mother had spent their childhood years there before they had been taken to Lagos and their lives had been overtaken by the war.

It had not been too long after they arrived that the first of the guests showed up. All that Friday evening and all day Saturday, there had been a constant stream of visitors. It seemed everyone was a cousin of some sort and deciphering who he was genuinely related to and who was just a neighbour who wanted to meet the visitor from abroad was impossible.

Certainly, Dorothy and the female members of the family, including Isioma, spent most of their time supervising the cooking and serving of food as every guest was attended to. Most of the callers were older and the predominant language was Igbo, though the few younger ones were comfortable speaking English.

One person who stood out clearly in Robert's kaleidoscope of memories was a particularly older man named Mazi Chiemezie, who conducted the official welcoming ceremony. As Vitus was later to explain, Chiemezie was an age-mate of his father, Okafor. They had been at school together and friends until Okafor and Abigail had set off for their new life in Lagos in the early 1960s before the Biafran war ripped them apart. Mazi Chiemezie may have been diminutive and wrinkled but his still clear eyes sparkled with humour below the rim of his red cap.

Robert had an approximation of the traditional custom in his head but was excited to experience the true ceremony. The kolanuts were quickly produced and passed around until they reached Chiemezie, who was the oldest person in the extended family and therefore had the duty to bless the kola. Although the prayers were in Igbo, (as Isioma explained, "the kola nut does not hear English"), Robert found the attendant ceremony moving: the splitting and sharing of the kola, the passing round of the garden egg and alligator pepper all washed down with a shot of Schnapps. Robert had already arranged with the Guinness sales team to deliver a good selection of Guinness, Harp, and Malta: an act that somehow became known and was approved of by his colleagues back in Lagos. The selection disappeared down the throats of the elders with alacrity.

Isioma had told him that like most of his generation, her father spoke very little about the war: about his losing his parents, becoming separated from his sister, and being thrown, as little more than a boy, into a vicious, dirty conflict but that evening, having Robert there triggered something. For nearly three hours after eating lunch on Saturday, the two of them walked around the compound before sitting together on a small bench. The rest of the family checked on them occasionally and topped up their glasses but otherwise, they were left alone, with Isioma and her mother happy to catch up with their news. As dusk fell, Robert hardly noticed the attention of mosquitoes as Vitus recounted the trek into the bush with his distraught mother after Okafor had disappeared on the way to Onitsha.

The older man's shoulders heaved with emotion as he described how they waited in the hope that his father might find his way home until they were forced to flee Ngwo from the encroaching federal troops. How his final memory of his mother was of her standing on the road with outstretched arms calling his name as he had been taken away by Biafran soldiers. Robert too would never forget the look in his uncle's eyes as he held his hand.

"I saw too much that I cannot unsee," Vitus said, turning away slightly and then, staring straight ahead, spoke as if Robert was no longer there. "There was something that happened. I think in 1968, around March because the rains had yet to come. I was sent on my bicycle with a message to deliver to an officer commanding troops somewhere along the road from Enugu down to Onitsha. When I arrived near Abagana township, I was told to wait quietly as something was about to happen. Suddenly there was an explosion so loud that my ears pained me for weeks to come. A wave of heat fried the air and all the bush shrivelled. Then more blasts, 'bham, bham bham'. It turned out that a rocket shell had hit an army tanker and the burning fuel had engulfed a whole convoy. Our troops were now firing at the Nigerian soldiers fleeing the inferno, many in flames. Picking them off like rabbits as they panicked in all directions. Despite the shots and the noise, I could hear the screams of burning humans. I lay in the bush and covered my ears, but I could not keep the horror of that sound from entering my head, no matter how hard I pressed my ears. After some time, a pair of boots stood by my head and a hand pulled me up. 'Go and deliver your message now, boy. The major is over there.' The stench of burnt flesh, the whimpers and moans of dying men pleading to be put out of pain and our troops just walking round finishing them off. Many were jubilating. Happily jubilating. How? Yes, they were the enemy that had done so much to us, but I could not feel any joy. I was taken to the major and handed over my paper. I was still fifteen and skinny with no uniform, just a satchel. The major, I was later to know that his name was Uchendu and he did not survive the war, read the message then looked at me for an instant and said *'O di mma'*. It is well. In my memory, I am always standing amid the choking stink of death. *It is well?* If these boys, these so-called activists for a new Biafra had seen what I have seen, they would never call for another war. Never. Never."

After that incident, Vitus explained that he had continued to carry messages until his bicycle was damaged in an explosion, and then on foot for some time, on bare feet, before he was able to retrieve a pair of boots from a dead soldier he came across. He explained how nearly two years later, at the end of hostilities, he was with a small, isolated troop in the bush near Owerri and described how, by the time he reached Ngwo, he was emaciated and wretched, only to find their compound, though intact and undamaged, was looted and empty. And then, to hear of his mother's death and burial in a mass grave.

Vitus spoke of the desolation and loneliness of those few months as he and a few surviving neighbours and returning soldiers scrabbled to survive until he was able to turn his thoughts to seeking out his sister. When Vitus described finally receiving Udo's first letter, and what it had meant for his determination to survive, Robert could barely breathe. The very weight of tragedy, and its implications, told so simply, was overwhelming.

In the days following their return to Lagos, Robert would catch himself staring out of the window at work or pacing around his Maryland apartment.

Reflections would suddenly come to mind, eliciting different sensations: Isioma's respectful relationship with her parents, the central attachment to the compound for the whole family, the feeling of the presence of their ancestors and, over and over again, burning shame at his previous failure to even attempt an understanding of what all this must have meant to his mother.

On the Sunday, before the rest of the family went to church and as they prepared to go to the airport for the only flight to Lagos that day, they called Udodirim back in Chiswick.

They had used his phone but Vitus spoke first, telling his sister what a wonderful son she had and how he was fully one of the family, occasionally lapsing into Igbo and laughing with the delight of connection. When it was Robert's turn, he could hardly speak. There was too much weighing on his heart to unburden himself all at once. He allowed his mother to sing her joy at hearing her son speak from the home that she missed, which remained at her core throughout the vicissitudes of her life. He had to explain that he would ring her later. Just telling her he loved her threatened his equilibrium. Sitting alone in his flat days later, he knew he had to make that call but he was still unsure what he would say.

Vitus came with them in the car to the airport. After the catharsis of the evening before, he seemed somehow younger. He had connected with his young nephew which brought him closer to his sister. He had sat with the youngsters at the back of the car and Robert could still feel the grip on his knee every time he made a point about something noticeable on the journey.

Robert particularly remembered them reaching a roundabout in which there was a memorial to the miners who died, as Vitus had explained the evening before, at the hands of their countrymen, albeit from the north and at the direction of the British.

Vitus asked Emanuel to drive around the central island twice so Robert could see the monument better. To Robert's eyes, the statue was a jumble of men raising their arms to the skies as helmeted soldiers stood by. It did not seem especially looked after as it was dusty and there were piles of litter around the plinth and plastic bags tangled in the legs of the figures. It was surreal that this was part of his family's history—one of those men was great-grandfather Agu.

Robert made a mental note to read up about the incident, including finding out what the Nigerian regiment was doing fighting alongside their colonisers. There were other places that his uncle had pointed out along the winding journey to the airport but trying to conjure them up later was beyond Robert's recollection.

Vitus' emotional goodbye embrace was something he could never forget. The old man's eyes glistened as he held Robert close and exhorted him to stay in contact and trust in their gods: "Nwa'm deeje, inuna? Ijeoma. Chineke nna ga e duru gi uno."

Before exhorting him to come back and bring his mother and sister with him, Vitus explained he had become the bridge between the family in Nigeria and the UK, almost between the past and the future. That was a responsibility he had not expected and never asked for, and struggled to understand how it had come about.

On the plane back, Isioma had been ecstatic.

"I cannot believe how much my father opened up to you, Robert," she shook her head in happy disbelief. "Mummy could not believe it either, or the other family members. It was as if you opened a magic door for him. Did you see how cheerful he was today? I am so happy we came. Thank you, thank you!"

He tried to be enthusiastic in return, but he was borderline traumatised by all the emotion and was drained by the intensity of it all, not to mention the lack of sleep.

"The thanks should go to you. It was your idea and I think I am grateful that you insisted. But honestly," he continued, "I have to say I have found it pretty exhausting and it is going to take me quite some while to process everything."

For some minutes he lapsed into silence, staring out of the plane window but seeing nothing.

When they landed and he reached up to get their bags, Robert shook his head to clear his mind. He had much to take in.

Chapter 17

Udo's Story

"When Efuru went home, Ajanupu could not help admiring her character. 'She is a woman among women. I like the way she is carrying her burden.'"

'Efuru' by Flora Nwapa

Udo lived her life in Lagos almost completely unaware of the tragedy unfolding for her family and her people. As she helped Simone run the house, no longer free to attend school or church or even leave the compound, she prayed every day that her mother and father and brother would soon return.

The Dukes knew more of the truth about what was happening than the government-controlled papers revealed. They feared the worst. As the months turned into years and the war came to an end, there were still no letters; no word from the family.

Winston tried to find out what he could through diplomatic channels with no success. Eventually, as Igbos returned to Lagos, Winston and Simone took Udo to the Catholic Church in the chance of hearing something. Few wanted to speak of what had happened. Fewer still could offer any news, or hope.

Finally, Winston was offered a promotion: a posting to London as the deputy there. With Simone's prompting, he pulled favours and strings and was able to persuade friends in the Federal Civil Service to issue Udo with a passport. He paid for her to accompany them to London. By then, she had grown into a young woman of seventeen and could earn her keep as a maid while they also helped her continue her education. Every night, her prayers went unanswered and her trust in God diminished a little more.

When they made their way to London by steamship and settled into the High Commission residence, Simone and Winston did all they could to keep their promise to treat Udo as their daughter. They helped find her a church attended by Nigerians and took her to as many events as they could. By day, she worked as their housekeeper and two or three evenings a week she went to night school and learnt simple bookkeeping and shorthand. Her life was somewhat lonely but despite her occasional days of deep sorrow, she was grateful for the love shown her by her surrogate parents.

Winston never stopped asking his colleagues back in Lagos for news and one day in 1972, an envelope was sent in the diplomatic bag. He took it home and he and Simone sat with Udo as she opened it. It was a letter via the High Commission in Lagos from Vitus. As soon as Udo realised who the letter was from, she excused herself and took it up to her room. It was around 6 o'clock in the evening and the Dukes spent the next four worrying hours waiting.

From time to time, Simone sent Winston up to listen at her door but there was no sound. They were just considering going to bed when Udo came down holding the letter.

With swollen and tear-laden eyes, she handed the pages to Winston and sank into Simone's outstretched arms where she stayed, her shoulders heaving as she sobbed silently for several long minutes.

How do you console a young woman who has waited years for the bitter confirmation that everything she ever feared has come to pass? Yet, not quite everything. Few of the family members she could remember from her childhood had survived. Only her beloved brother, Vitus, had come through. His letter, describing the agonising story of his endurance, tore her heart to shreds.

It had taken weeks after the cessation of formal hostilities for him to find his way back to Ngwo. Though not badly wounded, he had countless unhealed cuts and open sores from two years without proper sustenance or nutrition, culminating in an arduous and bitter trek back to what had once been their home.

If the physical scars were obvious but superficial, the less visible emotional wounds were deep and almost fatal. He was barely out of childhood but had already experienced more than any man should be expected to endure. At his age, he had not been pressed into the full army but had been used as a runner. As such, he had been present at some of the worst battle fronts. He had witnessed some of the profound atrocities of what had been a vicious war by any standard. He had been an onlooker at the terrible massacre of thousands of federal soldiers at Abagana when a rocket from one of the Biafran army's improvised ogbunigwe launchers had hit a tanker, exploding burning fuel all over a densely packed convoy. Then, as Biafra's youth was sacrificed for a cause that had become increasingly hopeless, he was forced to extreme measures such as scrambling over the dead in search of food scraps to save himself from starvation.

Having survived all the war had thrown at him, the peace had its challenges as he and a couple of other family members were reduced to living like squatters in their own compound. Looted by the federal forces and thereafter by anyone, including neighbours looking for anything of any value to barter for food, their home was a shell. It took months to grow some vegetables and cassava in and around the compound and almost as long to complete the formalities for the twenty pounds given to every Igbo adult as compensation for their lost assets as the Federal Government sequestered all Igbo bank accounts. He had already heard the news of his mother's death and burial in a communal grave and had no optimism that his father would ever return, though bitter hope can be a cruel and debilitating torturer.

During that period, the local economy struggled. Even the mines had been smashed and looted and there was little employment to be found there. There were a few days of casual labouring but many more spent queueing at the Red Cross station for barely enough food to keep those in the compound from starving.

Fortunately, Vitus' father had not only ensured his children were diligent in their schoolwork, but he had also taught his son to drive. A Catholic charity worker mentioned they needed a support driver for a few days a week and this allowed Vitus achieve a little dignity and a route to a future.

As his body healed, his mind turned to wondering about his sister. The mail service was hardly working. Sourcing paper and a pen was a major effort. The hours spent staring at empty sheets, forcing himself to conjure memories and commit the chronicle of their parents' last days to paper, were agonising.

Eventually, the tear-laden envelope, addressed to Winston Duke, found its way to the High Commission's mail room from where it was forwarded to London.

* * *

Udo's life progressed, measured only by the time between each letter. It was to be years before she was able to speak to her brother on the phone, so their correspondence became their way of healing, as much as anything ever could, and of charting a way forward.

Eventually, Winston retired, and he and Simone returned to their home just outside Port of Spain in Trinidad. Through the church, Udo had made friends in the West Indian community. Through them, she rented a room in a family house in Shepherd's Bush.

By then, she had passed bookkeeping exams and earned a decent living in the accounts department of Allied Lyons, the old tea company based in Hammersmith.

At some point, another lodger moved in.

Darren Railsford's family had emigrated from Barbados, his father having come across under the Windrush scheme. Darren was born in Shepherd's Bush but still spoke with a Caribbean accent, having been immersed in that culture. He was quiet and serious and taken with the unobtrusive and often solitary young Nigerian in the nearby room. They struck up a friendship and a relationship developed born of the love of God, the desire for a family, and a willingness to work hard.

Darren was a trainee mechanic for London Transport but dreamed of having his own workshop. Udo continued her studies at night school and achieved more accounting qualifications. They married in a modest service.

As she tired of explaining to his family that Udo was short for Udodirim, which was seemingly difficult for them to pronounce, she allowed herself to be known by the anglicised version: Peace. She was soon pregnant, and they qualified for a council flat in White City.

After Robert was born, she went back to work as soon as possible and the same again less than two years later when Cindy came along. They continued to work hard and save so that Darren acquired a small lock-up that became his workshop, soon building a strong reputation in the community. Many White-owned garages were seen as racist, and often suspected of deliberately failing Black-owned vehicles on their MOT tests. So Darren became the go-to person for the rising car-owning Black and Brown middle class.

Meanwhile, Udo, now known as Peace, gained promotion at Lyons as a supervisor, eventually becoming one of the few non-White managers running a whole accounting office.

In the evenings, she would do the books for Darren's growing business. Eventually, they saved enough for a deposit for a mortgage and bought a run-down terraced house between Chiswick High Road and the busy Great West Road. It was their ambition, based on the values so cherished by the traditional British middle class.

* * *

Peace, as we should now call her, and Darren lived a modest, family-focused life; pushing their children to succeed at school academically but also encouraging social and sporting engagements. They understood the benefits of being assimilated into what was becoming a middle-class, comfortable suburb of London.

There was one family trip to Ngwo but Darren had not felt comfortable. He also resisted too many visits from her family, particularly after her cousin Onyeka borrowed money from them. Over time, she became more detached from her Nigerian roots. The regular phone call to her brother and his family was the only real contact.

Robert and Cindy were brought up as Black British children, to integrate and progress at school. Their Caribbean and Nigerian backgrounds were never a focus. Practically all their classmates were White and their friendship groups reflected this. Neighbours were friendly, there was little overt racism in what was becoming a desirable area on the back of good school ratings and its real estate designation as "Chiswick Village".

146

In some sense, Peace was content. She shared her husband's values and her heart would burst with love and pride at Robert's football medals and Cindy's school drama awards. Both were strong academically and made it to university. Their graduations were two of the happiest moments of Darren and Peace's lives.

Yet, somewhere deep inside, she was still that woman who had insisted that her children have Igbo middle names: Robert Afamefuna, 'May My Name Never Be Lost', and Cindy Ndidi, 'Someone Who Is Patient'—reflecting her secret hopes and dreams.

She could never forget her father's stories of his upbringing, the bravery of his father and the wisdom of his grandmother. The memory of that night, watching her parents and her brother drive out of that Ikoyi compound and into a brutal war, would forever be ready to disturb her sleep.

Her own parents' desire for that which had long since been snatched from their family, even before the onset of that civil war, was reflected in their choice of name: Udodirim, Peace Be Upon Me. Yet, true peace had not come to be theirs, or hers either.

147

Chapter 18

How Comes the Time?

"For he was a shrub among the poplars
Needing more roots
More sap to grow to sunlight
Thirsting for sunlight
A low growth among the forest.
Into the soul
The selves extended their branches
Into the moments of each living hour
Feeling for audience
Straining thin among the echoes."

'For He Was a Shrub Among the Poplars'
by Christopher Okigbo

It had been a busy day at Pat's, culminating in the Rugby World Cup final of South Africa versus England. There had been alcohol-fuelled tension and testosterone in abundance but no serious trouble. Rugby afternoons and evenings were always boisterous, especially during the annual Six Nations Championship, England versus Scotland being the most vociferous.

However, afterwards, as the Irish would say, it was all about the craic, and Pat's regulars from across Ireland and the United Kingdom, with the odd Italian or Frenchmen thrown in, would soon settle down to drinking and bantering.

Whenever South Africa was involved, things would get more heated. It was not just that many of the Springbok fans were players in their youth, loud of voice and large of fist, but many had come to work in Nigeria because the post-apartheid government's policy of "positive affirmation" or Black empowerment, coupled with the weakness of the rand, had forced them to look for work away from their homeland. There were few Black South Africans in Lagos. Most were White engineers or technical guys, many of recent farming stock. They had generally learned to co-exist with Nigerian work colleagues but after a beer or ten, bitterness and resentment would sometimes creep in. The Rugby World Cup was a massive symbol for them, a reinforcement of their laager mentality and their manhood, so Pat had prepared by getting in plenty of security for the evening.

A narrow victory over England saw the South Africans in an expansive mood. Rounds of Castle lager were flying, and Afrikaner songs rent the air. Terry and the other English fans had been fatalistic from the outset so, apart from feeling hard done by because of a narrowly disallowed try, they accepted the result.

Terry had not been coming to Pat's as often or staying as long since he had promised Isioma he would change his ways. But given it was the final, he settled in after the match for a couple more with the usual crowd and some of their "saffer" mates.

Eventually, knowing Isioma was at his flat watching television and that he had already had more than he promised he would have, Terry stood up to leave.

"Ach man!" one of the South Africans cried out. "It's still early. Don't be a winging pom and stay for another."

One of Terry's previously regular drinking buddies laughed. "Don't worry about Terry, he's pussy whipped. Gotta get back to his honey."

Terry forced a smile. "It's true, I admit. Have to go."

The South African went to hold Terry's arm but just managed to grab a handful of his shirt. "Nah, you can't leave your mates for local poes, have another."

Terry pulled away. "Don't go there, mate."

His experienced boozing companions recognised the signs. "You're all right, Terry. Off you go. Catch you next week."

Terry turned to leave but the South African was not to be denied.

He stood up. "Hoosh Roinek, it's rude to stand up and leave your mates like that." And as he half-pulled Terry around, added, "Especially for some kaffer kut."

Terry's reaction was impulsive and instinctive, borne of countless army bar brawls. A sudden, short but intensely violent

149

movement and he had head-butted the South African, catching him perfectly on the bridge of his nose, instantly breaking it. The victim collapsed back on his chair, clutching at his face as blood dripped through his fingers.

Terry's mates were quick, holding him back from following up but they were not able to prevent one of the South Africans from grabbing a glass. In trying to hit Terry full on, it caught him with a glancing blow; enough to break and leave several bloody but shallow gauges down the side of his face, but not nearly enough to take a man of Terry's size down.

Before the general ruck could kick in, Pat jumped in, faster than his generally sluggish appearance would have suggested possible, and stood between the two groups. Almost at the same time, two or three of his massive bouncers stepped over.

"Now, now gentlemen," his experience telling in his calm demeanour. "You," he said, pointing at Terry, "leave now." Terry glowered at Pat but knowing better than to say anything, spun round and walked straight to the door. Pat turned to the other Brits. "You too, gents. Tell Terry he's banned until further notice." He gestured to the South Africans. "We don't use words like that here. My colleagues," beckoning his bouncers, "don't like that kind of talk. Look after your friend," who by now had been given wet towels by a waitress. "Wait ten minutes before leaving and do not come back."

As Pat would often sing to anyone within earshot, "Never smile at a crocodile", and he would know. Running any bar in Lagos required teeth; an expat bar even more so.

Pat's was of Lagos and Lagos shrugs off violence like a warthog in a puddle of mud. It was all in a day's work for the staff. Pat always claimed to run an unbiased and balanced establishment, but he was a shrewd operator and as his genuine long-term customers knew, he had his ways. He expected loyalty and gave it in return. The South Africans were never allowed back in. After a couple of days, he would send word to Terry that he was welcome but with a warning to behave. Pat was also ex-British army, and he appreciated the rough beauty of a perfectly executed Glasgow Kiss as much as the next street fighter.

By the time Terry got home, his polo shirt was covered in blood. The cuts looked worse than they were but it was a

150

shocking sight for Isioma when he walked through the door. As Benoit, the new steward, had closed for the day, she rumbled about in the kitchen and found some disinfectant and a pile of clean tea towels.

Most of the cuts were superficial. One or two could have done with stitches but when Isioma suggested it, Terry refused, so they made do with some plasters. A bruise on the side of his face was already swelling and he winced as she cleaned him up.

Even though Terry protested that the fight was for her honour, Isioma was unimpressed. She was no fan of Pat's Bar and Terry was supposed to be cutting down on his drinking. Even though he had gone for the occasion of the final, he had promised her he would come home straight afterwards. This was everything Isioma loathed about the expatriate drinking culture. Immediately she finished cleaning up his face and put his shirt in to soak, she asked him to call Saturday to take her home.

"But you said you would stay," Terry pleaded. "Benoit has made up the spare room." He thought of more reasons. "And Saturday would have gone by now because he is off tomorrow."

Isioma maintained an uncompromising expression. "Well, you are clearly fit enough to drive me home or I will just walk down and get a taxi."

"You can't do that."

"What do you think I used to do before you came along?" She picked up her bag and headed for the door, but Terry blocked her way. She stood staring up at him. "I am not doing this, Terry."

There was a stalemate for a few moments but Isioma held her ground until he moved aside. As she reached for the door handle, Terry said, "Please, Isioma. Please."

Despite her determination, something in his tone made Isioma waver.

He could be serious occasionally, but his usual response was to humour her or to make a joke. He had learned early on that any sign of his temper would be the end. But he was not a pleader. Nor a crier.

As Isioma turned around, tears were streaming down Terry's face. On the side where the cuts had reached his cheek, they mingled with the blood and ran down to his chin. He wiped them with the back of his hand and looked at her but said nothing.

She stood still for a moment then turned back to the door. This time her hand reached the handle then she paused again, standing still for several seconds until she loudly sucked her teeth and twisted to face him. Again, without saying anything, she examined his expression until, almost as a whisper, he said, "Sorry."

She dropped her bag to the floor where she stood, then without warning she punched him in the face. Not a slap but a hard fist-balled punch. She caught him right on the side of his face and opened up some of the cuts. He hardly flinched but she doubled up, holding her hand in pain.

"You bastard!" she cried, waving it to shake off the pain. "You've broken my hand."

Terry stood for a moment watching her then started to laugh.

Isioma did not see a reason for laughter. "It's not funny, Terry."

She took a wild kick at him, which missed as he jumped back. So wild was her swing she would have fallen but he caught her. She shook him off and slumped disconsolately onto the settee, still nursing her hand. He sat next to her.

She repeated, "It's not funny," then added, "I mean it, you understand?" They both sat there for a moment without saying anything until she broke the silence. "I am not going to put up with this kind of imbecilic behaviour."

This time the quiet lasted. He leaned forward, his head in his hands. Isioma sighed and sat back, tucking her legs under her. For a moment she closed her eyes, and then opening them she saw his shoulders were shaking.

She punched his back and flinched as her fist hurt. "It isn't funny, it isn't funny." But as she spoke, she realised he was not laughing. His shoulders were heaving from silent weeping. She swivelled to the floor in front of him and took his hands.

"Isioma, I can't help who I am. I am trying. I mean, it's what I am, it's where I come from. I am trying." He looked directly into her eyes. "See, you make me laugh, then you make me cry. No one makes me cry."

They sat in the same position for several minutes until Terry stood up, moved her gently to the side, walked to the balcony and opened the doors. There was a warm breeze that made the net curtains billow into the room as he stood and looked out into the darkness over the creeks. Isioma sat and watched him until, once more, she sighed.

Wearily standing up, she walked to the front door and picked up her bag, carrying it across the room and into the corridor and the spare room where she dropped it on the bed.

When she came back, Terry was still staring at the lights on the distant ships waiting to enter the creek into Apapa. She flopped back onto the sofa. Terry turned back into the room and went to the small bar. He stood by it for a moment as if he was going to pour a drink but thinking better of it, spun around and let himself collapse into an armchair. He stuck his legs out and with his head back, looked at the ceiling.

"When I go back, I am going to tell Rachel that I am leaving."

"No, Terry!" But before Isioma could say anything more, Terry interrupted her.

"No, listen. It's not about you. Well, it is in a way, but it's about me. Whatever happens to us, I have to change. I have to be different and if I go back to the same place and the same people, I never will. What is it your clever friends would say, 'a child is a product of its upbringing'? You haven't seen where I live or heard the people I hang out with, like my old schoolmates down the pub. It's shite. It's what makes us act like drunken, wife-beating, racist cunts."

"Terry . . ."

"No, listen. I have been talking to Tunde. You know, the older guy from work. He agrees I have to break the mould as he calls it. Avoid the old places and people." He continued staring at the ceiling. "I don't know. Maybe I should go back to school or something . . ." His voice trailed off before he sat up suddenly and looked directly at Isioma. "I can't ask you to be part of it. Well, anyway, that's for you to decide but you have already helped me open my eyes. You and Robert and Tunde and the guys at work."

She stood up and stood in front of him. He put his arms around her and she bent and kissed the top of his head.

Isioma spoke softly to the top of his head, "Well, they normally say 'you can take the man out of the bush, but you cannot take the bush out of the man'. But maybe that is not true. If you mean it, and try hard enough. . ." For a few moments, the only sound was the rustle of the wind through the curtains until she shrugged.

153

"Terry, I am tired. Let's go to bed."

He heaved himself up, shut the balcony door and switched off the lights. They walked together into the corridor and stood between the two doors: his bedroom and the spare room where she slept. She looked at him, kissed him on the cheek and let her hand fall away from his. He watched her step into her room and shut the door behind her before turning into his room.

The curtains were open and there was just enough light to see without turning on the bedside lamp. The air conditioner buzzed quietly as he padded around undressing, dropping his clothes on a chair. In the bathroom, he stood for a few moments studying his bloodstained face in the mirror and dabbed at it with a flannel before giving up and going back into the bedroom where he threw back the sheet and sat on the edge of the bed, his mind whirring. He sat slumped for several minutes without moving until, unexpectedly, the door opened.

"Isioma?"

He had not known it but while he was pacing in his bedroom, Isioma had been doing the same thing. She got undressed and put on the night dress that was in her bag. In the bathroom, she washed her face and put on some cream, then, stared at her reflection. She studied her face without her glasses, her mind almost empty rather than actively considering the situation. She too went back into her bedroom and sat on the edge of the bed. She leaned back on her hands, then restlessly leaned forward, her arms on her knees. "Why, why, why?"

Abruptly, almost subconsciously, she made the decision, stood up and walked to the door. Then she stopped, pulled her nightdress over her head and threw it on the bed, opened the door and crossed the corridor. As she opened his bedroom door, Terry was sitting on his bed and was startled as she burst in.

"Isioma?"

For a moment, she stood naked, silhouetted by the hallway lights. He tried to stand up but she stepped forward and pushed him back, putting her fingers on his lips.

"Shush," she said. "It's time," and allowed herself fall on top of him. "It is time."

Chapter 19

A Tokunbo Decides

"You cannot sing African music in proper English,"
Fela Anikulapo Kuti

As they crossed the junction at Gbagada, heading to join the Third Mainland Bridge, it was clear the traffic was already backing up on their side even though the rush-hour flow was against them. You seldom saw what the cause of a go-slow was: sometimes a broken down molue, a skewed and tipped over truck, maybe or even, occasionally, please-God-not-today, a burning petrol tanker.

Usually, of course, the trigger was just some dumb piece of driving, a moment of impatient idiocy that blocked a junction and created a gridlock. Or perhaps a shunt into someone's rear end that could generate a pointless twenty-minute face-off, in which both drivers got out of their cars to shout and gesture while a crowd gathered around to add their commentary or to take sides, only, without any apparent resolution or even the sharing of insurance details, for the drivers to get back into their cars and resume their journeys, allowing hundreds of vehicles queuing back for a mile to gradually start moving again.

Robert could sense Mathew's frustration. "Ah, sir, wahala dey for road," he said.

"Don't stress Mathew. I am not in a hurry."

Robert was in a quiet, reflective mood. Over the last week, he had been in conversation with HR in London and with his boss, the Finance Director, here in Lagos. His boss had wanted him to stay for at least another year but there was a position Robert wanted which was soon to be available at HQ. The compromise was a further six months, although with outstanding leave the reality would be less. He had called Isioma and arranged to meet her and Terry so he could give them the news.

"Turn the radio on, Mathew. Let's listen to some music."

155

He leaned forward to reach the lead from the radio to plug into his iPod and selected a Fela playlist. As the afrobeat rhythm kicked in and Fela's high-pitched sax intro on Yellow Fever flooded the interior, he idly gazed out of the Pajero's window at the dense water hyacinth that clogged much of the Oworonshoki end of the lagoon. The mud of the lagoon, the piles of discarded plastic bottles and the mountains of cleared drain debris created an impression of something grossly organic. Not from any healthy being but as if some toxic beast was decomposing on the side of the road. By the intersection, a changing point for many of those who had made their daily commute from Lagos Island, buses disgorged themselves of their heaving innards, seemingly impossible that so many people could have been squeezed into such a constricted space and then be squeezed out again into what to the untrained eye, is a formless, directionless pandemonium.

Yet, the noise and the confusion belied a kind of organised chaos. Bus conductors shouted untellable names for the next leg of their journey into Lagos' hinterland: Agege, Ojodu, Ikorodu, and even Ota. Customers jostled around bus stops as perpetually irate policemen and LASTMA officers beat against the danfos with truncheons or pieces of wood with protruding nails, threatening dawdlers to move on and stop blocking the traffic streaming off the bridge. Clouds of diesel fumes floated above the throng, enough to sting and water the eyes and cause spluttering coughs. Even for the practised Lagosian, this was an exhaustingly arduous process.

Fela was the perfect musical accompaniment on any journey through Lagos. His words were born out of and perfectly describe the reality that Robert was watching out there on the street. To Fela, this scene was just "katakata". His lyrics captured the mood of these people grinding out their tough lives with humour and dignity in the face of hostility and even oppression such that he was still a hero to many people so many years after his death. Robert had not felt Fela's music until he had heard it performed live. One evening some friends of Isioma's from UNILAG suggested they go to O'Jays, a small club in Yaba, where Fela's youngest son, Seun, was playing. Seun had started fronting his father's Egypt '80 band when the man everyone called Abami Eda—The Strange One—died in 1997. Seun was fourteen at the time and having stepped up when he was still at school, was now building a career in his father's footsteps. So much so that everyone who saw him came away convinced Fela was channelling through his son: the physical likeness, the movement, and the style were all so eerily evocative of his father. He even "yabbed" like Fela.

The evening had been a revelation. Packed into the dense club full of Fela Anikulapo Kuti devotees, all swaying and rocking to the call and response of the Afrobeat rhythm, the intensity of Seun's delivery of the lyrics made them explode into Robert's consciousness.

Even as much of the Yoruba and street pidgin had been beyond his cognitive understanding, the message was suddenly real, carried by the throbbing pulse of the music itself. Yes, he had been to ganja-filled reggae gigs in Brixton with his mates but he had experienced nothing like this. Maybe it was the clouds of weed and the closeness of so many bodies, or the shared response to the music, but Robert had felt somehow different.

Thinking about it later, he had allowed himself to consider that he had felt *African* for the first time. Though he quickly dismissed this as too much of a cliché and could not even tell Isioma about it, he had been listening to Fela's music ever since.

As the car crawled amongst the usual mix of smart Mercedes 4x4s, battered Nissan pick-ups, beaten-up trailer lorries and the usual danfos and Lagos BRTs, Robert wondered what impact his news would have on Isioma and Terry. While he was not entirely convinced about the future of their relationship, they certainly seemed comfortable together.

It threw his mind back to his first impressions of Terry at the airport and that first experience of this crazy traffic but his thoughts were less concerned for Terry than they were for himself. His expectation back then that he would complete a three-year tenure and somehow return unaffected by the country of his ancestors, now seemed unbelievably naïve.

However, one never knows how much you have changed without the mirror of other people. He was aware that he had become more worldly. He did not feel particularly different, he was still himself. But, somehow, people treated him differently. His relationship with his parents had already changed. That with his father in subtle ways. There was a sense of his father's pride in his achievements, of now being more of an equal. But his bond with his mother was on another level.

Even before his trip to Ngwo, she had been able to reveal more of her Nigerian identity and have it understood and acknowledged. On his last Chiswick visit, she talked a little about her childhood and asked him about certain places in Lagos she could still remember. His sister even announced one evening "It's like sitting down with Nigerians being with you two", not without a hint of irritation in her voice.

The Ngwo visit and Vitus' revelations had transformed his understanding of the true nature of what her family meant to his mother and the trauma of being torn from it. He had been unable to explain over the phone how his newfound respect for her journey created a whole different person in his eyes. He was looking forward to sharing that knowledge with her and making atonement for his previous ignorance while at the same time thinking, '*How could I have possibly known if no one had explained it to me?*'

When he first went back on leave, everything seemed the same with his mates, as if he had never been away. He was bemused by their apparent indifference to his stories. What seemed to him to be life-changing experiences failed to break through their football banter and sexual gossip. A couple had recently got married and he listened to tales of the stag parties and the weddings he missed with some envy. Yet, after a few trips, he began to feel detached from them, somehow frustrated that they seemed not to have moved on.

One evening, walking home after a few beers with the football lads, his mate, Chris, brought it up. After asking him if he was alright, he went on to say Robert seemed quiet and less engaged. Robert brushed it off with a joke but had to acknowledge to himself that it was true. He could not admit to his childhood friend that for the first time in his life he was suddenly more conscious that almost all his "crew" were White. He had always wanted to be one of the lads—the football team, the drinking guys. He still did, still was. They were still his mates. They had gone to the same school and had played in the same park but somehow, he knew that he was somehow different. He

158

understood now that he had always known that but never acknowledged it. Travelling to Nigeria not only triggered that acknowledgement but had set him to one side in his head. He had come to realise that his adventures, because that is what they were to him, had been so out of his friends' own experiences that he was better off not even trying to talk about them.

So, if he was not the same person who left the UK three years or so ago, who was he? That was something he had not yet worked out. He had never felt the need to before but, for the first time in his life, his sense of his own identity was in question.

* * *

The traffic trickled along. They were now adjacent to the waterside ghetto of Bariga that had spread on top of the lagoon until it was almost under the bridge itself. Shacks and lean-tos on stilts, fully lived lives of love and pain, of laughter and death, christenings and weddings and funerals, all floated above the dull, brackish porridge that formed that watery end of Lagos. Yet, above it all, as if by some miracle of God's paintbrush, the pollution would often cause a phenomenon that coloured the atmosphere and through it, the setting sun, into a ball of the deepest orange in a vermillion-streaked sky.

From where they were on the bridge it seemed as if the sun was suspended, just above the trees around the UNILAG buildings, a glorious postcard impersonation of an African sunset. Yet this was a misrepresentation, almost an abomination. The phosphorescent glow was made possible only by the tens of thousands of wood-burning and kerosene stoves of the slums of Bariga and Akoka, creating a smog that hung like a shroud over the scene. To open the window at that point was to inhale the almost indescribable smell of poverty and the desperate stench of effluence that came with it.

Normally oblivious to the contradiction of the visceral beauty floating above the contrasting humanity struggling to make a life in the shantytown, Robert's reflective mood and the slow pace of the traffic gave him pause.

His visits with Isioma to Orile and Enugu had taken him out of his comfort zone, prised him from the comfortable life of an expatriate and dumped him head-first into the reality that was the existence of millions of Nigerians. It might have just been possible to have completed his generous hard currency contract without engaging, but once his eyes had been opened, they could never be fully closed again.

By the time they reached Awolowo Road and turned into Ribadu to park the car, Robert was ready for a beer though his first act was to hobble up the stairs of Havana for a pee. Feeling more relaxed coming down and turning into the bar, he had to run the gamut of the regulars lined up in their usual positions. They had seen him hurry past as he came in.

"Evening, young Robert. Feeling better?"

By now, though not a full-on Havanaite, he was enough of a frequent visitor to be known.

"Usual Third Mainland nonsense," he responded. "Been desperate for a piss since the Ebute Metta turning."

Someone laughed. "Well, your family is waiting for you in the back."

Sure enough, Isioma and Terry were already settled with their drinks and, judging by the empty plate of what had been suya, had been there for a while.

"Even going against the traffic, Third Mainland was a crawl," he explained as he sat down.

"Yeh, I heard," said Terry, "I had a job on the island, so I missed it."

After they had caught up with the day's news, Isioma asked her cousin what had prompted him to come to the island mid-week.

As Robert explained why, he could see disappointment reflected on their faces.

"You know I was only ever on a three-year posting?" He looked at Isioma directly. "This was always going to happen, coz."

"I know," she replied with a side tilt of her head that suggested resignation, "but, I kind of guess, I was hoping in my heart that you would have learned to love us enough to stay longer. Especially after your visit home."

Robert reached across the table and squeezed her hand. "I have learned to love you. I confess the first few months were difficult but your patience with your Tokunbo cousin has borne fruit, Isioma. Thanks to you, I have at least some understanding of my background, my culture I guess, especially since our visit East. My tolerance for pepper has increased ten-fold and now, when I go home, my mum happily serves me swallow with pride. My sister keeps nagging me to bring her out and I will. Possibly before I go back, or more likely later, on a visit. Yes, like to your wedding." He nodded towards the silent Terry. "Though, obviously, when you find a nice Nigerian boy, not to him."

Though he was laughing, the comment was not entirely without a point.

"So, Terry, you look pretty glum. Wassup?"

Terry paused. "I dunno mate. I guess it was always gonna happen but I am gobsmacked, to be honest. Like Isioma, I just didn't think about it. It just kind of makes me think about my situation. I mean, my contract is an open one. I am assuming GTW will keep me on as long as I am willing to stay really." He took a breath and glanced at Isioma. "I don't want to go back."

For a few moments, no one said anything until Terry waved at a waitress.

"Well, I don't know about you, but I need another beer. Same again?"

He ordered his usual Star, Robert's small Guinness and after Isioma nodded, he ordered her a small Heineken.

"Oh, and three more sticks of suya."

Then as an afterthought, he called out to the waitress' retreating rear end.

"Aina, and a plate of chips please."

"Chips!" exclaimed Robert. "With suya? You're incorrigible."

"Why not, mate?" Terry shrugged. "You're always going on about me being bush and no one will ever stop me eating chips with everything or drinking my tea strong and milky in a proper mug."

"I don't know," Robert laughed and looked at Isioma. "Maybe you had better take him to the village, Isioma. A day in Ngwo might do him good."

Isioma sucked her teeth. "I am not taking him. A married man? Kai, what a disgrace."

She was laughing and slapped Terry playfully on the arm.

"No, seriously. He doesn't have to go with you, but you can send him down as a friend of mine. Terry, you can sort out the generators that are not working. I seem to remember quite a few air conditioners that need gassing and cleaning too. You have clients in Enugu anyway, right?"

Isioma was still not convinced. "Well, that would be handy but I do not see the point."

Robert raised his arms as if to say, 'Isn't it obvious?'

"Terry, you are always saying you want to feel more engaged with Nigeria and understand Isioma better. I can tell you from my experience that a visit there will teach you a lot. Plus, you can help her, in fact, our family, in a practical way. After all, you owe us."

"Owe you? Like what?"

Robert laughed. "I think you should repay the Ede family for shagging their daughter and abusing their son for the last three years."

He jumped up from his chair before Terry's swinging arm could land on him.

Isioma put on her sternest face. "Robert Railsford! You are no Ede talking like that. In fact, I am not going to miss you at all, and I am glad you are going."

At this point, the waitress returned with a tray loaded with their drinks, suya, and a plate of chips. Robert sat down again.

Isioma chuckled. "You can finish your stout before you go but you're not having any of our chips."

Chapter 20

Conversations

"Unwind the wind
Give rapid legs to the crouching leaf;
The horse of words has galloped
Through clouds, through thunder, through roaring
waters...
Throw open the door of your ears

Araba ponmbe ponmbe ponmbe
Araba ponmbe ponmbe ponmbe

The Word, the Word, is an egg
From the nest of hawk and dove
Its shell the sheath of anger's sword
Its yolk composted of bile and boon."

'The Word is an Egg' by Niyi Osundare

When Terry suggested Robert should have a big "boys' night out" before flying out, Isioma made it clear she did not think much of the idea. When she had called it antediluvian, Terry understood perfectly what she was saying without having a clue what the word meant. In the end, she persuaded him that they should all go for a farewell meal at Yellow Chilli where she had first encountered her cousin. Arranging the evening on the phone she could not believe it had been less than three years since that first meeting. Robert could hardly refuse.

Robert had already had "send-forth" drinks at work and a "leaving-do pool party" at the Maryland apartment, so he did not feel the need to invite any of his colleagues. In the end, it was arranged for the three of them plus Florence and Ezzy to go for dinner until Terry suggested they invite Tunde to join them.

Tunde was delighted but explained he might be a little late as he had a meeting that evening so they should not wait for him.

Terry and Isioma were already there when Robert turned up and it was sometime later when Isioma's housemates arrived, laughing at some joint hilarity, tottering on heels higher than their usual work shoes and fully ready for a social occasion.

They had become fond of Robert as their early teasing about his oyibo ways had morphed into genuine affection. He was always generous whenever they went out but not in the obvious way of many of their male Nigerian friends and without any ostentation. Equally, he appreciated their down-to-earth and good-natured mischievousness; what his mates back home would call "banter". Nevertheless, despite their best efforts, he had not been hooked by the many fishing lines cast by their friends. He also knew better than to expose his occasional dalliances to their scrutiny.

"See, Isioma, you have taught your cousin well. He eats his swallow like a true son of the soil."

"Not like the first time we ate here, Robert?"

He laughed. "I refuse to rise to the bait. Anyway, it is my going-away dinner so you should pick on him," pointing at Terry, who responded by making a spluttering noise of protest with a mouth full of chicken and by waving a thigh bone.

"He is a lost cause. I have given up!" Isioma handed him several napkins. "You are such a messy eater."

He swallowed his mouthful, then wiped his greasy fingers.

"The grub is always good here though."

Ezzy looked at his plate and sucked her teeth. "But Terry, you waste half your chicken. There's plenty of meat left on those bones."

He shrugged. "You can suck on them if you want."

Florence smacked him hard on his bare arm.

"Ouch!"

"You know you can be really revolting," she complained, feigning disgust. "But you can buy me a Baileys if you like."

"That's a good idea. Where's the waiter?"

Ezzy was quick to support her partner in crime's idea.

164

Before Terry had a chance to order more drinks, Isioma caught sight of someone coming into the restaurant. She waved. "Uncle Tunde!"

As Tunde came over, he was followed by someone else.

Isioma burst out, "Uncle Onyeka! What a surprise!"

Everyone stood up to greet the older men who waved them down and pulled up chairs.

"I had no idea you knew each other," Isioma said.

"Connections," winked Onyeka, double tapping the side of his nose in the gesture to suggest a shared secret or discretion. "Anyway, you know what they say: 'Lagos is a village'."

They all laughed. Tunde looked around. "What is everyone drinking? Onyeka, what are you having?"

"Egbon," said Robert, using the respectful Yoruba term, "you are incorrigible!"

To Onyeka, "Mazi, I assume yours is a Guinness?"

"I am impressed, young Robert. You have learned a few things and yes, I would like a Guinness, please."

"Uncle," Isioma said to Tunde, "we are about to go on to the Baileys."

"Speak for yourself," Terry replied. "I am sticking with Star."

Tunde thought for a minute. The waiter had come over and was waiting.

"Yes, large Baileys, and plenty of ice."

"So why have you never taken us there before?" asked Terry.

"Well," Tunde said, smiling, "Oti's Cellar is not a place you can take everyone. It is like a secret club really but as Onyeka and I are both members, or more correctly, fellows, it could be a farewell treat for Robert."

"But Uncle Tunde, Uncle Onyeka, are you both saying it is men's only?"

Isioma was giving Tunde as hard a stare as she felt she could to someone close to her father's age.

"Well Isioma, not exactly. But we cannot take too many as it is a small place. We could take you with the boys but not everyone."

The girls looked singularly unimpressed. "Well," said Ezzy, "If you are going to be so ungentlemanly, Mister Terry," giving

165

him a pointed look, "leaving your three favourite girls alone, you could at least buy us a bottle of Baileys to take away."

Isioma was going to tell her off but as she thought about it, it seemed like reasonable punishment for typical male behaviour.

"Yes Terry, I think it is the least you can do if you are going to dump us."

Onyeka laughed. "You see, mess with an Ngwo woman at your peril. I think that is a cheap price for a quiet life, young Terry."

Not long afterwards, Terry's man Saturday had taken all three girls and their bottle back to Keffi Street and Robert and Terry followed Tunde and Onyeka down a side road not far from Yellow Chilli.

It was a quiet residential area and down the bottom end of a cul-de-sac, a few SUVs were parked with several drivers sitting around looking at their phones or chatting.

As their drivers found parking spaces, the four men walked to a small door within a larger iron gate. As it opened, a face peered around, recognised the older men and let them in.

Inside, Robert and Terry were impressed to see a small, neatly tended garden with a Jaguar XJS parked in it. There were a couple of garden seats and a small bench with a couple sitting on it, who looked up and greeted Tunde and Onyeka.

At this point, a dapper Nigerian in starched jeans and a linen jacket with a silk handkerchief in the pocket came out of the door of what looked to be an extension on the back of a regular house.

Oti, the eponymous owner of the establishment, greeted his fellows with shoulder hugs and warm handshakes.

"Hey, hey, hey! Who do we have here?" he smiled, spotting the younger guys.

Tunde stepped to one side and allowed Robert and Terry to introduce themselves. As they did, Oti interrupted them. "Hey, I recognise you," he pointed to Terry. "Didn't we go to university together?"

Terry was nonplussed. "I don't think so, sir."

"Oh yes," beamed Oti. "The university of hard knocks. Am I right or am I right?"

Terry was not quite sure if this was a joke at his expense, but it was said so openly that he could not take offence. So, he smiled.

"Yes, I guess so, sir." As everyone else was chuckling, he joined in and laughed.

"Hey," Oti grabbed him by the arm, "Big fella, no need for sir or uncle here. Call me Oti. O. T. I. Oti. Anything else would be. . ." he stopped, pointed at Robert, and continued, ". . . uncivilised, right?"

The first time anyone entered Oti's Cellar, it was invariably a shock. They felt suddenly transported into what, for all purposes, looked like a miniature old-school, gentleman's club in Mayfair, or, given the hint of New York in Oti's accent, Manhattan. That there was nothing else like this in Lagos was a truism.

There was a long leather bench seat along one wall and just enough room for four or five leather armchairs of different sizes. At the far end of what was clearly identifiable as a converted garage, was a baby grand piano. There was one coffee table and a few stools to complete the furniture. There were three men, two Nigerian and one expatriate, sitting in the armchairs around the coffee table. An elegantly dressed woman was sitting on her own in the corner reading a book, though she did not stay long, waving a cheery goodbye as she left. On the walls were several artworks including portraits of Nina Simone and Fela, while piles of books and magazines covered whatever other space was available. Robert recognised the music playing to be jazz from the Blue Note era.

There were lowkey greetings in the manner of friends accustomed to meeting in the same place more than occasionally. Tunde took the only available chair left at the coffee table and Onyeka indicated that the boys could take two stools. A younger man in a white shirt and black trousers immediately put four fine wine glasses on the table and began to pour red wine. Before Terry could say anything, Onyeka leant over and whispered, "Only wine here, Terry, though Oti could probably rustle you up a cognac. But no beer."

The expatriate was sitting closest to Terry and reached over and held out his hand for Terry to shake. "It's Terry, I believe? And Robert?" he waved. "Sorry, can't reach that far."

"Good evening sir," replied Robert.

Tunde indicated the expat. "So chaps, this is one of my closest friends. He claims to have retired but has nowhere else to go. In any case, where else would he go given he is as much a Lagosian as I?"

He chuckled at Tunde. "Bros, I would not go as far as that." To Terry, he said, "Well, Tunde has told me a bit about some of your escapades so it is finally nice to meet you. And you too, Robert." He smiled across the table before turning back to Terry. "I have to say I was particularly impressed by Pat's description of your Glasgow Kiss. Sounds like it was perfectly executed."

"Wow, you seem to know everybody. How long have you been here?" asked Terry. "Sorry, what did you say your name was?"

"You can call him 'Chief'," laughed one of the Nigerians, puffing out a plume of cigar smoke.

"Seriously?" Terry and Robert looked confused.

The man they called Chief smiled. "It's true," he said. "And in answer to your questions: it's Thomas, and about twenty-five years off and on."

Oti came over with another bottle, leaned over and topped up Chief's glass.

"Don't mind him. He may as well be Nigerian. We have adopted him."

The evening broke up into smaller conversations, more glasses of wine, cigar smoke, and the general hum of conviviality, all orchestrated by the genial Oti. After a while, Robert found himself on a stool chatting directly with Chief.

"Well, it's a shame we did not get the chance to chat more before you go back to the UK, Robert."

Robert pulled a face in agreement as Thomas continued. "Over the years, I have met many returnees, some from the UK and others from the US. Often, I would say they needed more support than White expatriates. Often, I found they had expectations of coming back to their people and their motherland with an improbably idealistic point of view. The reality of life here then becomes quite a shock. On the other hand, the standard expat just shuts himself off in a compound before buggering off

168

back home when he has finished his stint. May I ask what your experience was?"

"A fair question," Robert said, and considered his answer before continuing. "I think my situation was dissimilar as I did not see myself as a returning Nigerian. Rather I was British. In fact, I used to be quite aggressive towards anyone asking the 'where are you from' question. However, my spell here, particularly since I have re-connected with my mother's family, has changed that stance. To a point. I mean, I would still say I am British but would happily add 'with a Nigerian heritage'."

He thought for a moment. "Or maybe an Igbo heritage? One of the biggest effects has been being exposed to the contradiction of calling myself British when I have learnt more about the impact of the British Empire on my community and, more directly, on my family. Just a few weeks ago, I learnt that my maternal great-grandfather had served with the British Army in Burma and was later shot by British officers for going on strike in a miners' dispute. If I am honest, I am still processing that. It is not an easy thing to understand, let alone come to terms with."

"I can imagine. I have been here for years, and only in the last few years have I thought about the deeper implications of being an expatriate Brit here. I mean, beyond the obvious stuff. But for you, as someone who looks like a Nigerian and has a Nigerian family background, the contradiction must be all the greater. Having run businesses here, I cannot escape the reality that I have been part of the modern colonial structure. For me, that's clear cut but I am guessing, for you, it is a bit more complicated?"

Robert shrugged. "To an extent. Yes, this trip has opened my eyes to the impact of colonialism on my life. Well, my mother's mostly. Yet her story is more about what the Biafran war did. I mean, that was Nigerian on Nigerian, a federal side opposed to a Biafran side. I don't see that as a colonial thing. Not anymore, surely?" Robert was aware that the others around the table were also listening to the conversation. "I mean, take Terry here." At which point Terry pulled a face. Robert grinned. "Yes, someone please take Terry. But seriously, Terry may be White, but he is here fixing generators. You cannot tell me he is part of modern colonialism?"

"I am not so sure. It is still a way of life, a culture. I mean colonialism. Today, in a way, we are all victims of it but obviously, some are more victims than others. These days plenty of people still benefit from it, including Nigerians. Call it what you want, 'economic colonialism', 'the American military-industrial complex', whatever. Some might just say it is 'the patriarchy'. I reluctantly admit that I have been a tool of it, unfortunately."

"You still are," came a rich voice from the recess of one of Oti's leather chairs.

"I admit. Guilty. But we cannot escape it."

"You don't want to." A grey-bearded face emerged out of the cigar smoke and a hand grabbed Chief's knee. "You see my brother Thomas here? I love him dearly, but he is still full of oyibo shit. First, he made money running not one, but two multinationals and second, though he is my brother from another mother, he is still a White Englishman in a privileged position in a former colony. He enjoys all the benefits that entails and not for a second would consider giving them up."

"What he is inarticulately trying to tell you is a contradiction. He wants to tell you that only the elite British ruling classes benefitted from the empire, that the European working man was coerced into being a soldier or a junior colonial officer and was as much a victim as the poor Africans working on the palm oil plantation. Only, that is not true." He paused and looked at Oti who was refilling glasses. "Bros, you don forget me na?"

Oti flashed his trademark smile. "Oga, no vex. I dey come. For you, my senior, the bottom of the bottle."

The younger man studied the face in front of them, waiting for him to continue.

The face belonged to a distinctive Nigerian with short grey hair and an equally short grey beard. Okey had been introduced earlier but he had been content to stay leaning back in his chair, savouring a Cuban cigar from Oti's humidor. As he leaned forward to reach his now replete glass, cigar in his other hand, they could see he was wearing a well-cut pinstriped suit. His white shirt was open at the neck and his outstretched arm revealed a monogrammed gold cufflink. Despite the serious tone of his voice and his obvious gravitas, he was smiling as if enjoying himself. Indeed, he was.

170

"You see. Some might argue that some poor army private, some colonial police officer, joined up to escape poverty and a working-class existence in Glasgow, Liverpool, or London. However, the truth is that their education, health service, social housing, pension and even the factories their parents worked in were only made possible by the proceeds of stolen resources or the labour of enslaved persons working in those colonies. Once out here, they received a degree of comfort and treatment that exceeded anything they could have anticipated back home and certainly more than any African could have expected.

"The entire structure of modern British society has been shaped by the proceeds and by the expectations of colonialism, by the extraction of resources from colonised people back to their home country. And, lest you believe this is a thing of the past, it is still happening today."

"Surely, sir," said Robert, "this ended years ago?"

"Don't you believe it, young man. Your people, that is if you call yourself British, are still extracting resources from Africa under the umbrella of the world's financial system: the IMF, the World Bank, and so on. Why is it that all this cocoa and palm oil from West Africa is taken back raw and cheap and turned into chocolate and other finished products back in Europe? Finished product that is then exported back to us at exponentially increased prices? Why is it that those factories are not here close to the source of their ingredients? The entire structure is set up to benefit those same people who, in their generosity, gave us independence. The same with the crude oil that we export and re-import as subsidised diesel. And now all the minerals for your computers and mobile phones that are being dug out by children in the Congo and exported to be turned into high-value, billionaire-creating, technology.

"Yet these same countries that provide the raw material for the industrialised nations remain in poverty. The raw materials that these economies depend on is extracted by the same people who refuse to invest in processing here, only allowing the value to be added to benefit the West and now, China. These African countries and what liberals like to call 'the developing world' are the world's most indebted. Indebted to guess who? You know the answer. So, young man, in short, in response to your question, it did not 'finish' years ago."

171

While Robert was listening intently well before this point, Terry's eyes had glazed over. Had he not been perched uncomfortably on a low stool, he would undoubtedly have been asleep. At this juncture, he jerked himself fully awake.

"This is too complicated for my brain this time of night."

Onyeka had been standing behind the boys during the conversation.

"Terry, let's get some fresh air outside."

"Bros Onyeka, you brought these young men in here. Have you taught them nothing, you old goat?"

Onyeka laughed out loud. "Robert, ask my brother Okey, what he is doing here sipping on fine South African pinotage and smoking his Havana cigar complaining about colonialism while I go out for a breather with Terry."

Okey laughed. "What Onyeka means is that as a Black man, I should be out somewhere being exploited or wearing a black beret and organising a revolution rather than sitting here pontificating. I have been very successful as a lawyer to those very same institutions I have been talking about, so I have the perfect window into their mechanics, and I am equally pleased to say I charge them an inordinately hefty amount of money in doing so. I am happy to play them at their own game. Anyway, enough of that. So young man, you seem to be doing well. From what I heard you are back to the UK on promotion?"

"Yes, sir. I have enjoyed my stint here, but I have been given a significant opportunity back at head office in London."

Oti was standing behind Robert and squeezed his shoulders. "What a shame. And we have only just met you. Our loss. Were you not tempted to stay with us?"

Before he could answer, Okey interrupted, "No, Brother Oti. Do not confuse the lad. Let him go away and make his money. When he is old and retired like you, he can come back and open a wine cellar to benefit his African people."

He stood up. "Ouch, these old bones are creaking. Robert, I sincerely wish you well. Despite what the cynical lawyer in me says, do come back sometime. We need young men like you." He shook Robert's hand.

Oti followed him to the door. "Let me see my egbon out."

Robert was still standing from shaking Okey's hand as he watched them saying goodbye outside to Onyeka and Terry. He realised it was late and he was now the only person in the room except for Chief.

"One of the things I so love about this place is the different late-night conversations. Okey there is one of the most formidable intellects I know, almost intimidating, and is a world-class lawyer to the very organisations he so disdains."

Robert looked about him. "I wish I had known about this place before." He thought for a moment. "No one seems to have paid for anything. Can I . . ."

"No. Olumide over there," Chief nodded over to a corner where the young man who had been serving wine was standing by a small bar, "sends all the fellows a monthly account. Some of us occasionally pay."

They walked out into the darkness of the garden, only dimly lit by a couple of lamp posts.

Terry was admiring the Jaguar and Oti was explaining that he occasionally took it out for a spin around Lagos on Sundays but he was currently waiting for some spare parts. Even so, he took off the cover every day and turned the engine over, putting the cover back on in the evening.

As they went out through the door in the gate, Terry offered to come back and help Oti service the Jag and supervise any mechanics.

Oti shook his hand warmly. "You can come again."

"So, when are you finally off, Robert?" asked Tunde.

"Next Friday, sir."

"We shall miss you."

"He will be back," said Onyeka. "He has to bring his sister and escort her and his mother to the village."

As the various drivers started their cars, they all shook hands one last time.

"Uncle Onyeka, I have a funny feeling you may be right."

Robert turned to Terry, whose pick-up had previously taken the girls back home with their bottle of Baileys.

"I will drop you off mate."

Chapter 21

Seldom by Chance

"A human feast is an indifferent morsel to a god."

Professor Wole Soyinka

Isioma had rung her parents to tell them a friend of hers and Robert's would be in Enugu and had offered to come around to look at the family's generator. Once they expressed their delight, it took Terry only a few weeks to make the arrangements. The day before he landed in Enugu, a crew of three had turned up and sorted out the main generator plus a couple of smaller ones used in the evenings to save the expense of diesel for the 20kva Mikano. There was nothing wrong with them that new filters and decent maintenance could not fix. The boys cleaned and serviced several air conditioners as well.

Travelling out of Lagos was now almost routine for Terry. GTW supplied generators and had service contracts with companies in most of the bigger cities and Enugu was no exception. His teams would go by road, stopping to service various installations, and Terry would fly in and inspect or supervise the more important ones. A couple of Enugu's larger hotels leased units from GTW, so it was easy to arrange to fly down, stay in one of those, and keep an eye on his boys.

He had long since stopped using a tout to check-in at the domestic airport, relying instead on his size and strength to push himself to the front of the queue. In contrast to the day of his first arrival, he was oblivious to any stares or complaints about his elbowing his way to the desk. His mixture of steely determination, strong elbows, and a disarming grin at the female staff, usually saw him being served quickly.

Once on the plane, he would cheerfully help lift elderly passengers' bundles onto the racks or wink at small children who stared at the bulky White man.

This flight was little different from any other: a short wait while some recalcitrant traveller had to be shifted to his proper seat, a bouncy taxi onto a bumpy runway, stale cake and the usual carton of juice, scattered applause at a successful landing, and half the people jumping up to retrieve their luggage well before the plane finished jerking its way to a complete stop at the terminal building.

During the commotion of passengers collecting luggage several seats away from where he sat, Terry noticed an attractive, smartly dressed, young woman reaching up to retrieve her bag. In truth, he was admiring her shapely backside when she turned to face him. Recognising him, she paused and then turned away. As Terry grabbed his bag and helped another woman with her bundle, he racked his brain trying to remember how he knew her.

"Thank you sir, have a nice day," muttered the stewardess as he reached the exit.

Lost in his thoughts, he noticed little as he clambered down the wobbly stairs and made his way across the runway. He had no baggage to collect but as he pushed through the people waiting to collect theirs, he noticed the same woman standing ahead of him. She turned round this time.

"Hello Terry. Long time no see."

She waited for his response before continuing, "As always, you don't remember my name, abi?"

"I am sorry, I recognise you but…"

"Pat's Bar. And your place behind Silverbird."

He coloured up. "Oh God, I am so sorry! Yes, how are you?"

"I am very well, thank you. But you don't remember my name."

Terry's face became even redder. "Comfort?"

She sucked her teeth. "Blessing."

"Wow," he said. "Blessing, of course. You look great. How are you? What are you doing in Enugu?"

"This is my hometown. I have come to see my parents to tell them I am marrying."

"Wow," Terry repeated. "That's nice. Who? A local guy?"

"No, a White guy. I don't think you'd know him. He only came into Pat's once or twice and he is more serious than you and your friends." Her look was cheerful but challenging him to respond. "He paid for me to go back to university, I should graduate next year. I also have a small shop in a mall in Surulere."

"I am really happy for you Blessing."

She smiled pleasantly because he sounded sincere.

There was a clunk as the baggage trolley was pushed against the conveyor. Despite the presence of what should be automatic equipment, a couple of porters started unceremoniously dumping bags onto the belt which started lazily circulating.

"I have to go. I have to go, and my father is waiting for me outside." She looked up at him. "You are not a bad man, Terry. I hope you have stopped drinking too much and find a nice girl to look after you." She noticed a heavy bag on the creaking conveyor, pushed through a few people, and hauled it off.

"Let me help you."

"No. Thank you, Terry. I do not want my father to see me with another White man except my Michael. But it was nice to see you."

A porter came up with a trolley and she indicated the bag and another bundle still rotating on the near-empty conveyor belt creaking around in the emptying hall.

"I am fine, you go."

"Sure, all the best. Good luck with the wedding," he stammered and then turned into the Enugu sunlight where he was soon met by one of his GTW team.

Samuel, in his GTW polo shirt, took Terry's bag from his shoulder and carried it to where a branded pick-up was waiting.

"Hello, Samuel. Thank you."

As he was about to slide into the front of the double cabin, Terry looked to the terminal building. Blessing was greeting her father, bending her knee respectfully before being given an emotional hug. There seemed to be other family members all excited to see the return of a prodigal daughter bearing, as suggested by her heavy bundle and suitcase, gifts for everyone.

"Where to, sah?"

On his first trip, he had stayed at the Presidential Hotel, once one of Enugu's jewels but by then sadly run down. They had been unable to pay GTW's invoices for servicing their generator so he had switched his loyalty to the new Nike Lake Hotel, another GTW customer.

"Let me check-in first. Nike Lake. Then we can check what you guys have done with their set?"

"What of your friends, Mr Terry?

"We can go there tomorrow."

After dropping his bag in the room, Terry inspected the servicing of the hotel's two generators and declared himself satisfied. Over the next three hours, they made several courtesy calls to clients around the city as Terry was wont—his way of maintaining relationships. He was always genuinely welcomed and he, in turn, was at ease.

Terry soon announced it was time for the team to share a beer and some pepper soup. This had also become a routine with Terry on tour and it gave him a chance to build on his relationship with his team. He had done his best to improve their working conditions, but improving their salary and allowances was above his paygrade. Though controlled by the head office, Tunde Adebayo, as a director, would have had some responsibility in this, yet he in turn, would complain to Terry about the deeply unpopular expatriate CEO.

Samuel and the other two junior members of the team appreciated Terry's natural ability to engage. At the same time, they knew that if, in his words, they "fucked up", his temper was not a pleasant experience.

At around eight o'clock, they dropped him off at the hotel. Terry more than suspected that they slept in the truck and gave him false receipts for their guest house so they could pocket the "expenses" but, as far as he was concerned, that was their business.

As long as they didn't take the piss.

After a couple more beers to wash down the chicken and chips in the half-empty restaurant, he headed to his room.

He was moderately tired, but he just could not settle. He watched a bit of TV, sent a couple of texts to Isioma, and then had a shower before switching off the light and getting into bed. But lying there, he could not drift off. Every time he closed his eyes, he saw Blessing dancing in front of him, teasing him. He remembered how she would strip off some of her clothes and then make him spray her with five hundred naira notes before taking off her panties. He would sit watching her while holding his bottle of Star with one hand and stroking himself with the other until he could no longer contain himself.

Now, as he lay on the bed with the gentle whirr of the air conditioning, time and time again he seemed to hear her whispered entreaties until, so aroused, he gave in to the impulse, shutting his eyes and imagining her open legs as he spluttered his load.

Several minutes later, cleaning himself up with toilet paper, he felt somewhat ashamed. Dirty. He did not know why. For the months before he and Isioma consummated their growing relationship, he had relied on the regular use of his right hand. Only this time, maybe because he was in her hometown, it seemed something of a betrayal.

The feeling of guilt lasted no longer than a fleeting second before he was distracted by a familiar buzzing. He switched the light back on but could not find the offending insect.

"Bollocks," he said, as he rifled through his overnight bag. He had forgotten his mosquito repellent. Back in bed, the incessant humming continued to distract him.

He leaned over for the phone, thinking to ask reception if they had any but he could not quite reach it without getting out of bed. Wearily, he swung his legs over, turned on the lights and dialled the front desk.

He sat slumped for several minutes listening to an unanswered ring tone until his inevitable "For fuck's sake". Now, his irritation turning into a strop, he pulled on his trousers, pushed open the door and marched along the corridor and down the stairs to the front desk.

As he stormed into the lobby, he was momentarily distracted by the sight of an old woman standing incongruously in the glass and tiled modern hotel lobby. She was dressed in a traditional wrapper with her light brown shoulders bare. She held a curved walking stick with a figurine carved into its top and just stood there. There was no expression on her face. She just seemed to be staring directly and pointedly, at him.

Before he could react, a voice came from behind the desk.

"Can I help you oga?"

Terry gave an involuntary shiver as he turned to face a security guard.

"So, you don't answer the fucking telephone in this place?"

"Please, sir, the receptionist is sick and has gone home early. I am on my own sir."

Terry muttered another "For fuck's sake" under his breath and more directly said, "I suppose you don't know where the mosquito spray is?"

The guard looked transfixed by the question. "Sorry sir. Please ask in the morning."

Terry thought of going off on a rant but at the sight of the guard who looked like he was about to burst into tears, he just shook his head and turned on his heels. There was no sign of the old woman he had noticed briefly and he thought how weird it all was.

He let himself back into his room, let his trousers drop to the floor, turned the light out and got into bed. Within seconds the buzzing started again. Grumpily, he pulled the sheet over his head. Eventually, he fell asleep.

* * *

"This is so kind of you, Mr Armstrong."

"Please. Call me Terry."

It was the afternoon after Terry arrived in Enugu. He had completed the morning's supervisory visits and had just driven into the Ede compound where he was met by Vitus and Dorothy. While located in a suburb of the city long past its heyday, it was a large airy compound comprising a few buildings in different styles and several shady trees. There was a couple of decommissioned vehicles rusting beside a scrupulously maintained 1979 Mercedes Benz saloon.

"I just wanted to pop around and check everything has been done properly, and to drop off some spare filters and bits and pieces."

Terry had his guys run the generator for a few minutes after topping up the tank from the jerrycans they always carried in the back of the pick-up. He listened to the running of the engines. He then asked Vitus if their air conditioning was working correctly now.

"Yes, yes. We are so grateful. We don't run the gen too often and the air conditioning is usually saved for visitors, but it is wonderful to have them all serviced and up and running."

They were standing outside the front door. "Dorothy and I would like you to have something to eat with us. Please. We have plenty for your team too."

"Well," replied Terry, "We don't have any more jobs for the day, and I fly back to Lagos tomorrow. So, that would be very nice, sir."

Before Vitus could respond, he added, "We can't stay too long though because my team leader, Samuel, is from near Awka and I promised he could stop over there for the night on his way back to Lagos."

Vitus smiled. "Why don't they have something to eat and then go off? I can drive you back to your hotel."

He turned to Samuel and the other two who were standing by the truck, "Biko, nwunne m, deeje nu. Enwere m nwa obere nri ndu beeke. Bia nu tinye aka ka ozugbo anyi fuo ngwa ngwa!"

Samuel looked at his companions who promptly nodded.

He replied to Vitus with an appreciative "daalụ", smiling with a slight tilt of his head.

Vitus turned to Terry and pointed to the same bench he had sat for so long with Robert a few weeks earlier.

"I like to sit here in the evenings," he said. "Dorothy will supervise the food. I hope you will join me for a beer."

Though the words 'Is the Pope Catholic?' flashed through his mind, Terry managed to restrict his natural inclination to "Thank you, yes". Within minutes, the house girl brought out the drinks and placed them on a side table in front of the men. There was a bottle of Harp for Terry and a small Guinness Stout for Vitus, alongside a saucer of roasted groundnuts.

"Robert brought some drinks when he came. I hope Harp is okay?"

"Any beer is fine sir, if it is cold. Thank you."

Terry drank straight from the bottle, smacking his lips.

"We bought ice. I know you expatriates like your beer like ice cream," Vitus said, smiling, as he poured out his Guinness. "I mostly drink mine warm."

Terry's team sat on stools and another bench on the other side of the doorway. The same girl brought them soft drinks and nkwobi.

"Terry, I was not sure how you like our food so my wife is preparing you chicken, but can I offer you more traditional fare?"

"No sir," Terry replied, laughing. "I am afraid I am not very adventurous. Chicken is perfect, thank you."

Vitus held up his glass. They clinked glass to bottle.

"So, my daughter tells me you came out to Nigeria with my nephew?"

Terry chatted happily about how he had landed at the airport for the first time and was collected with Robert, how they had a shared interest in football and had eventually become unlikely friends.

"And is that how you know my daughter?" asked Vitus.

Terry was not sure if this was a barbed or trick question and answered simply that he met her from time to time when he was with Robert. He was slightly taken aback when Vitus suddenly asked if he was alright.

"Yes, why?"

"You seem to be scratching quite a lot. Have you been bitten? Mosquitoes?"

Terry was relieved. "I seem to have got bitten to buggery last night!"

The food arrived then.

"We can go inside if you like. And I can put the gen back on and run the air conditioning?"

Terry demurred. The fried chicken, rice, and Nigerian salad looked appetising. He realised he was hungry. Though his teeth struggled with the chewy local variety of "running chicken", it was tasty and he ate with alacrity. His crew were also happily tucking into the more traditional stew and rice that Dorothy explained was ofe akwu. Vitus was eating that with rice and beans. He offered Terry a taste and he allowed him put a little on his rice.

"That's very nice," Terry said, coughing.

181

Vitus laughed and slapped Terry on his back. "We will allow you to stick to your chicken Terry," he said.

Eventually, the GTW crew asked to take their leave, offering their respects to Dorothy for the food.

Samuel was effusive. "Anyi ekene kwe unu, n'enu nri marumma unu ji nwe mere anyi ezigbo oji. Deeje nu o!"

"Owu anyi kwesiri ikele gi," replied Dorothy.

After Vitus had seen the crew off, he suggested one more beer before accompanying Terry to his hotel. Terry could feel himself being bitten again by mosquitoes but he was enjoying the relaxed nature of Vitus and Dorothy's hospitality.

A few minutes into the conversation Vitus said, "I hear you were in the army, Terry."

"Yes. Royal Engineers."

"Did you know that my grandfather, Robert and Isioma's great-grandfather, was also in the British army?"

Terry nodded. "Robert mentioned that he only learnt about that after his visit here. He didn't give me too many details, but I did hear something about the Nigerian Army still having an 81st Division to remember the 81st West African Division that fought in Burma."

"Correct," said Vitus. "My ancestor was with the 81st in the Far East. Like you, he was an engineer. I have tried to do some research but it is very difficult. All his medals and most of our family records and photographs were destroyed or stolen in the civil war. I am not very good with modern technology but Isioma's older brother has done some digging on the internet. So, I do know he was in the Field Engineers. After the Burma campaign, the unit was disbanded and he came back home sometime in late 1945."

Terry shook his head. "The Forgotten 14th are a legend in the British Army but no one I ever spoke to mentioned there was a Nigerian division."

"They were meant for logistics but were also trained in preparation for the fighting. By the time Mazi Agu returned, my father was still little more than a boy and he also died when I was barely a teenager. I remember some of the stories. But I do not know if you are aware that this same valiant soldier who fought for the British was later shot dead by them."

Vitus pointed over to the other side of the compound. "According to our tradition, he was buried here in our compound. My parents both lost their lives at the hands of our own people and I have not been able to bury them properly. It upsets me still."

Terry did not know what to say. He wanted to ask how Isioma's great-grandfather had died but Vitus had lapsed into silence. Eventually, the older man slapped his knees and stood up, somewhat wearily.

"Well, young man, we must count our blessings. I have two sons and a daughter. My business with my brother made enough money to pay for my children through university and then I was able to retire. So, they will bury me here, in the proper way." He looked at Terry. "But, not yet. The ancestors have not called me. Now, I will go with you to your hotel."

Sitting in the back of the Mercedes, a few minutes after receiving what he thought was a surprisingly warm embrace from Dorothy, Terry asked how Vitus' grandfather had been killed. Vitus explained.

"It is a long story, Terry. But, briefly: My grandfather, Agu Ede, and many former soldiers went to work in the coal mines near here. Experiencing the terrible circumstances in the pits after they had honourably served the British in the war, they joined those agitating for decent wages and better living conditions. The mine workers were not allowed to strike so they tried a kind of work-to-rule. The management, all White of course, called in the police and the army and there was a stand-off. My grandfather, a British war veteran, was shot dead while protesting for a new pair of boots."

Terry felt a lump in his throat sitting in the gloom of the back of the car.

"I am so sorry sir. I don't know what to say."

Vitus tapped Terry's knee. "Man is a terrible animal. Just a few years later, the atrocity at the mines was dwarfed by the banal stupidity of our civil war."

They were approaching a sizeable roundabout on the road. Vitus leaned forward suddenly.

"Emanuel," he said, "Pull over at the memorial. I want to show Mr Armstrong."

Being evening and after the busy period, it was easy for Emanuel to do so.

Vitus and Terry got out of the car and crossed the road.

There was a low link chain around the kerb that even Vitus could easily step over to reach the memorial which was on a large plinth several feet high. The monument was not well maintained and many of the surrounding streetlights were broken. It was too dark to read the plaque but Terry could see half a dozen figures made of some dull material. Almost full-sized, a couple of them had helmets on as if they were soldiers and were brandishing guns. Others, presumably miners, held up their fists and one appeared to have a shovel. There was one large man in a full agbada that Vitus thought represented an official.

They looked at it for a few minutes.

"So, there it is," Vitus said. "Ask most schoolchildren what it represents, and they will look at you in ignorance. Nor will they know any of the stories around this memorial. Twenty-one miners whose deaths helped trigger the fight for independence. Just as bad is that too many Nigerians do not know anything about their civil war apart from myths perpetrated by politicians or these idiots calling again for Biafran independence. What is it they say? History is told by the victors. It seems as if our family have never been the victors, but I thank God that my children can make a new life for themselves. And never be victims."

As they walked back to the car, Vitus continued, "It is a heavy responsibility being a father. To bring up your children with the values of their culture. You are a father too, I believe?"

"Yes sir," said Terry. "Three. Two girls, and a boy—Josh."

Terry was grateful they were getting back in the car so he did not have to continue what could become an awkward conversation.

"Thank you, Emanuel," Vitus said, tapping his driver on the shoulder. "Let us take this young man back to Nike Lake and save him from more of this old man's musings."

Back in his room, Terry rang Isioma to tell her about his visit. Then he had a shower before standing in front of the mirror. There were red bites all over his back and his legs and even on his buttocks. He rummaged in his wash bag and there was the butt end of a tube of bite cream which he squeezed out and tried

184

as much as he could to cover the blotches. He contorted somewhat to reach the big ones around his shoulder blades before giving up and getting into bed.

This night, his dreams were less of erotic memories and more a nightmarish vision of a Bosch-like inferno of soldiers and miners writhing into a bottomless pit of spicy pepper soup while giant mosquitoes teased him by eating a plate of chips he could not quite reach.

Chapter 22

What Shall Be?

"We are well,' Efuru replied. 'It is only hunger.'
'It is good that it is only hunger.
Good health is what we pray for."

'Efuru' by Flora Nwapa

Terry was restless all evening. Isioma was not sure what to make of it.

After his return from Enugu, he was strangely incommunicative. Isioma was so pleased when her father had rung to say that the nice friend of Robert's had serviced several air conditioners and a generator and had promised to send some spare parts, that she cooked dinner at the Keffi flat for Terry and her roommates. Terry did not eat much and left early, complaining of tummy wahala.

Now, two days later, he was pacing around the Roman Gardens flat complaining.

"Isioma, my guts have been iffy since I got back and now, I feel like I am going down with something."

She felt his forehead. "It does feel a bit feverish. I hope it's not malaria. Maybe you should take something, just in case. Have you got any paludrine or malarone in the house?'

"No, I ran out."

"Oh Terry, it's bad enough you're not taking them preventively but you should at least have some in the house. It probably is malaria, given how many bites you had on you. When you got back you looked like a pin cushion."

"It doesn't feel like the malaria I had before, but I do feel like shite so if I am not better tomorrow, I will pop in at St Francis for a blood test on the way to work."

They watched some television, but Terry could not settle. She could feel him tense and fidgeting on the settee next to her.

"You have not been yourself at all since you returned," Isioma said as she stroked his hair. "Is anything the matter, apart from not feeling well? Did anything happen?"

"No, work was the usual and your family were so friendly when I spent the afternoon with them. I just seemed to get bitten so much though. The bugs in Enugu must have bigger teeth. Even in the hotel."

"You didn't eat anything funny?"

"No." He pulled a face. "I told you. Your mum just cooked chicken and rice because she thought I might not like anything too local."

"Which is true."

"Copy that." He managed a wan smile. "To be fair, the beer was cold, though I had to drink Robert's bloody Harp." He was quiet for a moment as they stared aimlessly at some chance comedy channel on DSTV. "I did feel weird though. As if I had been there before."

"Well, you have been to Enugu several times, right?"

"Yeh, but somehow this was different. I don't know how to describe it. Even the hotel felt a bit weird. Maybe I am a bit run down." He paused. "Or just sad. You know I told you we passed some monument to some dead miners and your dad stopped so we could have a look. I didn't know that your great-grandfather was also one of them." She nodded. "It just made me think 'What kind of fucking eejits could do that?', I mean, shooting innocent people just striking for a living wage and to get boots for chrissakes."

"You were in the army though, Terry."

He gave her a gloomy look. "Yeh."

"Soldiers just follow orders, abi?"

"Yeh." He stared at, and straight through, the television for a moment without seeing a thing. "Yeh, but. . . I dunno. At least I was in the engineers. I fixed stuff rather than shoot people."

"Weren't you in Ireland? The British army were shooting people in the streets there, weren't they?"

"Well, yeh, but it wasn't me. That was before my time. I didn't have to. I was repairing Land Rovers. I don't know, baby. Anyway, maybe it was trying to think too much about this stuff that made me feel peculiar. You know that kind of brain work is not my strong point but . . ." his voice trailed off.

"But what?"

"It does kind of make you think, don't it?"

"What does, baby?"

"You know. I mean one moment I am on the dole in southeast London, just a normal bloke going on the piss too often and failing to be a decent husband and father, just like most blokes I know. Next, I am in Nigeria, a country that apparently fucked up my grandad. I have had my head turned inside out and started asking questions I never really thought about. On top of that I have fallen in love with my African Queen and my life is upside down. Maybe Africa has made me a better person."

Isioma stroked his head. "Or maybe it has just brought out the real you. Anyway, you still feel hot. I think you need to take some aspirin to bring your temperature down. Go to bed and I will bring a cold flannel."

* * *

That night, Isioma was aware of him getting up several times and by the sound of the constant flushing, it was not pleasant. In the morning he looked terrible: pale, sweaty, feverish. He only managed half his usual mug of tea before muttering that he was going straight to St Francis clinic for a blood test. His farewell kiss was clammy and perfunctory.

Twenty minutes later, Saturday pulled the pick-up outside the gates of a small but tidy building that was GTW's clinic of choice for their expatriates.

"I won't be long, Saturday," muttered Terry weakly.

"E pele sir," Saturday said, as his boss shut the door. Two hours later, he jerked awake as Tunde's driver Felix put his arm through the open window and shook his arm.

With a concerned expression, he pulled his seat back up and looked at his colleague.

"Wetin?"

Felix gestured with his head towards Tunde striding up the gravel path into the clinic.

Staff were not supposed to use personal mobile phones while at work, so Isioma had hers on silent. She felt it vibrate as a text came in so she took a sneaky look. It was from Terry. *'St. F keeping me in. on drip. All ok'*. She replied *'tanx 4 letting me kno. Will pop in after work. Luv XX'*.

Isioma managed to get off work a few minutes early to beat the rush and instead of her usual bus, she caught a keke to the clinic, ironically just a few hundred yards from the shared apartment on Keffi Street. She felt weak with apprehension as she approached the building. Terry was usually so strong, not missing work during previous bouts of malaria, so she feared that whatever had laid him low was serious. She was also worried because he had not sent her any more texts, which was unlike him. St Francis was a small but well-respected clinic, run by a long-term resident Lebanese doctor and a small staff. Most of their activity was expats coming in for a blood test, waiting for results, being prescribed malaria medications, and heading off home, but they did have a couple of private rooms for simple admissions.

There was no one in the waiting area but a nurse was at the reception desk writing something in a notebook.

"Good afternoon. I believe Mr Armstrong is here. Is it possible to visit?"

The nurse looked up and asked flatly, "May I ask who you are?"

"Isioma. A friend," she replied as calmly as her jangling nerves would let her. "He is expecting me to visit."

She received a long stare with what she felt was condescension, but she bit her tongue.

"He is asleep at the moment. You can wait there." The nurse indicated towards the chairs in the waiting area.

Isioma did not know whether to sit or to pace about. She flipped through a couple of old magazines and sent texts to her flatmates to let them know where she was. Eventually, she used some of her credit to let Robert, now back in the UK, know what was happening.

She was sitting staring at the wall when the Lebanese doctor came in, saw her and walked over.

"Are you Isioma?"

189

"Yes."

"Mr Armstrong, Terry, asked that you be let in if you came." His voice was sympathetic. "He is sleeping and must not be disturbed but you can look in."

He led her into a small, bright but windowless room in which there was a solitary bed. There Terry lay. She was shocked. His colour was awful, his flesh pudgy. He looked as if he was moulded out of pounded yam. He had a drip in his arm and despite an oxygen mask, his breathing was a shallow pant.

She turned to the doctor who signalled her to follow him outside.

"He has a very bad case of malaria, we are monitoring him very closely. I am expecting Mr Adebayo from his employer, GTW, shortly. You know we are contracted by them." Seeing the concern on her face, he followed up with, "Please, don't worry. We are doing everything we can. He is very strong so I am sure he will recover in a day or two."

Isioma sat back in a chair. She had to gasp for breath. Such was her disbelief at how Terry looked. She had her face in her hands, hot and tense, when the door opened and Tunde walked in.

She jumped up. "Uncle Tunde!"

Tunde gave her a small hug and said, "Isioma, I am going in to talk to Doctor Talib and then I will come out and let you know what's happening. I came earlier but had to rush back to the office. He is quite poorly."

"The doctor let me look in. I . . ." She could not finish the sentence.

"Ssshh, I know." He touched her shoulder gently. "Give me a moment."

He knocked on a door and walked in without waiting for a reply. After some time, each minute of which Isioma thought she would faint from tension, he came back out and sat down next to her.

"Isioma. So, it is malaria but there are complications, probably typhoid as well. They are worried that it may become what they call cerebral malaria."

She let out a gasp. "I know it."

He squeezed her hand. "We need to do more tests, so I am asking them to move him to St Nicholas. They have more facilities there. They are sending an ambulance to collect him shortly. You know I will do everything I can. He is poorly but he has the constitution of an ox so I am sure he will come through." He paused and looked at her before continuing kindly.

"You know his wife and children are his next of kin, Isioma? I have to keep them in the know. If his wife wants to come out, I will arrange it. You do understand?"

Isioma nodded.

"Would you like to see him again?"

There were no chairs around the bed, so she stood there for a few moments holding his hand. His skin was warm and clammy and did not feel like him at all. Terry stirred in his sleep and opened his eyes and, for a fleeting moment, she thought she saw a glimmer of recognition before he sighed and fell back into his slumber.

Tunde came back in and whispered, "The ambulance will be here in a few minutes."

As they walked out of the premises, Tunde gave her hand another squeeze. "I promise I will look after him and will keep you posted. Give me your number."

After he had put her details into his phone, he asked if she would like him to arrange a lift or a taxi.

She smiled wanly. "Thanks Uncle. I only live a few minutes away, along Keffi. I will be fine." She took a few steps up the path and looked back.

Tunde was still standing there. "Please, try not to worry too much. I am sure he will be right as rain soon. I will keep in touch, I promise."

Terry was not right as rain and for two days, Isioma could neither eat nor sleep. Ezzy and Florence did all they could to comfort her at home and keep an eye on her at work, protecting her from colleagues who kept asking, "What is wrong with Isioma?"

Just as he promised, Tunde kept her informed, by text and by the occasional call, but the news was never positive. The tests provided no real clarity. Yes, it was cerebral malaria but in a way that the doctors had not seen in such a healthy adult. It was not responding to the usual medications and they were having to seek further advice.

Terry had now been in a coma for nearly two days and was on life support. GTW's medical insurers had approved an emergency evacuation. Usually, they would have recommended South Africa but Terry's wife, Rachel, had asked for it to be the UK so she and the kids could be with him. Tunde was working with the hospital and the insurers to obtain the necessary flight permits and clearances. He promised he would arrange for Isioma to see him before he flew out but she could not travel with him. Apart from everything else, the ambulance plane only had a license for a doctor and a nurse. As soon as he had details, he would call.

Isioma was on her lunch break, sitting in the staff canteen with Florence who was nagging her to eat something, when Tunde called again. The plane was due to arrive at about ten o'clock that evening at the small private terminal next to MMA where the businessmen and politicians kept their jets. It was planned that the St Nicholas ambulance would leave the hospital around 7.30pm, to give plenty of time for the Lagos traffic. Tunde suggested that she meet him at the hospital just before then so she could see Terry as he was leaving.

"Can I come to the airport to see him off?" she pleaded. "Please Uncle Tunde."

"You can come in the car with me," he said. "I will follow the ambulance and make sure everything is going as planned. I will be speaking to Rachel, his wife, to keep her informed so. . ."

Isioma interrupted him, "Yes, yes, of course, Uncle Tunde. I understand. Thank you, thank you. Thank you."

Around seven o'clock, Isioma and Florence arrived outside St Nicholas Hospital in a keke. Despite being one of the most well-known and long-standing private hospitals, as well as being prohibitively expensive, catering for the elite and corporate health schemes, it was a tired and unprepossessing place.

Florence hugged Isioma. "You sure you will be alright? You have enough credit on your phone, or do you want me to send you some?"

"Flo, thanks. Honestly, I am okay."

Florence got back into the keke. As it made a U-turn and headed towards Obalende, she turned to look out at her friend who seemed so small and vulnerable standing outside the tiled frontage of the hospital.

An unhelpful and grumpy receptionist told Isioma to sit and wait until someone could attend to her but a few moments after she sent a text to Tunde, he came down to collect her, telling the staff in a tone that brooked no dissent that Isioma was with him.

"Isioma, I must warn you, you might be shocked when you see him. You cannot touch him but we can go in for a few moments. Then, they will start preparing him, putting him on the ambulance stretcher and so on, while we wait downstairs. When the ambulance is ready, they will let me know. I have arranged for a police escort so there are no holdups, and we will follow them to the airport."

The person lying on the bed attached to drips and monitors did not look like the Terry she knew. It was not much more than three days since she had seen him in St Francis but, in that time, he had seemed to have shrunk and lost half his body mass. His face was drawn and ashen and his closed eyes deep set into his skull. He had a mask over half his face, at least two drips attached to his arm and several wires leading to a monitor. She could not restrain herself from spluttering, "Oh my God!" as she put her hands to her mouth. It took her a few seconds to compose herself.

They stood there, side by side until Tunde beckoned towards a couple of chairs and whispered, "We can sit down for a while."

While they sat on the hard plastic chairs, Isioma looked around the room. She had heard that this was the best place to be brought to if you had money, but it did not seem so special to her. It looked utterly unhygienic. The once-white tiled walls were more a pale yellow or cream and various used swabs lay in an open bin by the side of the bed. The blinds on the windows looked as if they had not been dusted properly for months. This hardly inspired confidence for his treatment but she assumed that once in the UK there would be the most modern medicine and facilities available.

In the twenty minutes they were there, a nurse only popped in briefly twice to check Terry's vitals. So, again, she was unimpressed. Eventually, another nurse came in and said something quietly to Tunde, who excused himself and went out of the room.

Isioma stood up. She had spotted a small bag that she recognised as Terry's. GTW must have had someone collect it from his flat. She bent down and opened it. There was his wash bag and a few pieces of clean underwear. Quickly, she undid a small chain with a tiny crucifix on it from around her neck. She kissed it and tucked it inside some of the items in the bag. Before retaking her seat, she gently touched his hand and whispered, "Travel safe, my love."

After a few minutes, Tunde came back in with a doctor and said quietly, "They are ready to prepare him for the ambulance."

Isioma made her silent goodbyes and followed him into the corridor where a nurse and a couple of orderlies were waiting with a trolley.

As they walked down the stairs, he told her they would be ready in about thirty minutes. Sitting in the reception, it seemed like thirty hours. Tunde brought some weak coffee from somewhere and tried to be as positive as he could, but neither of them felt like talking.

Eventually, a nurse came and gestured to Tunde and they went outside to where Felix was already waiting with the car and a police pick-up. Almost as soon as they sat in the back seat, an ambulance came up a slope and turned in front of them. The small convoy started its journey to Ikeja.

After a few minutes of staring silently out of the window, Isioma spoke. "Uncle, I have to say I was disappointed at St Nicholas. It has such a reputation, but it just seemed so miserable, so rundown."

Without looking at her, he replied, "And you would not believe what they charge. That stay was probably more than your annual salary." She looked at him aghast and then he added, "Per day".

She shook her head and resumed staring out of the window. Eventually, Tunde heard her say, almost to herself, "What hope do ordinary people have in this country?"

Eventually, they arrived at the terminal gates around the side of the main airport buildings. They stayed in the car. Isioma watched as a doctor and nurse came down from the plane and helped the ambulance men and an orderly load Terry onto a special trolley while the nurse made sure the drip was fitted properly. The trolley automatically slid up a ramp into the underside of the small jet. Although they got out of the car, they kept their distance. She could hardly bear to look.

After Terry disappeared into the ambulance plane and the St Nicholas ambulance left, nothing seemed to happen. For what seemed an eternity the aircraft just sat on the runway without moving.

"What are they doing?" she asked Tunde. "Why aren't they going?"

"There are always protocols and often a wait for a clear runway."

After some time, the engines gunned to life and slowly the plane began to move.

They watched as it taxied off into the distance until just its lights could be seen on the runway. Tunde, standing beside her, put his arm around her protectively.

"Do you think he will make it?" she asked, almost impassively.

Tunde turned her round so he could look at her. He held both her hands in his.

"Honestly?"

Her answer was straightforward. "Yes."

"No. That is, I doubt it. I am sorry to say that even if he does recover, his health will likely be damaged permanently, and he probably will not come back. Certainly, our insurance would not allow us to bring him back."

She let go of Tunde's hands and dried her eyes. "I am sure you are right, Uncle."

They waited a few moments until somewhere in the gloom they assumed the plane had taken off, then turned to where Felix was standing by the car.

"Where would you like me to take you? Would you like to come home to ours for a while? My wife, Anne, is at home and expecting me."

"Uncle, I would rather be on my own. I don't even want to go home as the girls will smother me. Can I go to his flat please?"

"Of course, you can. I will drop you there." He smiled gently. "And I know you have a key."

She looked up. "Oh."

Before she could say anything else, Tunde winked and said, "Keep it for a few days and if. . . when, we hear from him, we can decide what to do."

Again, she wanted to say something, but Tunde just put his finger to his lips. "No wahala."

As they approached the car, Felix opened the door respectfully. Even though he was old enough to be her father he said quietly, "Sorry ma."

On the way back, Tunde whispered, "Sorry, Isioma, I have to do this," and called Terry's wife, Rachel, back in the UK. She listened to him tell Rachel that Terry was on his way and that arrangements had been made for her and the children to visit him at a private hospital somewhere near Gatwick Airport as soon as he arrived. Rachel asked Tunde how Terry was, as Isioma heard him say, "Well, he is very poorly, Mrs Armstrong, and is still in a coma. But he is in good hands, and I hope he will pull through."

After a few moments, he finished the call with, "You have my number as well as the insurance company's and the hospital's, so please feel free to call anytime. Terry is a very good man, Mrs Armstrong, and he is in all our thoughts and prayers here in Lagos."

In the dark of the back of the car, in the flickering lights of nighttime traffic, they looked at each other.

"The poor woman," said Tunde.

"And the children. Terry loves his children."

Isioma spent the rest of the journey staring out of the car window.

* * *

Being late, they got to VI from the airport swiftly. Isioma noticed the security guards at Roman Gardens opened the gates much quicker for Tunde than they ever did for Terry. As she dropped from the back seat of the black Mercedes, she felt a sharp stabbing pain in her abdomen. Enough to make her wince with pain.

Tunde too jumped out. "Are you okay, Isioma?"

"It's nothing. It's been a tough few days."

"You are not kidding," Tunde agreed. "Okay, then. If you are alright I had better be off. You have your key? Anyway, I am sure Benoit is around."

Isioma smiled at him, bending her knee respectfully. "E se gan sir", but then stood on tiptoe to hug him.

"Uncle Tunde, I cannot thank you enough. You have been such a friend to Terry, and I am so grateful for your kindness to me too."

"Isioma, my daughters are only a little older than you. Call me if you need anything."

He watched as she turned into the dimly lit doorway.

Chapter 23

Questions and Silences

"The casualties are not only those who are dead
They are well out of it
The casualties are not only those who are dead
Though they await burial by instalment
The casualties are not only those who are lost
Persons or property, hard as it is
To grope for a touch that some
May not know is not there
The casualties are not only those led away by night."

'The Casualties' by John Pepper Clark

As soon as Isioma stepped into the apartment, she sensed someone was there. The kitchen lights were on and, as she turned to the balcony door, she noticed, through the gloom, that someone was sitting on one of the plastic chairs looking over the lagoon.

She suddenly recognised the figure and gasped, "Papa!"

She ran to him and almost threw herself on his lap as he turned to face her.

On her knees with her arms around him, the shock of seeing him and the build-up of all the stress of the last few days culminated in a torrent of emotion. As she sobbed, he sat calmly, gently stroking her hair.

"Shush, little daughter, ssshhhh. It is well."

It was several minutes before she could say anything.

"Oh Daddy, I am so sorry," unleashing a flow of yet more tears.

Eventually, Vitus took her hands, "Come now, Isioma."

He stood up and then pulled her up in front of him. Isioma winced and doubled up, grasping her abdomen.

"Isioma?"

198

"It is nothing. I am sure it is just the pressure of everything. But how . . .?"

"First, make your father a cup of tea, please. Then we can talk."

He followed her into the kitchen. As she boiled the kettle and laid out a tray, he explained that the steward had let him in, and he had allowed him to close while he waited for her.

"But Daddy, how did you know I would come back here and how did you even know about this place?"

"In a moment, Isioma. Look, the kettle is boiling. Do you have any biscuits?'

A few minutes later, they were sat on the settee drinking tea: father and daughter.

"So, I went to your place in, is it Keffi Street? Your girlfriends could not hide the truth from me. I already knew so they told me about this place. At the gate, one of the guards is Igbo. He is not from our area, but he could still not deny a father looking for his daughter."

Isioma shook her head, almost in disbelief. She had so much respect for her father, but this was beyond what even she expected of him.

"But how did you even know to come now?" she asked.

"Your generation has learnt so much yet there is still some wisdom we old folk possess that you are yet to understand. First, to us, the world is an extension of our village and there are unseen threads that connect us. You know how, eventually, I found my sister and, look at the way her son Robert was brought back to us. It is necessary to exercise patience but eventually, everything that is, will come to us. Secondly, the ancestors still look after those who respect them. Lately, they have been sending me dreams. My grandfather and his grandmother have been whispering. I knew they were telling me something I should hear. I also rang your Uncle Onyeka. I know he knows a great deal. It is how we used to do our business together before I retired. He told me some things and some I learnt from what he did not tell me. So, I came."

"Oh Daddy, but that bus journey is so long. Why didn't you just call me?"

Vitus laughed wholeheartedly. "Bus journey? Are you mad? I am too old for that. We may not be as wealthy as we once were, but we can afford a plane ticket. Onyeka collected me from the airport and dropped me off at your place with your charming flatmates."

He reached forward for his cup and took a long swallow of tea. "You know we had our own teas, long before the British came but I must admit, I do like, what do they say, 'a proper cuppa'?" He took his time before speaking again.

"So, Isioma. Should I now ask the question I do not want to hear the answer to?"

She looked at him and took a deep breath but before she could speak, he put his cup down and took her hands in his.

"Isioma, first, let me ask. Will Terry survive? Onyeka said he was desperately ill."

Tears streamed down Isioma's face. She shook her head, looking directly at her father.

"Ndo," he said quietly. "Sorry. He was not a bad man. There is nothing more to be said now. When you are ready, we can talk."

* * *

It was a grey, overcast day, as Robert found his way from Grove Park station and headed towards Hither Green crematorium. As he walked, a black Mercedes saloon pulled up beside him, with the windows rolling down to reveal the driver.

"Robert." It was Tunde. "Jump in."

"So, do you know where we go in?" he asked Robert, who was now in the front beside him.

"I think it's just along here, to the right, Uncle Tunde. Thanks for letting me know the arrangements."

"No problem, Robert. It is nice to see you again. Though, horrible circumstances. How long have you been back?"

"It's only a few weeks really but suddenly Nigeria seems a long way away, in time and distance."

"How's Isioma?"

200

Robert grimaced. "Not great, if I am honest. But our family has been genuinely supportive. You know Terry went to the village?"

"I do," Tunde replied. "That is where he almost certainly caught the malaria. Though, having said that, the doctors remain flummoxed about it. It was completely beyond any experience they have of that level of virulence in such a healthy adult so they did a full autopsy but with no conclusions. That's why it has taken so long to arrange the funeral."

"It all sounds strange. He was such a strong bloke. Anyway, my Uncle Vitus and Auntie Dorothy guessed something was going on from his visit. Parental intuition or something?"

"Don't knock it, Robert. You never know. Anyway, Isioma told me her dad was already waiting for her when I dropped her at the flat."

"She told you?"

"Yes, they only stayed there one night then she called me to let me know she had left her keys with the steward. We had a quick chat, but I haven't seen her since. Though she did message me to ask if she could stay in the flat today."

"Well, the upshot was that suspecting something was wrong, Uncle Vitus spoke to Onyeka and decided to fly over. He had already felt something was strange about Terry turning up to service the compound's generator, even though she had told him, correctly, that he was a friend of mine. Anyway, he has been completely unjudgmental and even implied it was fate. He said it was 'as the ancestors have decreed'."

"As I said, you never know. I have seen too much unexplained to be certain of anything. Anyway, talking about ancestors, there are a few in here. . ."

As they turned in through the gates, there was a long sweeping drive past rows and rows of gravestones. Ahead was a nondescript 1950s building with a cement angel above a low balustrade. There was a group of about thirty people outside but, as they parked and walked towards them, a hearse came in. They stood and watched as the funeral directors' pallbearers professionally lifted what was undoubtedly a heavy coffin and took it into the crematorium. After family, friends and, judging by a couple of uniforms, a few former army colleagues, filed in, Tunde and Robert slipped in quietly and sat near the back.

Up at the front, Rachel was standing by the coffin with the three children. Seemingly, they were saying goodbye before they took their seats.

The coffin itself was draped in a Millwall flag. There were even a couple of blokes wearing football kits; much like the day Terry flew into Nigeria that first time just over four years earlier.

The service was short, with a minimum of fuss. There were no eulogies, and the only hymn was the unimaginative choice of 'Onward Christian Soldiers'. It was not sung with much enthusiasm. Finally, 'We Are Sailing' by Rod Stewart played as the coffin slipped gradually through a set of curtains. Robert whispered to Tunde, "They normally sing 'No one likes us, we don't care' to the same tune at Millwall matches."

As Tunde and Robert waited for the family to pass and then followed them out of the chapel, Rachel was standing by the door surrounded by her family. She was a slim woman of about 5ft 6in, in a black dress with her auburn hair tied back with a black ribbon. Her eyes, indeed, her whole face, was puffy from crying.

"Thank you for coming," she said, holding her hand out.

Tunde was ahead of Robert and took her hand. "I am very sorry for your loss Mrs Armstrong. He was a lovely man."

"Have you come all the way from Nigeria?"

Tunde nodded. "Tunde Adebayo. We spoke several times. I arranged the evacuation and wrote concerning his belongings and other things."

"Ah, Mr Adebayo." Rachel gave a wan smile, though her eyes were still red from crying. "Thank you for everything you have done. You were so kind. And your kind words too. They mean a lot. And, she hesitated, "thanks for trying – you know what I mean?"

Tunde nodded. "I do. Please, I am just sorry it didn't work out."

He squeezed her hand and then turned towards Robert. "This is Robert, one of Terry's friends from Lagos."

She offered her hand now to Robert. "You came all the way too?"

Robert gently shook his head. "I was in Lagos until a couple of months ago. I am back here now. I was shocked when I heard what happened. I am so sorry."

"I was asked to give these to you. From some of his colleagues."

Tunde held out a couple of cards. "I have the bag with Terry's stuff in the car. There wasn't much, actually, so I just thought I should bring it."

"Thank you so much. You are coming back to the house?"

Tunde and Robert both demurred.

"No, really. You were Terry's friends. He would've liked you to." She paused and looked at them both. "Please. I would like you to come, honestly."

They did not have the heart to refuse. "Can I park nearby?" asked Tunde.

Another family member said, "If you follow us, we can show you where to park. I hope you're not driving anything too swanky. It's a bit of a dodgy area."

"Hire car," said Tunde.

They followed some of the family's cars back to New Cross but, as finding somewhere to park took a while, most people were already settled by the time they walked up the short stairs from the street and through the open door. Tunde dropped the hold-all with Terry's few possessions by a coat rack. They paused in the hallway until someone they did not know ushered them into a room with chairs pushed around the wall and a dining table at one end with a buffet covered in cling film.

It sounded as if most people were in the kitchen, judging by the hum of chatter and the chink of glasses. There were just a few elderly neighbours or relatives sitting down. No one spoke to them apart from a cursory hello.

Eventually, a cropped-haired teenager came in and said generally, "Would anyone like a drink?"

He brought Tunde and Robert cans of beer. "Wanna glass?"

Eventually, people filed in self-consciously. Someone took off the cling film and the usual sausage rolls and sandwiches were passed round.

No one said much to them until Rachel came over and greeted them for a few moments before someone else needed her attention.

There was a hard clink on a glass as someone who announced himself as Terry's brother stood up and thanked everyone for coming before handing over to Rachel.

Struggling with emotion, she too thanked everyone for coming. She explained that she didn't feel up to speaking at the service but wanted to say a few words here among close family and friends. She knew everyone here knew Terry could be "a real sod at times". He ran his mum in circles when he was a kid and she and him had their issues but underneath all that, he was a gentle soul and loved his family. Then she paused.

"I especially want to thank Tunde and. . ." she hesitated, "Robert. . .?" he nodded, "for coming today. They brought a card from some of Terry's team in Nigeria and I want to read it."

She opened the card that Tunde had given her outside the chapel.

"Dear Mrs Terry. We are very sorry for your loss. Mr Terry was our oga. We appreciated him. He was the only White boss who would listen to us and eat our food with us. He was a good man. We remember him in our prayers. Our condolences please to you and the family and his pikins." She looked up. "It is signed: The engineering team."

There were murmurs of "That's nice" and "Bless 'em".

As soon as she finished, several friends huddled around her making reassuring noises. Most people seemed to drift back to the kitchen.

"Hello."

Tunde turned to his side and there was a young girl dressed in what seemed to be an unaccustomed smart dress, with a ribbon around her waist.

"Hello young lady. You must be Dolly?"

Dolly stood, head slightly to one side as if she was thinking hard. "How do you know my name?"

"Well, your father told me."

"My dad?"

"Yes, your dad. He would talk about you a great deal and he told me your name. He also told me you liked Spiderman, just like your brother."

"Were you my dad's friend?"

Tunde had sat through the crematorium service without feeling particularly emotional, but he found Terry's daughter's simple questions stirred something within.

"Well, Dolly, I worked with your dad. But we were friends too. I liked him."

"I have a coloured friend at school."

"Do you?"

"Yes. His name is Anil."

Robert was listening to this conversation.

"Is he nice?" asked Tunde gently.

"Yes." Dolly thought again for a moment before saying, "He hasn't been to my house though."

Tunde and Robert instinctively knew why but Tunde had to ask. "Why is that?"

"My nan doesn't like coloured people."

"Oh dear," said Tunde. "That's not very nice."

There was another pause before Dolly asked another question.

"What's your name?"

Tunde took Dolly's hands and pulled her closer, between his knees.

"My name's Tunde and I am very pleased to meet you, Dolly."

Dolly smiled dreamily as if she wasn't used to being told by people that they liked her. She looked up into Tunde's face. "Tunde."

"Yes, Dolly."

"Why have you got such black lips?"

Tunde so wanted to pick this innocent child up and hold her in a hug, but he was aware people across the room were watching this exchange. Instead, he just held Dolly's shoulders gently. "I don't know, Dolly. Let me ask you a question, where do you think the colour of your hair comes from?"

Dolly answered proudly, "My hair's ginger, same as my dad's. My dad told me if anyone at school called me 'ginga', even though I was a girl, I should punch them."

"There. You see! I got my black lips from my dad too," Tunde laughed gently, "but he didn't tell me to punch anyone." At which point he stroked Dolly's hair and gave her a gentle mock punch on the jaw.

Dolly giggled and looked up to see her grandmother, who had come over. She was a woman in her late fifties, with short dyed-blond hair; she had the wrinkled face and thin lips of a person who did not need effort to frown.

"I like Tunde," said Dolly. "He made me laugh."

"That's nice," came the flat reply, then, "Doll, do me a favour and go and ask your Mum to make me a gin and tonic."

The girl skipped away with an, "Okay, Nan."

"I'm Linda, Terry's mother."

Tunde and Robert both jumped up, but she stopped them. "Don't worry," she said and pulled a chair from the nearby row of dining chairs. They both managed to say "I am sorry" at the same time as she interrupted them.

"I am not normally a fan of Nigerians," she said, bluntly. "But, to be fair I thought that was decent the way you handled Dolly there."

Robert looked at Tunde who said, neutrally, "I am a parent too, Mrs Armstrong. My wife is British, so my children and grandchildren are mixed-race. I am used to questions about colour."

"Fair enough." Her tone was polite but there was a hint of an edge in those words and in the way she leaned forward. "So, you are one of the bosses at the company where Terry worked?"

"I am, yes."

"I hope you people are going to do the decent thing for Terry's family."

Tunde's voice was even, unruffled. "Of course. There was a death-in-service benefit. I put the details in a letter I wrote to Rachel. There are just a few formalities to go through with the insurance company."

Linda sat back, apparently relieved. "My son loved his kids, you know."

It was a statement, not a question.

"I know he did," said Tunde.

Robert chipped in, "He often spoke about them."

Linda looked at him. "Yeh, why wouldn't he?"

At that point, Rachel came up with Linda's drink. "Here you go, Mum."

Linda stood up to take it. She turned to Tunde. "You know, I have grown up believing Nigerians are . . . well, my old man went to Nigeria after the war—his name was Phillips. He was a senior copper and accepted a job out there. He was there for just a few weeks, and something happened that he would not talk about, and he got sent back. He had a breakdown and got kicked out. I was born after that and I was told that before he went out there he was a strong bloke, but all my memories of him are of. . .

"Anyway, my mother always blamed Nigeria. She said he would have nightmares about it and shout stuff she could never understand. Now this."

Tunde stood up. His voice was emollient, soft. "I am very sorry, Mrs Armstrong. I do not know what to say except Terry did a good job. He was a very good engineer. His Nigerian team were fond of him, and Robert and I liked him."

They looked at each other for a moment until she simply said, "Thank you", turned and walked back into the kitchen where several more of the pub regulars seemed to have congregated.

Rachel came and sat in the now vacant chair. "Okay?" Her question was loaded with concern that her mother-in-law had said something unpleasant.

"Fine," smiled Tunde, also sitting down. "No problem at all."

"Didn't Terry ever tell you his family had a history with Nigeria?"

Tunde and Robert gestured in a way that suggested they knew a little but not much.

"Linda's dad was a policeman in Glasgow during the war and then went out there, to Africa. Something happened to him there in the coal mines and when he came back he was a mess upstairs apparently. He never spoke about it. After they let him go, he and his wife moved down here looking for work, but he drank a lot, was always sick, and could never hold down a job for long. He was an alcoholic and basically drank himself to death. Terry was just a kid then."

There was a pause as neither Tunde nor Robert could think of an appropriate response. Yet Robert had noted the one word Rachel had said so incidentally—the mines.

"By the way," she shrugged, not noticing their reaction, "I did mean to ask you a slightly strange question."

"Go ahead," said Tunde, arranging his face.

"Did Terry get religion when he was in Nigeria? I mean, he never mentioned it."

"Not to my knowledge." Tunde looked at Robert who shook his head. "Why do you ask, Rachel?"

She fingered a small crucifix hanging on a silver chain around her neck. "This was in a few belongings that were in a bag that the hospital gave to me. They must have brought them over on the plane. It was on a shitty cheap chain, but the cross is nice, so I got a decent one to hang it on. I mean, it's a bit weird but he had so few things of his own so I thought I would keep it."

"He never mentioned anything remotely religious to me," proffered Robert.

"In fact," added Tunde, "I once suggested he should attend church as a way of meeting people. You can imagine how he responded."

"Exactly. That's why I thought it was weird. Anyway," Rachel stood up, "Tunde, Robert, thank you for coming."

They took that as their cue to get away. Standing up, both said something about needing to get going.

Rachel paused and said, "You know, I was never happy when the bastard buggered off out there, but I am glad at least he had a couple of mates like you two." She smiled. "I'll see you out."

As they took their leave and said goodbye to Rachel and assorted family members and pub regulars, there were few handshakes and mostly neutral nods and "alrights".

They were not unhappy to be leaving. Just as they got to the front door, the three children ran up. The two girls came close, but the taller Josh hung back a bit.

Dolly put her hand in Tunde's and asked, "Are you leaving?"

Tunde looked down at the three faces and felt a frisson of compassion. He leaned over and offered his hand to Josh. "I am pleased to meet you, Josh."

The young lad looked a little taken aback before apprehensively taking it, saying, "Thank you."

"And me," said a little voice.

"And yes, you too, Jade," smiled Tunde. "You too, of course, Dolly."

"Will you come back to see us, Tunde?" asked Dolly.

Before Tunde could reply, Linda appeared. "In you go, kids," and the children turned and skipped back in. Dolly waved as she twirled into a room down the hall.

"Goodbye Mrs Armstrong," said Tunde dispassionately.

"Mrs Armstrong," echoed Robert.

"Safe journey." She lingered before nodding to Tunde in a kind of recognition. "Thanks for coming, gents."

* * *

Robert looked at Tunde as they reached the bottom of the steps.

"Uncle Tunde where are you staying?"

"I am in a hotel near Heathrow. Tomorrow I am driving up to Manchester where I have some family. You are still in Chiswick, aren't you? Isn't that on the way? I can drop you off."

"More or less," replied Robert. "Thank you."

They walked to the car, relieved to find it unscathed. Tunde fiddled with the SatNav and they headed off.

Little was said as they both absorbed the day and Tunde, who did not know this side of London, had to concentrate.

Finally Tunde asked, "Do you think she knew? Had he told her?"

Robert looked at Tunde and pulled a face. "He told me he had. Promised me, in fact, but after today I am not so sure. I guess now I hope not." He paused for a moment. "I mean, you know?"

"I do," replied Tunde simply, then, "Have you heard from Isioma?"

"Briefly. I messaged her earlier and she said she was okay."

"You know," Robert continued. "I keep thinking how unlucky Terry was. I mean, Isioma said he was covered in bites when he came back from Enugu and she is sure that's where he caught it. Yet I was there not long before. I got bitten plenty but nothing happened to me. Jeez, you never know."

"Terry's mother mentioned the mines. . ." Robert said, looking directly at Tunde before his eyes settled back on the streets ahead of them. "Do you think he was one of them? My great-grandfather was killed at the Iva Valley mines in 1949. Do you think Linda's father, Terry's grandfather, was there? Was he one of them?"

Tunde, suddenly world-weary, took his eyes off the road a second and looked at Robert. "Yes," he said. "I do."

They drove in silence for twenty minutes until they got to the West End where Tunde had a better idea of his location. Robert's phone beeped. He looked at it. "It's a text from my mum. She is cooking egusi soup with eba and has told me to invite you."

"Please, let her know I accept her kind offer with pleasure," Tunde said, smiling. "Are you back at home with your parents?"

"No. I have a small flat nearby in Acton but once a week Mum cooks me a Nigerian meal to tempt me back home."

"Sounds great. I am looking forward to it."

Chapter 24

There is No Answer

"A ma ka mmiri si were baa n'opiugboguru?"
(Who knows how water entered into the
stalk of the pumpkin?)

Igbo proverb

Isioma decided to take the day of the funeral off and spend it on her own. In the three or four weeks since Terry had been evacuated, Ezzy and Florence had been supportive and kept her entertained with their camaraderie but she knew their cheerfulness would have grated on the day.

When the news was announced that she had been given a significant promotion at work, which would involve moving to the east to become a manager at a small community bank branch, she secretly welcomed the chance it would give her to leave the flat without upsetting them. But as she waved them off that morning, they protested that she should let them stay at home and keep her company but she was having none of it.

It was with a sense of relief that she turned back into the flat after watching them enter a keke marwa. What she had not told them was she had already arranged with Tunde that, as Terry's old flat was still empty, she could spend some time there. She had returned the key but Benoit, the steward would be around to let her in.

There was much she had not told them.

Isioma dressed leisurely, preoccupied with her thoughts, and then headed out. She hailed a keke on Keffi but as they got to Awolowo Road, they hit traffic. There had been rumours of another tanker driver strike so queues of vehicles caused roadblocks at every petrol station on the road. It had taken nearly thirty minutes squeezed next to a mother and her grizzly child and they were not through the worst of it. When they crawled past the Yoruba Tennis Club and approached Onikan, she paid the driver and got out. Though it was humid, the heat of the day had not built up as she strolled through the fumes amidst the many others who had given up on the bus to trek to their destinations on Victoria Island.

On the bridge over Five Cowrie Creek, she stood for a while watching several men dangling fishing lines over the side. Occasionally, one would pull up a small fish, hardly large enough for a meal, unhook it and throw it into a small basket. For a few moments, it would flap, gills gasping open, until finally exhausted, it joined its brethren lying silver-still, drying out in the open air. Isioma could not imagine the toxins in these immature fish, absorbed from the polluted coastal waters around Lagos, yet still a source of protein for the impoverished families that bought them. If it wasn't the noxious water that poisoned the fish, it would be the vapours from the broken exhausts of buses marooned in almost motionless traffic that finished them off.

Isioma took out a handkerchief to cover her nose and mouth as she headed past Bonny Camp and The Federal Palace Hotel. Lost in her thoughts, an altercation between several bus drivers and yellow-shirted LASTMA officials at the junction with Adeola Odeku escaped her attention. Skirmishes such as this were so frequent as to merit no more than a sideways glance from disinterested passersby. Better to avoid the small rent-a-crowd that would inevitably gather with the potential for pick-pockets or phone snatchers. She felt comfortably anonymous amongst the inevitable throng at bus stops or places where it was safe to cross the busy road, places where no one took any notice of you, intent as they were on their journey.

After Silverbird Galleria, Isioma turned right. Passing the gaudily domed shopping centre, she allowed herself a chuckle at memories of Terry's first experience of Naija-style audiences in the cinema there. Used to sedate oyibo watching habits, he had been taken aback by the response of the other spectators shouting their disapproval of the villains or cooing with audible pleasure at the romantic scenes. She reminisced at his startled reaction when the guy sitting next to him threw his popcorn in the air at a particularly loud explosion in a Die Hard feature.

She soon realised she was just standing on the side of the road staring. She shook her head as if to return to the present and soon rounded the corner into the residential neighbourhood dominated by the sounds of multiple generators.

The security guards had not been forewarned to expect her at the gate but she received a sympathetic reception as they let her through: "Sorry for your loss" and "May he rest in peace".

Benoit kept his eyes respectfully lowered as he asked if she needed anything. She didn't, allowing him to close for the day.

Feeling warm and a little dry after her twenty-minute walk, she checked the fridge and found a bottle of Fanta. The kitchen looked just as she had left it and she had to remind herself that it was just a short time in which so much had changed. The night with her father had been a world away. She opened the door onto the patio, flopped onto one of the plastic chairs and swallowed a few mouthfuls of the fizzy orange, allowing her mind to carry her back to that evening as she and her father sat in the darkness sipping tea until the sun rose somewhere behind them.

Isioma had explained how she and Terry had met, how his rough simplicity had somehow touched her heart, and, eventually, that while he had been in Enugu she had found out that she was pregnant. Waiting for the right time to tell him, he had fallen ill and died not knowing that she was carrying his child.

Isioma remembered the still expression on her father's face in the pallor of the dawn: concerned, gentle, with no trace of judgment. Since that day, she had told no one else. Not her girlfriends, not Robert, and certainly no one at work. She had already made up her mind, even before that conversation with Vitus, that she would keep the baby.

Sitting by her father's side, she did ring her mother who also took the news stoically and supportively and they had spoken several times subsequently. The news that in a few weeks she would be moving to a branch in Abakaliki, a market town within easy travelling distance to Enugu, confirmed her decision. The new position came with a car to make it even more possible. She knew Ezzy and Florence would tell her to have a termination, easily accessible for a small fee at a discreet private clinic. But she equally knew that was not her fate. She had known the potential implications of her liaison with Terry. Even though they were not

213

the ones she would have chosen, to seek to avoid them would somehow denigrate their time together. That was not her intention.

Staring across the view that had become so familiar, her mind fluttered between the past and the future. She had resolved that she would not allow herself be dictated to by events. She had to look forward positively for herself and her child. The opportunity provided by the Abakaliki job was not just luck, she told herself. She had worked for it and if the powers that be, human or divine, had been looking out for her, she was determined to make the most of it. The branch was just a little more than an hour's drive from home so she could stay in the family compound until she found somewhere more suitable to live.

A text from Robert broke her reverie. She replied briefly, knowing that she owed him a longer call.

She had been sitting there long enough to get stiff so she stood up, stretched her hips and neck, picked up the tepid, half-drunk Fanta, and turned back into the flat.

Pulling the sliding doors shut, she allowed herself one last lingering look towards a soon-to-be setting sun, then, in the knowledge that she had things to do, sucked her teeth decisively. As she pulled the door shut behind her, she stood on the threshold of Terry's apartment and prepared herself for the Keffi flat, to tell her roommates that she had no one to thank for her choices but her own will and a belief in accepting consequences.

"O du mma," she said to herself as she pulled the door shut for the final time and turned to the stairwell. "It is well."

As Isioma approached the gate, two different security guards came out of the hut and she recognised one as the Igbo man who had let her father in that night. She knew it would be the last occasion she saw them so she thought she should give them something. As they held the small gate open for her, she stopped and pulled out her purse.

Just as she sorted out a few notes, something caught her eye and she looked up across the compound. Standing by the door of the block, she was surprised to see a venerable old woman dressed in traditional Igbo wrapper and top. She was staring hard at Isioma, slowly shaking her head in a way that could have reflected sorrow or disappointment. Isioma was completely thrown.

"Ma?"

214

The guard brought her back to her senses, so she pulled out some naira and gave them a thousand naira each. They were both grateful and thanked her. She looked back over to the apartments but there was no sign of the old woman.

"Biko, onye vu agadi nwanyi ahu?" she asked the Igbo guard.

He was surprised at her question and replied in the negative.

"Onweghi agadi nwanyi no na ebe a."

There is no elderly woman here.

Isioma thanked them once more and stepped out into the street. She was sure she had seen an old woman looking at her but it was true she had never had an inkling of her before, and the guards had never seen her. And what was that expression on her face? The way she shook her head. Was that a look of sorrow or disapproval?

"Ridiculous," Isioma thought.

Not for the first time that day, she shook her head and moved on.

Having dashed the guards some naira, Isioma realised she was now short of cash.

Many places on the island accepted cards but markets, taxis, and small shops, all wanted payment in cash. She remembered there was a Zenith Bank ATM in Silverbird Galleria so she decided to pop in there. She could use any ATM at all but employees were expected to use Zenith's. Plus, there was a small grocery store upstairs where she could buy a few bits towards the supper she had agreed to cook for the girls. After collecting the crisp new notes from the cash machine, Isioma made her way up the marble stairs to the shop.

The Galleria complex had opened as an ornate mall with pretensions to architectural grandeur. However, after just a few years, it was already becoming rundown. The cinema on the third floor was still popular but the shopping arcade on the second was far from busy. Though it claimed to be a supermarket by UK standards the store was little more than a corner shop with just a couple of aisles.

Isioma had most of the ingredients back at the flat but she knew she needed some more rice and a few other condiments but the badly lit shelves were particularly disorganised and it took a while to find them. As she reached the back, there was a mother and young daughter in earnest conversation and Isioma could not help herself as she hung back and listened to their tete-a-tete.

The child had asked for some sweets which the mother had refused to buy. Isioma could hear the mother explaining patiently that too many sweets would make her teeth go bad. This explanation was far from acceptable to what appeared to be a precocious five-year-old. Hormones kicking in, Isioma could not help but feel emotionally connected to the long-suffering parent who was far from the often-accurate clichéd portrayal of the Nigerian mother, quick with a slap to any back-talking youngster.

"I know you clean your teeth before you go to bed, my child, but sugar still rots your teeth, no matter how much you clean."

The girl remained unconvinced. "But mummy why? Daddy eats chocolate and he has strong teeth. How do you know that I will get bad teeth?"

By now even the sainted parent's patience was wearing thin and she took her daughter's hand and started walking up towards the small checkout, pulling her recalcitrant child along.

"You know what Grandma always says to you when you keep asking questions? What an elder sees while sitting down, a child can never see while standing up."

They paid and left the shop, Isioma was not far behind, smiling to herself at the mother's response.

Later, as the keke made its way up Awolowo Road towards Keffi, Isioma considered the exchange. Watching the exchange between mother and daughter reminded her of her parents' patience with her constant questioning as a child and made her think of what qualities she would have to display as a single mother in the future. The last few months had led her to respect both her mother and father even more than she already did. She knew she would have to rely on their experience but as wise as they were, they could not foretell how her life would unfold.

The keke pulled up outside the flat. She picked up her small bag of shopping, paid the driver and let herself in. Even the ancestors would struggle to handle her two friends when she told them her news, she thought to herself, as she closed the front door behind her.

"O du mma," she sighed. *It is well.*

THE END

216

Acknowledgements

Nigeria being so outrageously unique it is almost unnecessary to make anything or anyone up. Almost every incident in the book is based on something I have directly experienced, something I heard about second hand or something historical. There is also a real person lurking within every character, while many .... indeed, why would you make up people when you know Francis the Fixer, Pat, Mouin or Oti? I hope those that knew and loved KOP recognise my affectionate homage to him in the personality of Tunde. I cannot think of Lagos without Olu and Val Priddy. The incredible people of Nigeria are simply my constant inspiration; from the ordinary humans who, despite all the challenges, live their lives with humour and dignity to the extraordinary poets who I have started every chapter with.

Closer to home I have received support and encouragement from so many. Those that read sections and proffered advice such as Charity Simpson, whose early interventions from her own experience were pivotal; to Andrew 'Chip' Chipchase, whose literary ideas were matched only by his accommodation (cheers too to Charlie, Bartley and big Alex). Sister Anne also proffered the support/accommodation combo in Orgiva, as did the MacDonald family in Skye and Lucie and Jean Noel in Chamballan. A productive stint in Paris courtesy of Gaya's parents Savitri and Peter, made me feel like Ernest Hemmingway. My friend Anne Harte, who sadly passed away just too soon to see the finished article, was always encouraging as were; Seun, Ade (Oloye), Natalie, the PNG boys, all the Priddies, my bros Richard and the Akerele family, the omnium boys and the Beehive café, Raven pub and Pitanga restaurant fraternities. Kayode and Lynn kept my FES supply going. My two sons, Tom and George, were always engaged and ready with critical encouragement.

Bankole, you are not forgotten as my friend, fellow imbiber and bibliophile as well as being my Nigerian publisher. A shout out to all the Bookcraft team. Nkechi, 'copy editor by night, dispenser of justice by day', thankyou too. Renike's cover illustration is just a bonus.

Two people stand out in the 'but for them this book wouldn't have existed' category. Ed Emeka Keazor (not forgetting his rock, the indefatigable Muni Keazor-King) provided so much encouragement despite his own backbreaking workload, sharing his research and historical nous (it was he that suggested the Iva valley link when I had been thinking of the Aba Women's riots as the backdrop), as well as Nwgo-Igbo translation. He provided musical accompaniment and then introduced me to the final recipient of my gratitude. Richard Ali's editing has turned what I think was a decent read into something I can be truly proud of. Along the way through email and Zoom conversations (as I write this we have never physically met) between London and Abuja we found so many shared connections and mutual contacts (thanks Kadaria for bringing me my first taste of Richard's Tigray Coffee) and have become friends. You two guys are a representation of everything that gives me hope for Nigeria, thank you.

Chief Keith Richards
2024

About the Author

Chief Keith Richards brings a wealth of experience to his writing, having spent over 30 years working in developing markets across Africa. His leadership roles at prominent Nigerian companies like Guinness Nigeria and Promasidor Nigeria are matched by his deep engagement with the community, earning him several chieftaincy titles and a place on prestigious boards. He was recognised for his work and awarded an OBE in the 2010 Queen's Birthday Honours List. His Memoirs, "Never Quite The Insider" received critical acclaim but this is his first novel. He lives in London, UK.